Drilling through Hard Boards

133 Political Stories

ALEXANDER KLUGE

With Guest Contributions by
REINHARD JIRGL

TRANSLATED BY WIELAND HOBAN

LONDON NEW YORK CALCUTTA

This publication was supported by a grant from the Goethe-Institut, India.

Seagull Books, 2019

Originally published as Alexander Kluge, *Das Bohren harter Bretter.*
133 politische Geschichten
© Suhrkamp Verlag, Berlin, 2011

First published in English by Seagull Books, 2017

English translation © Wieland Hoban, 2017

ISBN 978 0 8574 2 701 4

British Library Cataloguing-in-Publication Data
A catalogue record for this book is available from the British Library

Typeset by Seagull Books, Calcutta, India
Printed and bound by WordsWorth India, New Delhi, India

CONTENTS

FIGURE 1. *Homo volans*.

PREFACE

The political is an especially high intensity of everyday feelings. One finds it wherever there are people. In this elemental form, it drives history. The measure: trust.

Then there is also politics as a profession. It is about power and its preservation. Here too, one pays in trust; but it is also used up on a large scale. The question is this: Whom do I trust not to abuse their authority? That sounds relative.

In January 1919—the First World War had just derailed the twentieth century—Max Weber published a speech with the title 'Politics as a Vocation'. He defines this profession as 'drilling through hard boards with passion and sound judgement'. Thus he combines the two spheres of the political: the ABSOLUTE, which is where humans themselves live, and the RELATIVE, in which they let others administer what is most important to them. How can one tell stories about it?

I asked Reinhard Jirgl to contribute a story about the encounter between Khrushchev and Kennedy in Vienna in 1961. Telling stories is sociable; I don't like to be alone when I work.

ON A WINTER'S EVENING

The Politics of a Dog

It is an old lady. In its youth, this Jack Russell captivated observers with its energy. Half a metre high, it leapt through the grass. On beaches it ran in the wind. Meanwhile it knows the members of the household, knows how to ensure that its needs are satisfied. Everyone serves this dog.

It belongs to the species of warm-blooded animals, interested in the distinction between good and bad sources of warmth. Where are the most pleasant places—and the heat-preserving positions—in the house? This dog is an expert on the subject. Shifting by mere millimetres, it corrects its resting position in the segment of sunlight that reaches the floor from the high windows and wanders every minute. The dog follows the daylight to ensure that not a single spot of its fur is deprived of it.

Four times a day it is taken for a walk for the projects 'number one' and 'number two'. Today the rain cuts the trip short. The left eye seems to be blind; it is inoperable. The right has a cataract. Its range of vision is roughly 4 metres. The cathedral of smells it brings home from its outdoor excursions, or rebuilds in the house in every position, remains immense. We think it can see its image in the elevator mirror if one holds it close to it, but it doesn't recognize itself. Its image of itself often seems to change: sometimes it is a giant, sometimes a dwarf dog. That depends on who happens to be sniffing at it. In relation to us, the people who accompany its existence, it probably takes itself for a human being who is denied a seat at the lunch table as a jest by its colleagues. When we proceed to our meal, the dog goes to its bowl. Immanuel Kant speaks of a peculiarity of apperception: the 'transcendental dog'. According to Kant, there are differences between dogs both outwardly and in their inner lives (between, for example, a Pekinese and a St Bernard), which do not suggest that humans should distinguish between this species and others (cats, for example) without prior agreement. This heterogeneity evidently does not disturb the concept which the dog inhabits. The concept of the dog, Kant continues, is more clearly defined than that of human rights, considering that slaves, aristocrats, travelling people like gypsies, Indians and citizens have very different legal claims. Our dog lies contentedly in its basket.

The Federal Chancellery Steamboat Jetty

A number of tourists arrive at the Federal Chancellery steamboat jetty. They do not want to visit the Federal Chancellery but, rather, the HOUSE OF THE CULTURES OF THE WORLD. In front of this heritage-protected building, two stalls offer baked potatoes and *Bratwurst* respectively, accompanied by beer. A band is rehearsing loudly for the evening on the roof of the building. They already knew how to use the loudspeakers before they started rehearsing. The rehearsal serves to mark their territory in the cultural garden.

The visitors to the Federal Chancellery have not come from any of the steamboats that landed here. From the rear of the chancellery, which faces the steamboat jetty, one cannot see the government's activities. How would one recognize them anyway, for example, from the front? There would be no signs from the outside. Nor would a visual impression inside the building be informative. And one hardly hears the government's activities either.

A spy who had researched everything that went on the in the Federal Chancellery (though this would be no easy matter, either physically or technically) would still not know what happens in the way of governance. To find that out, he would have to DO THE ABOVE and explore the circumstances, and hence the OBJECTIVE POSSIBILITY that circumscribes all actions and decisions. He would have to gather experience of how decisions are made. Perhaps he will say: This is a FEDERAL OFFICE OF HESITATION. Some of the efforts of the apparatus as well as the management go towards avoiding or stopping wrong decisions. The structure of the chancellery illustrates the work of the ministries in the form of functional units. With the aid of this structure, it keeps a restraining organ at the ready that reduces the surplus of impulses, similar to the human brain. This too is only seemingly the place where decisions are made. In reality, according to brain physiologists, this organ inhibits the turbulent desires that come from bodies.

That is why the GOVERNING EFFECT of the chancellery reaches its utmost fruition when the chancellor and her head of office are away on travels. Today, of a potential 2 billion wrong decisions, 60,000 are thus prevented in *a single* day, simply because the chancellor and her senior staff, held up in Lisbon on the way back from the USA owing to an ash cloud coming from Iceland, cannot reach their headquarters. An attempt to fly south around the lava cloud the following day was successful, and the chancellor's plane landed in Rome. From there it only took two days for the buses to reach Berlin. It goes without saying that the buses, despite being rented as an improvised measure, are equipped with communication devices. The Reich chancellor of the Third Reich would have had to order for the train to be stopped (he never travelled by bus) in order to speak to his headquarters. Things are different today. But no one expects the head of state to 'give orders while driving around'. On top of that, one of the buses got a flat tyre upon entering South Tyrol. Politically, it was the right decision for the chancellor to wait for the damage to be repaired rather than splitting her group. That would have called for a distinction between a 'group of the superfluous' and an avant-garde; with the wealth of pending decisions, it would have been one too many. One night at a hotel in Bolzano. A substantial period of six additional days (between leaving the USA and arriving in Berlin) that gave the function of the chancellery some reserves and was due to a natural occurrence in distant Iceland. The causal chains in the globalized world form a wide-meshed net.

In this time of intense performance at the chancellery, outside observers from orbit would have heard a shrill, very high note on the audio tracks of their devices, an angelic concert of crisis-avoiding politics. The sluggishness of the morning required the band on the roof of the 'House of Cultures' to draw out their experimentation with sonic fragments until noon. Simply to show that they were filling out the rehearsal time that had been paid for. After all, they could not retire to their hotel and simply wait and keep quiet after lunch until their late-afternoon performance, when they were being paid for DOING rather than REFRAINING FROM something.

On a Winter's Evening

It was on a winter's evening. On 28 January 1919, roughly a hundred people gathered in a bleak, narrow hall in Munich. A black curtain was hanging behind the dais from which the guest was speaking. A stenographer, hidden behind this curtain, was writing down the speech. Thus Max Weber gave his lecture POLITICS AS A VOCATION.

Later on, Weber revised the shorthand text. He formulated the subsequently famous manuscript afterwards in his study, as Cicero had done with his speeches against Mark Antony. Had it been read aloud, the published text would have been four and a half hours long.

Outside, the Bavarian revolution. None of Weber's trains of thought consider this attempt at a new political approach. He found the events amateurish in their execution.

Lord Ralf Dahrendorf wrote the afterword for the Reclam edition of Weber's speech. He comments on Weber's idea of the politician. Weber is concerned with a POLITICAL TEMPERAMENT. Dahrendorf compares the ACCESS OF THE POLITICIAN (according to Max Weber) with the entry of a space capsule from orbit into the atmosphere. If the capsule approaches at too shallow an angle, it will be flung back into outer space. In Weber's account, this is the fate of purveyors of the ETHIC OF MORAL CONVICTION. Some spaceships, Dahrendorf continues, enter the air mantle too steeply and burn up: those are the POLITICAL BUREAUCRATS. Only a few of those who want to reach earth succeed in entering: those are the LEADERS and HEROES.

The comparison to the space capsule comes from Dahrendorf. The identification of the three ideal types of political practitioner, however, refers to Max Weber's terms. They are no longer common in this form.

Drilling through Hard Boards

The experienced politician Gertrud Reinicke, currently an assistant in a parliamentary party faction, advised distrust towards the magnetic effect of catchphrases. On the other hand, she said, one could not do without expressions entirely. But the formulation 'drilling through hard boards', she continued, did not correspond at all to how she worked in the business of politics. The first virtue of the experienced politician was 'letting things happen'. Only through contact with the matter itself could an opposing movement, a political intervention, be initiated. Politics is not action but reaction. People themselves are active.

And again: if the answer was too hard, one looked for the soft spot right next to it where a compromise was possible. In that sense, she added, it was never really a matter of trying to operate on something rigidly resistant. She would not liken political practice as she knew it to drilling away at something hard. That would be uncommunicative.

The image of someone sitting like a carpenter in front of the object they are working and drilling at, that is to say, acting as an individual, also contradicted the role in the network that politics constitutes. Even if it was the chancellor or the head of the budget committee in agreement with the Opposition spokesperson (those are strong powers), they could not simply say 'I' if they wanted to arrive at a result. The politics of a territorial state, according to Gertrud Reinecke, had outgrown the artisanal stage.

The messengers were still coming with their trolleys and putting files on the shelves reserved for that purpose. This happened in cases where a personal stamp or signature was required. The rich flow of information and CC: documents, on the other hand, took place in e-mails. Between that, the text messages and calls, or the direct exchanges of words when someone peeked into the hubbub or a visitor interrupted the stream of messages and thoughts. You could say that one gets out of step, Gertrud Reinicke states, if one misses even three hours of this stream, which one 'does not step into twice': how is one supposed to put a drill to these flowing waters—streams, floods and sewage moving both uphill and downhill? What would be the point of that?

Nor could one compare their practical work, she proceeded, to the back and forth of weaver's shuttles, if only because it was unlikely that any of the communicators in the German capital had ever seen a loom. It was equally common, according to Gertrud Reinicke, to use such expressions as 'call a spade a spade' or 'drain the cup to the dregs', which extended from an earlier world into everyday political life. 'Drilling through hard boards with passion and sound judgement' was another one of those, she said. Here the word 'passion' recalled the Deutsche Bank motto, 'Performance out of passion', and in that sense it could be understood in a contemporary way. The catchphrase 'sound judgement' was also plausible. The rest of the sentence, on the other hand, was only useful as the polar opposite of the lightweight who only drills through thin boards,[1] so it would make more sense to speak of 'drilling through thick boards'. Further steps and quick results were only ever achieved by avoiding hardness, not by trying to attack a wall at its thickest point.

Boards at Halberstadt Open-Air Swimming Pool

At Halberstadt Open-Air Swimming Pool, hard boards formed the side walls of the changing cubicles. To drill through them with one's gaze, one had to push in the knot-holes. A large number of young bathing guests had done this in previous years, such that there was lively eye contact between each cubicle and the next. This remained the case on all summer days during the Second World War and the subsequent time of hardship. The gazes fed off the opposite sex, off the same sex too, as if the knot-holes were mirrors.

Boards on the Foreheads of the Patriots

Prussian Uhlans, accompanying the Duke of Brunswick's army in 1792 as it advanced to France, wandered into Alsace. In some cities they rounded up the municipal officials, whom they identified by their caps as Jacobins, and nailed boards to their foreheads. They borrowed hammers and nails from the local artisans under threat of violence. In some cases, they hammered the nails into the skulls so clumsily that the officials died.

Mussolini Shies Away from Drilling through a Hard Board

The surroundings of Il Duce Benito Mussolini, the 'master of determination', expected him to drill through a hard board at his meeting with Hitler in Feltre in 1943. The Allies had landed near Naples, and had evidently not been driven away from this beachhead by the German divisions. Mussolini had promised his staff to take Italy out of the war; he wanted to inform Hitler of this. Let no one underestimate me, he said, not my courage, not my intelligence.

Only two months earlier, he had refused to let the German Reich send more than three divisions to Italy. As a dictator, he knew what freedom of action meant.

He found the meeting place guarded by Waffen-SS men. They had arrived in an aeroplane that accompanied Hitler's. Assessing Hitler's brutality and recalling situations from the Renaissance period now summoned up by his vivid imagination, he could not find the right words during the meeting. His surroundings were horrified. It was not fickleness, let alone cowardice but, rather, realism that seduced him into a violent act of hypocrisy.

He succeeded in tricking Hitler, who, when the talks were finished, annulled the preliminary orders to occupy Italy that he had issued before his departure to Feltre. He believed in Il Duce's loyalty, he said. The next day, Mussolini promised the king in Rome to lead Italy out of the war by 15 September. But it did him no good; he was arrested a few weeks later.

In his first place of imprisonment, in Sardinia, he told a confidant: there was no chance to be hard in Feltre, nor any chance to be un-hard—there was no chance for me at all. After 22 years of ruling beautiful Italy! Though a prisoner, he could still give his face an expression of determination through mere willpower.

The Honour of the Stock Exchange

There was something known as the Lucca–Pistoia share dispute, which stemmed from an event in (Habsburg-ruled) Tuscany in 1853. A railway line was supposed to be built from Lucca to the town of Pistoia, and shares had been issued with a life of 99 years and a state-guaranteed interest rate of 5 per cent per annum. The state guarantee had the condition that the construction had to be completed within two years.

The railway track was not completed. The company went bankrupt. The bank Goldschmidt & Co. had sold shares to customers without expressly mentioning the limits of the state guarantee. This resulted in a legal dispute that dragged on for 10 years.

In this legal dispute, the renowned legal scholar Rudolf von Jhering (*The Struggle for Law*) issued a scathing legal opinion against the bank. Max Weber's doctoral supervisor, Prof. Levin Goldschmidt (unrelated to the bank by blood or marriage) formulated the counter-opinion: *pacta sunt servanda*, he wrote, regardless of any possible errors when the agreements are made.

In his response to the counter-opinion, Rudolf von Jhering introduced an unexpected legal argument: the stock exchange and the bank had colluded to violate their honour, and could therefore no longer be considered the SUBJECT OF A VALID STATEMENT OF DEFENCE. It was not a matter of formal legal reasoning; rather, anyone who destroyed their own honour forfeited their right. And for a member of a law faculty, it was defamatory to arm such an illusory defence with legal opinions. For legal scholars, there was a barrier of honour when it came to defending stock-market transactions.

Now under personal attack, Levin Goldschmidt asked his student Max Weber, who was pursuing a legal career at the time, for public support. Weber was unable to oblige; as he told his doctoral supervisor, he shared Rudolf von Jhering's position. After that, his academic relationship with Goldschmidt was ruined. Honour, according to Max Weber, is a phenomenon of universal history. The stock market (of which the bank is merely a derivative) constitutes a community founded through the free choice of the money owners. All communities possess honour. If this honour is destroyed, it loses its legal capacity. Just as a state system without honour becomes indefensible, a dishonest stock market, and hence the bank being sued, lost its right to make a statement of defence. At some point, Weber adds, argumentation comes to an end.

The 'Invisible Hand'

The internationally respected exploratory geologist and doctor of engineering Malte Wiegand was one of the experts provided by the parent company BP for legal defence in the USA. He was considered thoroughly rational. But one cannot use one's experience and be passionately active in the scientific world yet shut oneself off narrow-mindedly from the impressions which the examined material presented to the eyes of the senses and the mind (the eyes of most of the senses and the mind are not visible themselves). And here, in the documents on the disaster that had taken place in the Gulf of Mexico, he encountered connections between facts that he could not adequately interpret using the simple distinction between cause and effect.

On 20 April 2010, at 28°44′12″N, 88°23′13.8″W, the oil platform had all but completed its drilling. A few hours earlier, the well belonging to the Halliburton company had been secured by pouring in special cement. It was to be sealed shortly; a different platform that specialized in this would pump up the oil in a few months.

A pressure increase in the well at Mississippi Canyon Block 252 led to a blowout. The fountain of drilling mud, gas and oil was ignited and set the oil platform on fire. The central valve system at the bottom of the ocean (the blowout preventer) was activated, but did not work. The manual emergency shutoff for the blowout preventer, which was supposed to close it and separate the oil platform from the well, was only activated seven minutes after the blowout, but it too failed to respond. Up to that point, Malte Wiegand noted, it was a consistent chain of causes that one could describe after the event.

These were augmented, however, by exacerbating factors that suggested the guidance of an invisible hand. 'I am familiar with such accumulations of coincidences from historical accounts about past wrongs or a curse,' wrote Doctor of Engineering Wiegand, 'but have never encountered them in the technical reality of drilling work.' The escaping gas was sucked in by the platform's diesel generators. This increased their rotation speed and performance (a mystery to the technicians), even though the fuel intake was restricted. The electrical systems burst. The power cut caused the generators to explode. The security doors of the generator rooms flew off their hinges and injured the crew. The CO_2-extinguishing devices discharged their loads into areas where the ventilation had failed. The repairmen could not stay there, and attempts to start the standby generator instead failed. The oil platform sank on 22 April 2010, two days after the eruption.

'I don't want to attribute some demonic character to the sea, or claim that the deep geological layers we scratched with the drilling have a consciousness,' Malte Wiegand summarized his reflections. 'Nonetheless, I would advise a closer investigation of the context; it seems to me as if there were some writing hidden in the events. Here I am leaving aside the fact that both the curse of the Mayas on April 2010 and verse 1026 of Nostradamus' prophecy contain predictions for this region. Nor do I consider it significant that this is also the date of Hitler's birthday. But the phenomenon that massive clouds of coincidences circle the planet, leading POWER EMERGENCES that obey the connection between crime and punishment to break out of the relationship between cause and effect, is something I feel I have often observed in my explorations which are only requested after the disaster. BP considered my report inadequate and did not pay for it.'

Swarm Intelligence

During the last 700 million years of the development of life, swarm intelligence went through a process of refinement. One sees shoals of sardines in the waters off the horn of Africa. Predators break into them. The swarm closes around the predators. The swarm departs.

Birds or sea creatures find more food in such a constellation than an individual animal does. One sees helpless sharks—confused by the multitude, so to speak—hovering in front of their prey as it moves past in close formation.

At the congress in Ottawa, the Darwinist Fred Ockham presented the thesis that there are no altruistic or collective motivations in this swarm intelligence. In that sense, even taking into account the current state of research, the teachings of the old master Darwin in the area of swarm intelligence remain intact. For the highly varied behaviour of the animals (which becomes apparent as soon as more than three of them participate) follows three simple rules that can be simulated in the computer at any time and for any swarm formation: (1) KEEPING CLOSE, that is, the crowd stays together; (2) the impulse of repulsion, which means there has to be a sufficient distance from each neighbour; the principle corresponds to ELBOW FREEDOM and, according to Ockham, is the root of all ownership; (3) the FORWARD DRIVE. The bodies cannot turn around within the swarm. Human beings also follow this intelligence as soon as they join crowds to search for good fortune or flee. Fred Ockham presented impressive PowerPoint illustrations.

Now, however, one such shoal of fish had been observed heading into the oil-polluted sea in the Gulf of Mexico with the appearance of uniform behaviour, in fact following the customary three rules arrived at by evolution—and that meant death. This did not correspond to the technique of successful self-assertion which the species had developed for itself so long ago. ON THE FILM OF OIL, INSUFFICIENTLY INTERRUPTED BY SALT WATER, THE DEAD INTELLECTUALS FLOATED BELLY UP. The television networks in Florida kept showing the scene all day.

The Social Origin of Intelligence

One sees primates that have hunted cooperatively and fed over the course of the day. Now they sit close together, prepared to defend the group. The proximity creates stress. To reduce the tension, they treat one another in a friendly way. They scratch one another, pick fleas out of their fur, 'play'; they do the things that would be 'chatting' or 'conversation' among humans. The evolutionary biologist Olof Leimar, who works at the Institute for Advanced Study in Berlin, tells us that our human brain, which is four times as large as theirs, is a result of this compulsion to be sociable. The stress of proximity has to be reduced through anticipation of the other. One is mirrored in the other, and that—with all its echoes—forces the multiplication and increased connection of synapses, the NEW BRAIN.

Josef H. Reicholf augmented this information with the following observation: the original millet examined by bioarchaeologists was unsuitable for the production of bread. Our ancestors used it to make intoxicating drinks. Sedentarism and farming, which presupposed fences, gatherings and a community, were a result of DRUGS. The stimulation of the brain was the precondition for tolerance of all things: first beer, then bread. This was the historical sequence.

—Do you mean to say that intelligence is an intoxication that enables us to tolerate being close to one another?

—It's the fuel.

—There can't be any progress without it?

—Not even a human being.

—No politics without drugs?

—Politics is one of the drugs.

The Powerlessness of Politics

At the handover of intelligence officials agreed on by the USA and Russia, which took place at Vienna International Airport, I had a chance to chat with our counterparts at the airport bar. The president had integrated me, his assistant, into the handover squad to avoid any disturbances in the implementation of this agreement. As long as I was there and kept my eyes open, no one would dare to sabotage the handover. 'We would,' said my counterpart, who held the rank of lieutenant-general, 'fill up the well in the Gulf of Mexico, currently your number-one worry, through a nuclear detonation according to our maxims. We have experience in such operations. There's no chance of shovelling sand into a hole with a bulldozer at a depth of 1,500 metres. One has to set the rock layers 5,500 metres down, that means the sediments and plates, in motion to "make them dance". One puts a gravestone on a dead person's coffin to make sure they don't get up again. Here it's different: one shifts an excess pressure zone in the rock to the side by 30 kilometres as the crow flies. One can only do that by nuclear means.'

'We can't publicly follow your suggestion in a marine area that touches the coastline of the USA,' I replied. 'How are you going to explain the nuclear mushroom that'll be all over the media?'

'You've got the wrong idea,' my counterpart responded. 'You don't see any explosion. You set a rock wave in motion around 5,000 metres under the seabed. This has been a tried method since Chief Engineer Davidoff's experiments in Siberia. Even the most thorough measurement won't register the radioactive material.'

'No,' I replied, 'that's too violent for my president. The scientists wouldn't comment on it politically, I mean, not with a shared voice. Then there'd be the fantasies of people sitting in front of their TVs and imagining a nuclear explosion, even if it's not visible. Something invisible seems especially dangerous. And the president can't pretend to the public that he's speaking on the matter as an expert.'

On that day President Obama, as I heard at the embassy, had ordered by way of precaution that no American military authority should participate in closing the well. Iraq and Afghanistan were sufficiently great tasks. This contributed to the impression that the president trusted the BP engineers. As far as I know, that did not reflect his actual thoughts; he did not trust BP and its engineers any more than his own staff. In the light of the disaster, he did not trust anyone. He observed a 'powerlessness of politics'. How was he supposed to talk about that at a press conference?

Is It Risky for Obama to Follow the IDOL KENNEDY?

During President Obama's electoral campaign, one strategist raised the question of whether it was useful to base the format of the young presidential candidate on Kennedy. An argument *in favour of* this was that the idol was easily identifiable and very famous; there is no better example in US history of the dawn of a new era, a paradigm shift towards youth. An argument *against* it was Kennedy's tragic fate at the end. Did that not suggest how quickly a president who did not have the same skin colour as the majority and committed himself to reforms could be eliminated through an assassination? That might keep voters from voting for him. Either because they considered him useless if dead or because, if they liked him, they did not want to risk losing him? It was dangerous, said the strategists who presented this line of argument, to recall the lesson from experience that in history, every idol who personifies daring and new beginnings dies. They presented a list of precedents.

From this list:

—The Gracchus brothers

—Alexander the Great

—Walther Rathenau

—Henri IV of France

—Rosa Luxemburg

—Charles the Bold

—James Dean

—Albert Leo Schlageter

—Gustav II Adolf

But this was ultimately beaten out by the arguments that using Kennedy as a model would allow one to take over a degree of pre-existing public relations and emotional intensity that made any mere 'idea' (and the warning example of the assassination remained an idea, as no one wanted to hold on to the accompanying emotion for long) powerless in comparison. Expediency was what counted.

Night of Decisions

In honour of the German federal chancellor Schmidt, an after-dinner performance of an operetta by Sullivan in the rose garden of the White House had been prepared. Sitting in armchairs that had been moved to the garden area, the guests and their wives, the president, a few senators and some foundation presidents sat facing the small orchestra and the singers. The space was tight. Thanks to the midsummer twilight, the light faded very slowly. Many of the event's visitors wished there could be a clear decision between the remaining sunlight and electric light.

Outside of this tiny venue where the ruling circle was spending the evening, dramatic events were taking place at the same time.

In New York there was an electricity blackout. In the skyscrapers the lights went out by the millions. People were trapped in elevators for hours. The governor of New York State declared a state of emergency. For a while it was unclear whether the accident had been caused by an attack or a failure of   long-distance lines that had escalated into a disaster. News of this was brought by messengers across the narrow strip of turf between the orchestra and the first row of seats to the assistant sitting on the president's right, then by mouth to the latter's ear.

Only a few moments later, still before the singers had launched into what was meant to be a humorous potpourri, the president's national security advisor entered the scene with inappropriate haste, knelt down at Jimmy Carter's feet and conferred with him in this posture (Brzeziński is a tall man) about a dangerous state of affairs (the other guests only learnt the reason for the conversation and its content later on): there had been an exchange of fire with a US warship in the sea off North Korea; a Soviet ship had also been involved. The question was whether this constituted a provocation that required a military response.

In terms of possibly triggering a war, Zbigniew Brzeziński told the president, it was just as dangerous to react to fire from an insufficiently identified side as it was to show weakness and cause an escalation for that precise reason. So the result was almost the same whatever one decided, the president replied, as it was risky either way. Impossible, the federal chancellor rudely interjected after listening to them; one option was never as dangerous as the other, there was always a third way. A response was needed quickly, the security advisor exclaimed; every further word or argument was wasting time. Would it be better to make the wrong decision than to waste time? the president asked reluctantly.

The president, who was not interested in the music, still pretended in front of the guests that he was listening. In the present situation, he was unable to contribute anything in response to the urgent questions that were conveyed to him. The operetta by Sullivan from 1929, at any rate, did not contain any clues to solving political problems. For a moment, Carter weighed up whether he should get up from his chair and summon his staff to the rooms of the White House. As an interruption of the programme that would have been a dramatic step, itself a preliminary decision that a decision by the US president was imminent. Now three military men also brought the news that US citizens in Iran had been taken into custody in addition to the embassy staff who were under siege by the country's authorities. At that moment, there was daylight on the near-eastern side of the planet. Events were rushing along while America lay down to sleep.

Is there anything bothering you, Mr President? Federal Chancellor Schmidt politely asked. Nothing worth mentioning, the resident replied. But the troublemaker Brzeziński, completely in his conspiratorial element, was still hovering close to the president's ear and speaking insistently to him. For the guests, the situation was unclear. Sullivan's operetta dealt with a billionaire's daughter who could not bring herself to divorce a boy in Brooklyn whom a schemer had accused of being UNFAITHFUL to her. It was unclear, as the singer explained, whether he loved another or only her—having repeatedly promised her the latter. This remained the problem until the end of the performance.

Conflicts at the Seam

Henry Bierlich, a resident of Washington State in the very northwest of the USA, discovered that starlings from Canada were eating up the corn he fed his cattle. As well as that, they were spoiling the animal feed with their droppings. Blueberry plantations were likewise being plundered by starlings from Canada. Bierlich is therefore convinced that starlings have to be caught in traps and subsequently gassed.

It would be good, he says, if that would happen on the other side of the border, already in Canada. But the Canadians think one can keep the starlings, which have meanwhile taken on the character of masses and form flocks, away from the border to the USA with irregular cannon shots and scarecrows.

This lax attitude among people who have as much land as they like to the north is unlikely to convince US citizens who manage slimmer properties, for example, Henry Bierlich. The mere fact that Canadians are not fellow citizens but, rather, foreigners, already sets him against them. Half a million starlings were killed in the USA in 2004. How many in Canada? No one knows the number. The official figure: 28 starlings.

Seams or national borders are the zones in which different accounts, opposing attentions surge up like waves against a dam. In the course of a hundred years, these small elements accumulate into a *casus belli*. On the other hand, according to the border scholar Prof. Dr Hanslick in Stanford, it has so far been one of the seven wonders of the modern world that there have been no military conflicts between the USA and Canada in 230 years.

—What you call a 'seam' is the place in which two opposing forces collide, a separatrix?

—That's exactly it.

—But there is nothing being sewn between Canada and the USA. The border is a relatively arbitrary line, drawn on paper over 200 years ago, where two forms of civilization face each other.

—That's right. And such seams hold the danger of inattentiveness, viewed from the two headquarters that fixed the border.

—But the two headquarters in Washington DC and Ottawa no longer know anything about how the border was drawn back then.

—More's the pity. I say: No attention is paid to anything at the seam.

—The mistakes happen at the seam between two institutions?

—Exactly.

—A situation is ignited at the seam of an earlier operation?

—Certainly.

—The opponent breaks through at the seam between two powers of command?

—Always.

—The adulterer intrudes at the seam which resulted inadvertently from the creation of a love story?

—No, love is not an organization.

—Earthquakes come about at the seam between the continents and the tectonic layers?

—With or without observation of these seams.

—Why is it so typical that the diabolical seams which cause disasters and irruptions in organizations almost always go unnoticed?

—Because organizations only pay attention to the main issues.

Chancellor in the Wrong Place

None of her teachers or professional advisors would have predicted that she would one day take the salute in Moscow on the day of Germany's defeat, sitting between the Chinese president and the Russian head of state, Putin. And yet this advantaged position into which she had been forced was a misfortune at that moment. Her presence in Brussels would have been needed more, or at least in Berlin or in a Moscow hotel with a telephone and computer connection to Belgium.

The work timekeeper A. Trube would have confirmed that on this weekend (8 May was a Saturday; the crisis was recognizable by Friday 7 May, and it was expected to escalate on 10 May), every minute, hour, even group of seconds counted.

The chancellery advisor for world markets had already passed a file memo to the top on Thursday. The US president made a call for the same reason, which the chancellor answered. That was back in the days when the Bundestag agreed to the bailout for Greece. Messengers brought the bill to the federal president for signing.

What happens when the US president calls? He wants to exchange ideas about the impending crisis. His time is also very scarce. He has to make peace in the Middle East, he is deciding the future of Iraq, the measures that will be needed to compensate for removing the US troops, he is occupied with the question of how to present his position about the mosque that is to be built near the ruin from NINE ELEVEN, there are people who want to speak to him whom he can't turn away. Now he is calling the chancellor. He does not really have time for the call. He would have to speak with seven tongues; if humans were simultaneous computers, the US president's job could realistically be done adequately.

By comparison, the chancellor's attitude on the aforementioned Friday is *calm*. She answers questions. She has to fly to an election rally in North Rhine-Westphalia and reach Brussels from there. Are there translation services for phone calls between heads of state when it comes to technical terms? Would it be better for rulers to communicate via text messages instead of the telephone? This would provide time for reflection and would even be quicker, as A. Trube measured, because there would be no filler words. These are questions of work organization that governmental systems take care of at the roots of the matter.

Before leaving Moscow, the chancellor decides that the interior minister should be flown to Brussels by the Special Air Mission Wing to represent the German finance minister, who had been taken to the intensive care unit of a Brussels clinic. Until then, the secretary of state would conduct the negotiations in a delaying manner.

FIGURE 2. A. Trube, work timekeeper

Resurfacing in Reality on Monday Morning

'Mind you, the devil is old
So grow old to understand him.'

We were shocked on the morning of 10 May 2010, a Monday. Now we saw the results of the weekend. None of it can be returned to the state it was originally in when we travelled to Brussels on the evening of 7 May.

We, the responsible parties, woke up early in our hotels and rooms. Now it was a weekday again. Our departure to our respective capital cities was prepared. As if we had awoken from a bad dream, because the weekend—the absence of millions of souls working outside and the mere presence of the specialized meeting participants that we, the EU politicians, constitute— had seemed unreal to us, we warmed ourselves with the reanimated GENERAL WORKING WORLD, whose humming should always accompany our political craft. It is a fine thing that humanity is together again on Monday morning. Joined by stronger bonds than the agenda of a conference.

He Is Full of Concern

I call Jürgen Habermas the day after his birthday. He is appalled by the delay with which the European Central Bank has admitted that during the crisis from 7 to 9 April 2010, an even greater fiasco was on the horizon than the scenes that unfolded after the fall of the Lehman Brothers bank. The public should have been informed! How could the political have a chance if such facts remained concealed in the present moment while decisions on an immense scale were made by unprepared politicians partly on the telephone, partly in great haste during three meetings at the weekend? Habermas spent his birthday in Dublin. Now the family is planning to go on holiday in the South of France. He is full of concern. The thin coat of civilizatory tradition, comparable to an ice layer that becomes transparent, revealing the gruesome course of realities beneath! A philosopher will reflect from any place in the world.

The Trio of Deauville

The cooperation between Russia and NATO is, according to the work timekeeper A. Trube, one of the TOPICS OF THE

CENTURY. The relevant decisions have to be made in four weeks. Two hours are available for the prior agreements in Deauville. The small circle of three deciders—the Russian, the Frenchman and the German—the so-called trio format, is favourable for making use of every minute.

Regarding the planned deployment of the NATO missile system, which Russia resists, Sarkozy speaks of a 15-YEAR 'FIELD OF EMPLOYMENT' (10 years for setting up the missiles and 5 years for working out a tolerable practical solution with the neighbour Russia). The accelerated development of the German High Sea Fleet in 1900 took 14 years. In two years, one can expect a new US president who could be a member of the Tea Party movement. What if the relationship between the German and French heads of state and the current Russian president in 2060 is not particularly friendly, and the world powers move apart from one another? How many chancellors fit into 50 years, how many French and US presidents? The burden of possible consequences lay like lead on the minutes in which the three negotiators took their walk across the wooden planks of the sea promenade. Today a thousand-year wind from the English Channel, which had whistled from west to east on this coast constantly since Roman times, and was only a little gentler for a few days in summer, was grim and stormy.

China's confidant in Paris (many observers in the inner circle of delegations in Deauville have to report to him) gained an idea of the final result of the preparations on the previous day. He reports to his headquarters in Peking that to support the euro, states that violate the guidelines will be forced by automatic penalties to exercise budgetary discipline; regarding

Russia, there will be no prior agreements for the NATO conference on account of US resistance. There will, on the other hand,
be a probable consensus on questions relating to the use of the
Norwegian Sea. Both the chancellor and Sarkozy will advise
the Russian president not to visit the Southern Kuril Islands as
intended, as this would unnecessarily anger Japan. Next day, the
top spy had to revise all this. Some topics had not been raised
at all, and the formulations in the final record were not in line
with the previous day's information.

Deauville, said a high-ranking German diplomat, had gone
right past the Foreign Ministry. It was much the same for his
French colleagues at the Quai d'Orsay, he continued. In the Paris
ministries, up to 8,000 employees prepare a summit. The plans
are sent to the Elysée Palace, where roughly 20 staff members
start from scratch. They rewrite the plan. All that reaches the
president himself is what Jean-David Levitte, Claude Guéant
and Xavier Musca present to him (or what he hears if he
encounters an advisor in the hallway and questions them). In
Deauville, what the president makes of it depends on the
moment. The structures seems chaotic, the diplomat com-
mented, but the French line is 'always especially well prepared'
at every summit.

We diplomats have a hard time with the Chancellery! We
had developed the negotiating plan in a balanced manner. The
bulk of the documents had been fine-tuned. Then there was a
telephone call between the bosses the chancellor listens to—
Heusgen (Foreign Ministry), Corsepius (EU), Weidmann (economic affairs), Asmussen (finances)—and their counterparts at
the Elysée. Our plans were unrecognizable. There is no way to

prevent the top group from talking to pieces what we had prepared. The trio line-up of Deauville was new, but the procedures used are old: billiards with 23 balls.

The public does not see our work, the diplomat continued. How much negotiating time do you think we need to coordinate a breakfast or a lobster dinner at the beach with three protocol departments and security services, all with diverging mentalities? You can see (in the picture below) that the Russian president's suit is under tension because the button is placed too high. And his trouser creases are too heavily ironed. We pointed this out to the other side in a diplomatic form, but the politeness of the formulation prevented the advice from being understood and acted on. The plan to trim the agenda down from seven items to three was discarded by superiors. What's the point of all our conversations? What are we paid so much for?

FIGURE 3. The heads of state are set up for the group photo. There is a helper on the far left.

Fishing with Hand Grenades

Like many West German officials, Executive Undersecretary Wilfried F., a high-ranking member of Wolfgang Clement's staff during the time when the latter, as minister for economic affairs in North Rhine-Westphalia (NRW), was waiting urgently to become Governor Rau's successor, switched in 1991 to the TREUHAND which had moved into the offices of the former Reich Ministry of Aviation. He sat at Borchardt's very often. Buried in work, he spent sleepless nights. Investors antechambered in the house, the country's prosecuting natives—each one an unmistakable individual, yet sometimes hard to pinpoint in their exact position between REALITY and FICTION.

In a political phase which no one was prepared for in the East or the West, said the enterprising official, one had to rely on a focus and on dynamism. That's why we were imported from NRW—as a YOUNG SCHOOL, so to speak. We followed a rule from freshwater fishing: one throws a hand grenade in the water, and the fish come floating to the top, belly up—one can collect them. Later, fried in butter, no one can see how they were caught.

You can wait a long time for success with a fishing rod, bait and patience, continued the energized employee, who enjoyed presenting his way of working. Wilfried F. was responsible for the industrial combine Magdeburg which produced marine engines for deep-sea freighters. I saw at once, said the official, that the human and mechanical material gathered in Magdeburg wouldn't have a chance on the Western market. He was proved right after reluctantly (and to avoid even greater delays) 'accompanying' the sentimental rescue attempts. They could only cover up the fiasco, which was certain with the first balance based on the exchange rate of 1:2 Deutschmark to East German Mark when converting the combine's debts with the former head-quarters, now its legal successor, the FEDERAL GOVERN-MENT. He felt like an advocate of actual conditions faced with the sluggishness of heart that clings to people who are thrown from one life story into another. Being THROWN like that makes people slow, said Wilfried F. He saw that, but certainly did not condone it, as it was not RATIONAL. He was considered incorruptible. He did not favour any party. Rather, he considered himself responsible for the IMPLEMENTATION OF EVERY-THING, for the REALISTIC WITH NO IFS OR BUTS.

The Minister Behaves in an Uncontrolled Fashion

Twilight falls over the cities of the Ruhr region. Cloud masses from the northwest, the city lights more radiant, the bushes and gardens more wan. The executive committee of the NRW Social Democrat Party convenes in air-conditioned rooms, abstract in relation to the dusk. The minister for economic affairs, medium-sized businesses and technology leaves the room, evidently agi-tated. His assistant follows him. Friends hesitate. They follow the powerful man down the hallways. The meeting is presided over by governor and party chairman Rau. He continues the negotiations. The minister's walkout is an affront to him; his irate colleague will have to return and give a reason for his behaviour. He will have to apologize. It is the hours of such conferences that are missing at the end of one's life. 'Age ain't nothing but a number.'

Time is running out for the governor. But he has made a provisional gain in this time: he cannot yield to a minister who makes demands so brusquely. In that sense he has gained time.

Outside, the minister's friends surround him.

—Come back inside, Wolfgang.

   —I'm sick of it.

   —Sick of it, of what?

There are no two factions, says the minister, there's no factional dispute among NRW's Social Democrats. The one side committed to the people and their surroundings, and the other side serving the big businesses: that's precisely what there isn't. Naturally, the job of the minister for economic affairs is to promote RHINE CAPITALISM. It's beside the point if the minister for schools has her fears that the minister for economic affairs is not doing this with 'the restraint appropriate for a Social Democrat'.

The minister has 'hardened' facial features. One can't imagine him growing portly in old age and getting round cheeks. His gaze is uncertain. He cannot bear to be unpopular.

The crowd of friends pushes him imperceptibly towards the negotiation room, forcing back journalists who want to question the minister. The minister goes back inside, the comrades there knock on their tables. I had to go outside for a moment, says the minister. Now you're coming back inside, everyone has to go outside sometimes, says the governor. He is the older seafarer; he has the better nerves.

—What was up with Wolfgang?

—He's emotional.

—But there was hardly any reason. We were just talking about the 'two factions'.

—It tears him apart inside. He bottles too much up. It's bursting out of him.

—Well, it's obvious that he's displeasing the Green Party. He's a servant to businesses. How is he a social democrat?

—You see, that's the accusation that's preoccupying him.

—But you can see the magpie in his eyes as soon as a CEO or a globalist, preferably from overseas, approaches. It's like a drug.

—He doesn't want to hear that.

—And then he loses his self-control and runs away, and shouts: I'm sick of it.

—Yes, sick of it. That can mean anything, and the chairman knows what he means.

—But he pretends he's not hearing anything.

—What else is he supposed to do?

The Instinct of the Politician

The bar stools were upholstered with mauve leather, and a designer had managed to give the bottles, which were placed among the wooden panels like books, sparks flying deep inside the liquid. The assistants had already waited two and a half hours for their masters.

—I've never really noticed that.

—Noticed what?

—An instinctive reaction from a politician.

—Oh, come on! If someone shoots, they duck.

—I wasn't there that time.

—Maybe you're taking the word 'instinct' too literally? One also speaks of 'FULL-BLOODED' or 'THOROUGHBRED POLITICIANS', even though it has nothing to do with being descended from an Arabian horse. To me, at least, it's unlikely that a politician's blood should have a higher quantity or a different quality, and that this distinguishes them as a politician. Pure blood makes you ill.

—I mean instinct in the sense of having quick reactions. And that would be very much be a civilized quality.

—*Formerly* quick reactions?

—There's no such instinct in nature. No human living in the wild is inherently political.

—And animals?

—Never. One could only see politics in nature after the fact.

—So what makes up that quality I sense in a politician of real calibre as soon as they walk through the door, which I called 'political instinct' before?

—It's a mixture. By itself, each element would be politically disastrous. Everything together makes the man fast and unerring. It wouldn't be suitable for harvest work or jungle warfare.

The two assistants enthused. The majority of scenes they saw in their mind's eye corresponded to an observation that was hard to sum up in a single word. The descriptions 'adapted', 'experienced', 'hard-working' and 'unerring' were all too narrow. The homogenized sphere of the political has no designations of its own for its virtues, presumably due to lack of time.

What Does It Mean to Judge by Eye?

The human eye reacts most nervously to an unexpected sideways movement. The fastest measurement is made in the corner of the eye. The clearest can be expected at the centre of the view. Essentially, the ophthalmologist Konrad Winkler reports, the view is then the 'measure of all things' when the hands are dealing with an object roughly at diaphragm height—a clockwork, for example—and the eyes control this movement.

But the eyes, Winkler states, are extremely easy to deceive on account of their greed; they are also easily impressed by terror. They become blind at important turning points of fate. 'I would not recommend the eye as the organ of balance,' Winkler said, 'the seat of measurement, but, rather, the ear. Yet no one speaks of judging BY EAR.' He considered the lips a fairly reliable and well-balanced sensory source; nothing that the body and spirit consider poison enters by them. Nothing that belongs to the secrecy of the heart leaves through them, for example, the 'enduring measure'.

The eye is also forgetful, he states. It is not an organ for durations.

A Lover of Hard Boards

Accompanied by 16 people, who would also have fended off an attacker if necessary, Thilo Sarrazin made his way through the crowd which was amazed to find the celebrity so close. He was coming from the television programme *das blaue sofa* [The Blue Sofa] and pushed his way through the halls of the book fair. 'I'm the cleaner fish,' said the reporter from the *Frankfurter Allgemeine Zeitung*, who had been accompanying him all day. Why cleaner fish? 'We want to report in full,' said the *FAZ* journalist. 'Cleaner fish are polite animals,' I replied. 'They are known for treating their customers differently in the coral reefs, where they clean the parasites of larger fish. They are considered intelligent.' 'I just snapped up the phrase "cleaner fish",' said the reporter, 'because it sounds vivid. I wanted to explain that I was accompanying the gentleman throughout the day.' We got into conversation. How would Jürgen Habermas characterize Sarrazin? After the historian Hans-Ulrich Wehler had given a new twist to the debate about the highest-selling book, Sarrazin's *Deutschland schafft sich ab* [Germany Does Away the Itself]. 'You think Wehler and Habermas have been on the same level since the historians' dispute?' 'I think Habermas would term Sarrazin a DECISIONIST. Sounds negative. But it means "lover of decisions". One could say that about every paragraph in the book, but also about many episodes in Sarrazin's career.

'There is always something to be decided. If someone has an appetite for it, it can become a drug.'

'Do you think that Sarrazin can be excluded from the party? And that the chancellor will continue to distance herself?' 'We don't know any of that,' I replied. But I knew that this highly controversial man had held decisive positions in the country for a long time, and shown a similar determination and tone. He had never shied away from drilling through hard boards. Unlike surgeons, who apply their scalpels themselves and are only handed them by their assistants and nurses, great politicians require 'masters of the instruments' at their side, that is to say, artists in decision-making who not only pass on these instruments but also use them autonomously. Like two police officers, one of whom speaks in a friendly manner to a delinquent and the other threatens him, drilling through hard boards in politics is carried out by ONE person who presides over it like an 'unbiased observer' and a SECOND who applies the drill. If one doesn't want to tolerate such a character, one must attack them and exclude them from the party or the office while they are still occupying the key positions, not when they write a book about it. 'You think Sarrazin has always been the way he comes across in his book?' 'How does he come across in this book?' 'Have you read it?' 'I intend to,' replied the head of the Institute of Social Research at the Johann Wolfgang Goethe University. 'Our institute will be reopening in January of next year. You are invited to come,' he added.

I had the opportunity to ask Thilo Sarrazin some questions.

—What was your position?

—Undersecretary.

—And until '89–90 you were responsible for inter-German relations.

—No, first I had the Department of National Monetary Affairs. I had already studied money and credit as an elective course at university, and was also a delegate of the Ministry of Finance at the International Monetary Fund for nine months in 1977.

—A proper delegate, in America?

—Yes, sure. Through my activities at the minister's office I was always dealing with international monetary questions, for the minister too.

—What languages do you speak?

—Quite decent English, or if I practise, very good English, and thoroughly poor French. And then there was Horst Köhler, who followed me as director of the minister's office. He headed Minister Stoltenberg's office, that's how we knew each other. He then became head of my department, and switched to head of the monetary department. I joined him in the summer of 1989, taking over National Monetary Affairs. That was before the Wall was opened. I wanted to have a go at something different.

—Then you were in the right place at the right time.

—Yes. We dealt with the topic of the European Monetary Union and the report by Jacques Delors, and right in the middle of the time in which I was adjusting, the Wall came down. And it soon turned out that hardly anyone in the Ministry of Finance had clear ideas about what that meant for us and how we should deal with this situation. At that time, Köhler was becoming a closer advisor to Federal Chancellor Kohl. He then became secretary of state and relied heavily on my services. As I had a close connection to inter-German matters on account of my family history, and discovered that I was also in a place where I had strategic leverage, I then developed the conception for an inter-German monetary union in just a few weeks. (Finance Minister) Waigel and Köhler then made it their own and presented it to Kohl. Thus my conception was the basis of the offer to the GDR to form a monetary union—naturally, I was in the eye of the storm there, although I was in the wrong party. But it was simply a great time. Now I'm grateful to Köhler and Waigel for trusting me.

—This was the decision about the 1:2 rule? One Deutschmark to two East German Mark issued by the German Central Bank East?

—Yes, I supervised the inter-German monetary union intensively, I was in charge of it. A new sub-department was set up for that purpose, the Work Group for Inter-German Relations, and I directed that. When German reunification was complete, I was responsible at the Ministry of Finance for the legal and functional supervision of the Treuhand privatization agency, which devolved upon us. And then I set up the legal and functional supervision of the Treuhand agency by May 1991.

—Did you do that from Berlin?

—From Berlin. All significant events had to be approved by us.

—How many people would that be, apart from you, who were involved in this complicated question of the monetary union?

—Back then in the first phase it was my humble self, my head of department Haller, who passed away recently, the later secretary of state (at the Federal President's Office).

—Which is probably why the federal president left.

—Yes, exactly, he was a close confidant. And Minister Waigel. And it was the four of us—I didn't involve anyone at all from the ministry, that was much too dangerous.

—Who was your counterpart? On the other side?

—At first there was no counterpart; it had to be decided politically. Then the counterpart who turned up at the Federal Chancellery was Johannes Ludewig, with whom I worked, who was a close advisor to the chancellor.

—One could say that at the Federal Chancellery, the functions of the ministries are repeated as inside a brain?

—But he was a personal confidant of Kohl at the same time. Mr Ludewig and Köhler were now old friends. So I became part of that, if you will, and then there was the first contacts with the Bundesbank which was insulted that such important decisions had been made without their involvement.

—And then he resigned.

—Yes, but only many years later.

—What was his name?

—Karl Otto Pöhl. Then we had a joint expert committee with the GDR, headed on our side by Secretary of State Horst Köhler. I was there, the Bundesbank was there. Tietmeyer was appointed as the chancellor's personal representative. Köhler was more involved in European monetary affairs, and I accompanied Tietmeyer in this way until the contract was finalized.

—One sometimes speaks of bifurcation, that is, when there's a crossroads and the development goes one way or the other. Where there any discussions about choosing exchange rates like 1:6 or 1:8, say, rather than 1:2?

—There were discussions about the exchange rate. I believed from the start, and that was how it ultimately turned out, that current payments, prices, rents and wages could only be exchanged at a rate of 1:1. The money reserves and debts would then be exchanged at a rate of 1:2. There were long discussions about it. Weeks of decisions. I don't know if there were two ways or 50 ways in the end. I simply realized that we would either bring about German unity now or never.

—That's how Kohl put it too.

—That was my position in all aspects. And in that context I viewed the economy as an instrument, not a goal. It was a pure toolbox that I used here, and that was how I advised the others. The political always came first.

—One later learnt that the debt levels of the businesses which needed repairing, but might still have had a chance, drove them into bankruptcy through the enormous debts with the central government, which were astronomical because of the 1:2 rate.

—In my draft, I had drafted a 14-page paper before the offer which proposed cancelling all internal GDR debts, because I said that the substance was worthless and the debts were just . . .

— . . . ordinary debts . . .

— . . . I would have cancelled them all. But I couldn't win out over the Bundesbank.

—The Bundesbank said one shouldn't do it?

—Well, the Bundesbank was mortally offended that it wasn't present when the offer was worked out. To pacify the

Bundesbank and keep them on board, Köhler then said—after the offer had been submitted and the political decision made that would now coordinate things with the Bundesbank as far as possible.

—The legal supervision, that's a demanding task.

—The legal supervision is formal, the functional supervision was the main thing. Then I said which criteria would be applied to streamline businesses, to sales, where we set the limits for approval, what state directives the governance of this authority followed.

—You were able to do that?

—All of the rules followed by the Treuhand agency came into existence at my desk. I began with a staff of three, and in a few weeks I had built a team of 70 people. I conceived the entire structure of the functional supervision during those weeks.

—You find one industry in each centre of a GDR district administration. In Erfurt there are cars, in Leipzig you have a different focus. In Brandenburg you have the steel works. In the later Mecklenburg you have the dockyards, in Magdeburg the ship propellers.

—SKET. *Schwermaschinen-Kombinat 'Ernst Thälmann'.*

—Exactly.

—The publicly owned companies were changed into corporations or limited companies, already during GDR days. But they had no functioning industry. They had no functioning pricing, they had no functioning cost calculation. A lot of things were lacking, and they had too many employees on board. And my nightmare—I had experienced it during the many years I had inspected the Federal Railway—was a business with 270,000 employees costing the federal budget 13.5 million Deutschmark per year. Now we had 3.5 million employees in businesses run by the Treuhand agency, and my nightmare was that if we didn't downsize, sell or liquidate them rapidly, the West German state would go broke.

'One would,' explained Dr Widukind Hildebrand, former assistant of Karl Otto Pöhl, 'have had to halve or completely cancel the value added tax for the East German states, just as Count Lambsdorff suggested: freeze the wages, put a price freeze on food, rents and medical care, and then streamline the GDR through the EU in Brussels (with reference to the railway and telephone networks). Then the industrial substance might have been preserved.'

'Would such radical decisions have been sustainable?' I asked him. 'For example, in relation to the West German trade unions, the media or the populace's urge to have the Deutschmark, which was very general and not tied to any sacrificial devotion? Perhaps a second Switzerland would then have resulted?' 'All I am saying,' replied Dr Hildebrand, 'is under what circumstances the industrial substance of the Eastern states could have been preserved.' 'Do you hold Sarrazin, that is, the WILD FOUR in the Ministry of Finance, responsible for the DEINDUSTRIALIZATION of the East German states?' I probed further. 'I only blame him for one detail,' Hildebrand responded, 'namely, that he didn't push through his correct idea to cancel the businesses' ordinary debts to the central government. Sarrazin was not *decisive* enough on that point.'

'Shouldn't one be *against* deciders?' I insisted. 'Habermas warns fundamentally of DECISIONISM. It is not in line with the "spirit of participation", it is not very republican.' 'That's not my accusation,' Dr Hildebrand replied. 'On the contrary: his decisions were not decisive enough. If I am a driller of hard boards, I have to be godlike. Mistakes are only forgiven if there is participation on all sides!'

The Return of the Wolves as a Political Problem in Valais

Two wolves reached Switzerland by crossing the eastern border. Wolves were exterminated once in Switzerland 100 years ago. In subsequent years, animal farming saw a major increase. After the elimination of the highest predator in the food chain, the wild animals become less disciplined, writes Kurt Eichenberger of the biodiversity group at the WWF Switzerland. They then become estranged from their species and cease to be shy.

There was a sensational photo in the press showing the remains of a sheep that had been killed by a wolf. Eichenberger, on the other hand, collected numerous pictures of fallen animals, creatures cruelly executed by the circumstances of nature—fallen into chasms, suffering for days between the rocks. Every year, writes Eichenberger, 10,000 sheep fall victim to accidents. In contrast, up to 300 farm animals are killed by wolves over a period of several years. The wolves are not the problem; what is far worse is that numerous sheep in the mountains are not shepherded.

The Swiss government, Eichenberger continues, spends 43 million francs on sheep farming in the whole country, but only

830,000 to protect the herds. Funds have to be made available to enable a coexistence of wolves and animal farming.

Instead, Swiss politics is trying to use the media-compatible topic of danger from wolves for its own ends. In the National Council in Bern, agenda items are being developed to loosen the protection of the rare lupines and facilitate shooting them in future!

For the wolf to have a future here, Eichenberger writes, three things are necessary: new regulations for animal farming, not 250,000 sheep in the mountains but half as many; a proper expansion of herd-protection measures, which, above all, means better training for shepherds in wolf areas, equipping them with instructions for herd protection and providing further training courses; and finally, as in France, 'far-sighted planning'. With the words 'far-sighted' and 'planning', Eichenberger means observing the interaction of the animals among themselves and human interventions. Eichenberger demands a ROUND TABLE on the subject of wolves.

Incessant Killers Are a Rarity

'I know of no predators, except for martens and stoats, that "surplus kill", that is to say, kill their prey without being hungry. The incessant killers constitute a rarity.

'That means they are a phenomenon,' the animal tamer from the Moscow Circus continued, 'that would surprise the circus audience. Though it is terrible to watch the killing.'

—They are probably too small as well. They would already be almost invisible from the boxes on the edge of the ring, not least because of the speed of their actions.

—What one sees is the blood. The whirl of feathers, if it's birds they're killing. Or the hopelessly fleeing, likewise small prey.

—Do these killers also take on larger animals?

—Foxes. But duels would still not be enough of an event for an effective circus performance.

—You doubt their entertainment value?

—One sees a rapidly unfolding chaos. One doesn't see anything exact. And it's also very gruesome.

—One couldn't train them?

—Training killers is impossible.

'Exercises with well-fed tigers, on the other hand, are always interesting. Even when their stomachs are full, the powerful bodies show high levels of elegance,' says the trainer. 'They are not only prepared to jump through hoops of fire, but even—this is a special success of our training—to let themselves fall into a transparent basin and then shake the water out of their fur. After that they do the "group". There is nothing more good-natured than tigers that have got rid of their hunger.

'Traditional performance: a group of wolves chases a group of riders. Or even better: the wolves chase a carriage with a woman and children. The precondition is that the wolves are sated and the alpha female has been separated from them.'

—Are wolves good-natured?

—When they're sated.

'A Man Is a Wolf to Another Man'

In his book *Leviathan*, Thomas Hobbes starts from the assumption that human societies necessarily require a sovereign who prevents them from attacking one another in civil wars. On the page opposite the book title there is a figure representing the ruler. Inside the royal body are countless human beings—they fill up the body. Only the monarch's head is reserved for himself. Hobbes had experiences of the English civil wars in mind when he developed his sceptical thesis: *Homo homini lupus*.

Two friends in Scotland, Adam Smith and David Hume, objected to Hobbes' analysis roughly 100 years later. Why, they asked, had wolves been taken as an example of creatures that are dangerous to their own kind? Wolves are pack animals and thus willing to tolerate and cooperate with one another, even without a constitution. This contradicted the claim that a wolf kills another wolf.

In addition, a human—as a *zoon politikon*—could be cruel, dangerous, a hunter, but hardly possessed of the abilities of a wolf. At the same time, humans were capable of more concentrated aggression than wolves, as the (metaphorically speaking) 'predator man' even hunts when it is not currently hungry. One had seen aged landlords who could not possibly live long enough to consume the harvest of their estates, yet were still greedy to amass property. So humans were undoubtedly worse than wolves. But the following observation revealed a difference:

there were two striking human characteristics that opposed one another, but always found a way to come together. The one was OBJECTIVITY (attitude of the impartial spectator), and the second empathy (involvement). Neither of these qualities had been observed in wolves. But these, according to Adam Smith, gives every human society a natural constitution. They ensure the end of civil wars, prevent them from dragging on interminably. A sovereign, by contrast, would be useless for this purpose because, in order to tame the cruelty resulting from such qualities, he would have to be crueller than his subjects.

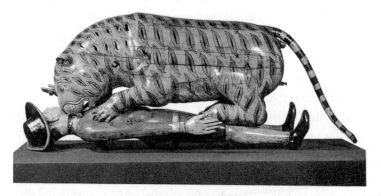

FIGURE 4. Tiger overpowering British mercenary from the East India Company. Porcelain figure made for the maharaja of Jaipur.

Temporal Forms of Afghanistan

Afghanistan is an unusual structure; even I had first of all to learn what it actually was, said the security expert Egon Bahr, who had already occupied himself with Afghanistan over Christmas 1979.

Geologically, this 'roof of the world' (the description competes with the Tibetan Plateau) is a slow event. I have been told that, in this zone, the great Pamir to the northwest, the Hindu Kush to the east and the Baluchistan plate, beneath the sediments of the Indian Ocean, drift towards one another: a slow-motion earthquake with a duration of 10,000 years.

I often mention that when field officers ask me to describe the nervous opposition between political powers in Kyrgyzstan, Kashmir, northwest Pakistan and Afghanistan—the political time lapse, as it were. Here it is a matter of months and days.

At the same time the mining minister in Kabul, a confidant of Karzai, badgering me: mineral resources have been found underground—namely, copper, cobalt, iron ores and probably gold. If there were not a war in progress on the surface of the country, one could extract these resources. I like to point this out in my conversations with clan chieftains on the northwestern Pakistani border. Here there is an objective possibility for the country to live off mineral exports rather than opium. It is unbelievably long ago that Berliners were singing the hit song: 'Afghanistan, Afghanistan, das geht Dich Aff' gar nichts an!'[2] That was on the occasion of King Amanullah's visit to the German Reich president. A photo of Erich Salomon went around the world. One could see an illuminated window in Hindenburg's official residence, and behind it—the caption stated—he was hosting the king.

FIGURE 5. Massoud checks a weapon.

FIGURE 6. Afghan anti-Taliban troops in 2002. What became of them?

FIGURE 7. South of Marib, Afghanistan. 'The Valley of Kidnappers'.

Some time after that, the statement of the Bavarian governor Franz Josef Strauss about the Kabul–Nairobi–Cape Town crisis belt. At the time we quipped, Egon Bahr continued, that one only needed to phone a travel agent to establish that there were no direct rail, naval or flight connections between the three places—in fact, no conceivable contacts. We knew the latter from our secret services. It was during the time when apartheid was still in force in South Africa and South Rhodesia was still subject to the dictatorship of the fighter pilot Smith. As far away from us as the Stone Age. What made Franz Josef Strauss mention Kabul?

When the Russians invaded, said Bahr, which was a dangerous moment because Marshall Tito's thigh was also amputated around the same time, so there was a risk that Yugoslavia would be destabilized, we only had a single advisor at the Foreign Ministry who was responsible for Afghanistan. At the security conference in Munich, which Egon Bahr took part in, the focus was the question of how many years it would take after the presumed withdrawal of US combat troops for the country to be consolidated. What does consolidation mean? came the counter-question. At any rate, said Bahr, this is a temporal form that cannot be compared to the course of an individual person's life. The prudent security politician, indispensable in his wealth of experience, was 88 years old at the time. He moved quickly.

The Destructive Character Is Young and Cheerful

'What does the "destructive character" you mention consist in?' The question was directed at a lawyer from New York who was representing the office of the inspector general at the Pentagon here, to the US troops in Afghanistan.

—It's a novelty that's harder and harder to explain psychologically. A new type of human being. The development of human aggression depends on an other, an object. But there are people capable of turning this aggression against themselves; this not only torments them, it also leads to the development of a 'second' aggression that can be used 'aspecifically', the way one pulls a banknote out of one's wallet, at any time and with a cool head, anywhere in the world. One could call it 'stackable aggression'.

—Which goes against their nature as such?

—It's not a feature of biological nature.

—Could one say that it's a kind of 'defect'? Viennese psychoanalysts around 1912 would have made countless appointments to treat a patient like that, yet doubted every possibility of recovery. Is this novelty a modern characteristic?

—It's not as if a new character were emerging: our choice of leaders simply results in a higher frequency of this character at switching points.

—You say these young people enjoy their own aggressiveness because they can act it out in a field where they are not afraid?

—They've banished their fears and teach others the meaning of fear.

—Young people enjoy being employed abstractly?

—That's exactly it.

—Are they cruel?

—If need be.

—Because they have experienced within themselves how to end the inner civil war?

—How should I know what goes on inside them!

—Do they multiply naturally?

—Only through our selection.

—And why is cheerfulness, as you say, a hallmark of this character type?

—He is relaxed. We have always misjudged the violent type. In the past I would have described him as thin-lipped, used to sitting at a desk, as 'tight-hearted'.

—Completely wrong?

—He's a content young man. He has 'arrived beyond himself', as it were, active on an emotional colonial territory, an ADVENTURER IN HIS OWN SELF. Why should he have thin lips? He has left the days of self-torment behind, he has escaped.

—He has escaped from himself?

—From himself, the way he was.

—And lives in the future?

—Not the future either: he is indifferent to time and place. He is capable at every moment.

—Escaped from the prison of his soul?

—He has become a pure body.

—Are there any known side effects?

—We don't have enough experience of the new character type yet.

—If he now remembers his childhood, the events that produced his character, does he break down?

—No. The system he belongs to (the network of colleagues)
holds on to him.

—And if he encounters a person with normal aggression?

—Something bad will happen.

—To the one who encounters the 'new person'?

—Almost always.

Those who were pulling the strings here, 10 time zones away
from the headquarters in Tampa, were young. They needed
cheerfulness to survive in the infernal heat. What was even worse
was that they realized the HOPELESSNESS OF THEIR
ACTIONS and had to endure that. They operated in an environment of 'frozen conflicts', as they put it. If one touches such a
conflict (it might look like a crowd, a residential area), it
unleashes unpredictable forces. That could only be mastered with
youthful elan and cheerfulness. It had a destructive character.

The battlefield of Afghanistan was an example of the 'new
obscurity' (Habermas). The troops' assignment had changed
several times (removing Al-Qaeda hiding-places, driving away
the Taliban because of their fundamentalism, stymieing opium
production, NATION-BUILDING, adopting the method of liberation developed in Iraq, isolating centres of resistance around
Helmand, pacifications in the border region between the northwestern Pakistani border and Afghanistan). First the strike
brigades had been developed for these deployments; now it

turned out, according to the man from the inspector general's office, that a new type of human was needed, and not only for an improved mode of military organization.

In the Belly of Future Monsters

I have neither blue eyes nor red hair. My skin is yellowish, not pink. I also lack freckles. But I do have Irish ancestors. My genetic make-up is mixed, with Norwegian, Italian and Galician forefathers. An examination of my DNA and a comparison with that found in Ireland in the bones of the prehistoric King Niall, however, recently showed that I am related to that royal family through a single ancestor. I am proud of that. Like a good house-keeper of a country estate, I intend to pass on my hereditary qualities to generations of my particular kind. Such lasting survival, however, demands (as was once a condition of loyalty to a successful tribal chieftain) that, of the surroundings one serves, one chooses the one with the highest possible chance of survival. It would be entirely wrong to treat racial distinction as a way of guaranteeing the clan's survival.

Rather, we cling as loyal followers to those institutions which somehow promise to have an eternal life. In the past that meant Chicago's fire department and police force. Today it is multinationally consolidated businesses like the firm N. Inc., which I serve as a factory security officer.

I risk my life to guard the security of my firm, which in turn ensures that my children and children's children, who will naturally offer their services to the firm N. Inc., will pass on their genes to the future 'in the shadow of ever-young industry in flower'). Now I am not only a security professional (which takes up my nights) but also a lecturer in sociology at a community college.

—When do you sleep?

    —The times are too precious to sleep.

    —Seriously. A human being has to sleep a certain number of hours. One dies without sleep.

    —With the necessary training, three hours of sleep are enough.

    —You take those in the daytime?

    —On the threshold between day and night.

My speciality is *Leviathan*. What does that mean? It is a book in which the author describes the composition of power. Power is a floating animal that has humanity living on its back. Thus parcels of land and a few towns and villages turn into a world power like the USA as soon as they are augmented by railway routes, mail-order companies and a constitution. In Europe, similarly, country estates and their expansion gave rise to the territorial states.

—Cruel structures, some of them. They wage war. Their only means of communication is the narrow corridor of international law, which they don't follow.

    —And today they are losing this authority they once had.

According to the vision of this sociologist and gene carrier, a new kind of power formed, more plainly than in the formation of the state, around the transnational companies (and their factory-security departments).

—Stronger than the People's Republic of China?
　　—This isn't a republic.
　　—A super-state?
　　—We need some other term for it than 'state'. It's privately organized, but penetrates all general areas of humans and objects. In that sense, it's a 'new public sphere'.
　　—With no constitution?
　　—With a works constitution.
　　—Which applies everywhere and nowhere.
　　—After the first major crises there is sure to be a constitution.
　　—With human rights?
　　—Or maybe just with an objective orientation.

The Irish gene carrier did not view such a future negatively. It is inappropriate, in fact, to speak of an erroneous development if one is an occupant of that development. From what perspective do you want to call it a 'mistake' or 'error' when humans lose rights while Leviathan takes them effectively through the dangerous waters on his back?

—One can't err in the belly of the whale?
　　—Whether someone errs or not doesn't initially matter if they're in the belly of the whale.

—And you hope that you'll be able to preserve the scanty DNA samples you share with the High King of the Irish especially well by being loyal to these future institutions, which resemble neither the Roman Empire nor the USA?

—It's worth it.

—The genes guide your respect in that direction?

—I feel that clearly.

—What will be at the head of these new, powerful entities? A president? An advisory board?

—Maybe a device.

—The same way the highest representative of the largest world business has to subject himself to an annual examination by electrocardiogram?

—Substantially more complex.

—An oracle?

—More or less.

The Politics of Teeth

In the Cambrian Revolution, bones developed—and, fixed in mouths, the teeth, so that creatures could feed off other life forms, privileged attackers, predators. Since then, offensive and defensive weapons have confronted one another.

Spectral and Actual Economy

Marx, who died in 1883, still lived to see the rise of 'scientific social policy' at German universities. It was the response to the GREAT DEPRESSION which lasted until the 1890s. Marx was busy editing his writings, as well as organizationally involved through meetings and writing calls for the First International. He was no longer a freelance researcher as he had once been in Paris.

But he followed events on the markets. In the wake of the upswing in Germany, a real-estate bubble had formed on the Viennese equities market in 1873. The Vienna Stock Exchange was seized by panic after the insolvency of a Budapest bank. Even good papers lost 90 per cent of their value within a few days (the nobility lost their cash assets).

What made an even greater impression on Marx than the Viennese fiasco was the collapse of the New York bank Jay Cooke & Co. On 18 September 1873. When it helped the government to finance the war against the South in 1865, it had used up its reserves. It was involved in speculation on the Northern Pacific Railway. To keep a stock-market launch attractive, the costs—as with almost all large-scale projects—were calculated too low. Now they exploded. Prices exploded. The New York Stock Exchange was closed. In Berlin the collapse began when the Quistorp'sche Vereinsbank declared bankruptcy. Of 900 new corporations founded after 1870, 700 were insolvent by 1873.

—Why didn't Marx write about that?

　　—He observed it.

　　—He could have had some publishing success by explaining the crash in his usual perceptive way.

　　—He didn't see the boom beforehand or the depression afterwards as real things. Those are the DREAMS OF THE ECONOMY, he said, I'm not an interpreter of dreams.

—What really interested him?

—Production. That's 'the overarching'.

The man speaking so confidently (and faithfully to the master), Henning Tacke, lived in Magdeburg: no college or university wanted the comrade any more. In a room connected to a kitchen, he sat between books like Marx and wrote. Only in 1989, however, he had bought previously unknown manuscripts by Marx for the party at an auction in London. His essay MARX AND THE GREAT DEPRESSION OF 1873, which was based on this source, had been translated into English and printed in Canada.

—Did Marx write anything about the railway projects leading all the way to the Pacific?

    —Well, that was the subject of the London manuscripts.

    —Which are now the property of the German state?

    —They wish!

    —You've appropriated and hidden them?

    —Secured.

    —And does Marx view the construction of railways in the USA as PRODUCTION or DISTRIBUTION, considering that their construction was more of a pretext for stock-market transactions?

    —You've got that all wrong. For him, production isn't about the rails or building locomotives, it's about the change that takes place in the essential powers of humans, in their heads, as soon as the track sections from the east and the west collide.

—He didn't think those were dreams?

—No, that's production. The stock market didn't really interest him.

—Even though he could analyse and, indeed, mock its movements like almost no other?

—He felt his time was too precious to write about it.

The Auditor General of the People's Republic of China

Liu Jiayi, PhD, member of the People's Congress, felt that he was 'sitting on mountains of numbers that were moving about underneath' him. 'You can only understand me,' he continued, 'if you've experienced an earthquake, and you've felt the earth losing its stability under the very soles of your feet.' 'Or like swampy ground?' 'Like no ground under your feet at all,' answered the high-ranking functionary.

'It's an inappropriate image anyway,' replied the visitor, likewise a high-ranking comrade, 'someone who is responsible for checking accounts "standing" anywhere. After all, he can't set foot on the valuable commodity he administers: the genuine data and numbers underlying the gigantic body politic of China. What kind of "picture of the tyrant" would that be? He is trampling on something that should be viewed properly and with respect at the computer or as a stack of papers!'

Occasionally, Liu Jiayi entertained himself by letting one of his advisors give a lecture on the HISTORY OF NUMBERS AND ACCOUNTING WORKS IN EIGHTEENTH-CENTURY CHINA. Those were works by earlier rulers, pleasantly readable overviews of debit and credit. They were antiques. The accounts of the Red Army's companies and regiments were similarly precious singularities, as well as those of the workers' and farmers' inspections from the early days, for example, the spring of 1949. There was a special museum dedicated to them on the grounds of the Central Audit Office.

There were also scattered bits of handwritten bookkeeping from smaller branches (of which the agglomeration that is China consists). Whenever the auditor general encountered such a case it warmed his heart. These residues of tradition had meanwhile been covered by deeply layered SEDIMENTS of economic action that the boom had left behind and kept piling up anew. One could only estimate it, not calculate everything individually, because the figures followed different standards and norms. An audit deals with events five years or more in the past. The same authority decides on the profitability and economy of projects extending up to 10 years into the future. In such cases, spot checks are the only realistic method. It filled the auditor general with dread to think what masses of numbers were excluded from the audits. There could be monsters moving around the broad terrain, which remained unchecked; but if they were dragons, there could also be favourable dragons among them. Liu Jiayi ruled that out, for how could muddled, presumably corrupt structures generated according to chance and local ambition provide favourable results, in the same way that there were interesting treasure finds in 1949, on the escape routes of the defeated Kuomintang? This all related to the category 'judging by eye', which was the euphemism for the inspection principle in the audit office's presentations to the party and state leadership. 'More like the category "pulling the wool over people's eyes",' said Jiayi and continued the conversation with the visitor.

'Our accounts are not based on experience. That's why there was a confidential super-dossier in which the office worked with excerpts from economic reality and real numbers—a seismometer, so to speak, that served the party leadership and was used without consideration for the useless official instructions for audits. This dossier was fiercely contested. Because no one knew what this SECRET INQUISITION inspected and what it "knew", no one dared launch an open attack. At the same time, attempts were made to interfere with the instrument or do away with it completely.'

Roughly speaking, the economic zones in the south and the fairy tale of Shanghai were not represented in the economic figures. The same was true of the debts incurred by the local administrative divisions. That included the practically bankrupt industrial belt in the northeast. If the interested parties were in a position to get together and reach an agreement, the central audit would be swept away. The important thing was to deal politely with the BONDS OF DEBT. The disguised form of slush funds, debts outside the budget and corruption in the highly developed south; a deluge of data. There were virtually no concrete accounts from the west and northwest, on the other hand, so the cunning of the indebted or corrupt lay in being so obliging as to provide checkable data at all. The figures of the People's Army and the navy were taboo. It was only just possible for Liu Jiayi to meet with the internal financial comptrollers of the armed forces over dinner and agree on a final figure, noted down on a bit of paper, for expenses and revenues.

'Is there a physical phenomenon in which a swamp can be as solid as rock and as insubstantial as a cloud?' Liu Jayi, a professor of physics, interjected that the earth's core itself had such properties. In the middle, the earth's centre (and China is also known as the Central Kingdom, after all), the iron is under such high pressure that it becomes extremely hot, and thus resembles a liquid more than a solid. Surrounded by wide rivers of melting iron, and out of step with the earth's rotation (and as swampy or mobile as mud, and as lacking in solidity as the ground during an earthquake). The earth's core, incidentally, melts away on one side and grows on the opposite side; it is no longer spherical. 'These are all geological metaphors, not applicable to the body of China, even if it corresponds to the planet Earth,' the visitor replied. Was there a physical phenomenon that determined the states of water (in which the partisans swim) in other terms than solid (ice), liquid (water) and gaseous (air)? 'I have tried to answer that. Swamp or corruption are not states of matter, and if you are looking for conditions as monstrous as those at the earth's core, those are not a swamp.'

The theft starts with local authorities who work together with speculators and need the land on which citizens are living for big construction projects. Alongside the NEW OBSCURITY, this was the second nightmare that preoccupied the auditor general. 'The leases,' he said, 'can quickly be terminated on a pretext. But by living on and cultivating the leased land (so-called "public property"), the people have long since developed a subjective sense of ownership. There are more and more cases in which citizens of our republic defend their land or their buildings with their lives. For example, a woman who defended the second floor of her condemned house—with the presence of her living body, with her unyielding purpose, so to speak—was caught by the shovel of a bulldozer and dashed to the ground. Of course that gets people worked up,' the visitor confirmed.

'One has to resettle the neighbours to calm the source of unrest.' This physicist was not only Jiayi's comrade-in-arms but also the minister for building. The circle of reliable people who silently formed a faction within the party was not large, so there was a danger of an accumulation of offices.

In the 24 hours of the day, from which one must subtract times for quick greetings, climbing stairs, taking the elevator, pressing buttons, getting dressed and undressed, for washing oneself and sleeping briefly, as well as further portions in the category of 'living', the central minister (and likewise the national CONSCIENCE OF NUMBERS, the auditor general) can only ever witness a small amount of what happens in the country directly, let alone participate in decisions about it. The politician is almost legally obliged to preside over what is just and unjust, and wait for his own punishment.

We Are the Eye of the US Congress

We are what the scribes were for the rulers of antiquity: auditors of the Senate, already the third generation. We auditors exercise the only active right of Congress. It would be an exaggeration to say that we serve the people, but lictors of a Senate, helpers of committee chairpersons we certainly are, and even our masters would not dare display their slight corruptibility openly to us. Thus we exert authority in two directions: upwards to our superiors and outwards towards the world.

When I say 'outwards', this refers to a view like that from a prison window of a few clumps of grass and the beginning of a garden which is itself out of view. This is because I look out of basement windows in the White House, from a room where gardening tools used to be stored. Thus a substantial view is not to be had through this porthole but, rather, by looking at the computer and the files. These insights, however, show me the innermost gears of the country. You can conclusively analyse a state system by examining its expenses!

Now our department—consisting of 16 specialists, there are 86 such departments in total—has cut a swathe into the practices of the Pentagon. Today we are presenting the Senate committee with our report on LOAN VIOLENCE, the work of the private security firms that have left their marks in Iraq and Afghanistan. They take pay from us, then sell their weapons. They fight among themselves—at the American taxpayer's expense. They recently attacked ISAF troops.

'When you write such reports, aren't you afraid of acts of revenge by those affected? You have a family living unprotected in a Washington suburb. The people whose activities you expose are armed and, in a certain sense, uninhibited?'

I reply: 'We're not afraid as long as we're in the service of Congress. I also consider our enemies intelligent; they know that someone else will immediately take my place if I am murdered. If I were blackmailed, on the other hand, they know I would give up my position at once and expose the blackmail. So I am working, as I said, in the third generation. When I work, I am watched by my father, who was an auditor, and my grandfather, who held the position of auditor general. People like us bear "all wounds on our chest".'

The Gains and Losses of Translation in Music

In the management of a major aircraft manufacturer, consisting equally of German and French members, fine-tuning was required among the bosses. Heartiness and joint excursions with the wives were not enough to achieve that; rather, the messages exchanged in order to keep the entire company running had to be precisely coordinated the moment they were formulated, and then collected and recorded at the end of the day. The German had been assigned a French-speaking assistant and the Frenchman a German-speaking one. The conversational language was English. Nonetheless the assistants, like prompters, were meant to pick up and rework all the texts, as they could have different nuances in each of the three languages, in English, French and German. It would have been better for the gentlemen to speak to each other using interpreters. Thus they improvised as far as their language skills allowed. The crack was hidden by the millions of lost fragments that accumulated in the back-and-forth of words between the bosses. The communicative deficits marched separately while the contrasts in management struck as one.

In a different case, where two female, Cuban-trained interpreters mediated between Chavez and Putin, the initially uninspired words of the Russian president and the badly prepared replies of the Venezuelan president, narrow-minded deliberations, took on a radiance that struck the souls of the politicians. They spiced their translations of Chavez's words with Russian sayings that transported the fatigued Putin, who had travelled a long way, back to his childhood in St Petersburg, summoning the six-year-old in him; thus the seven baskets developed by the political technicians on both sides (each basket contains one part of the problems at issue) were 'sorted in the spirit of personal commitment'. 'The good ones go into the pot, the bad ones go into your crop, cudgel in the sack.'[3] To the opponents, no problem seemed unsolvable that day. That was due to the translation method which had been taught at the Russian department of the University of Havana for a while by one of the tutors ('empathic translation'). The two interpreters had acted 'free-handed'. But they had tried not to change the essence of the information. That was why the assistants of the two politicians tolerated the unusual negotiating style of the two beauties, one of them specializing in Spanish–Russian, the other in Russian–Spanish.

—Could the two have exchanged places, and translated just as well on the other side?

—That's out of the question! They were specialists. They would have refused to improvise.

—How did this 'special school' of translation come into existence in Cuba?

—The department for translation training was part of a school for agents. There, however, the method of IMPROVING INFORMATION would not have been allowed.

—How do you explain the fact that they used such a method nonetheless?

—One always learns from the opposite of the teaching aim.

The Politics of Tone

In the night of 28 December 1942, Kurt Zeitzler, the army's chief of general staff, managed to persuade Hitler in a private conversation to recall Army Group A which was fighting a losing battle in the Caucasus. So far, the dictator had been unwilling to allow that for strategic reasons. 'It would go against the whole purpose of the summer offensive, even of the war itself!' He acknowledged the predicament in operative and tactical terms, but as a commander he always found a pretext to wait at least another day. He did not want to tell anyone that the war was lost.

The decisive point was that Zeitzler had found a tone in which he could smuggle himself into the Führer's nocturnal, gloomy train of thought. One could say that it was a shared stream of feelings, facts, hesitation and decision-like ideas (of late, whenever thoughts had come about as a result of conversation, it had become impossible to distinguish which ideas had come from the one person and which from the other) to induce the dictator to make a statement of his own accord, so that he would dictate the ineluctable result to his helper from his own head, as it were. As if in a dream, Hitler agreed to recall the army group. The following day Zeitzler was able to present Hitler with his concession.

A tone had established itself between the two 'comrades in crisis' that one also finds described in the stenographic record of Heinrich Berger, which relates to the escape of the Sixth Army from the pocket of Stalingrad. Those were the beginnings of their teamwork, but it could only succeed at night, not in the briefing while looking at the big map with a scale of 1:300,000, that is to say, before witnesses. When addressing a large meeting, the dictator had to appear both as a thinking person and an actor.

Influence via the ear, as when the Holy Spirit speaks the sacred texts into the monk's listening organ in the guise of a dove, only works for a short time. The dictator noticed that he was being 'pushed around'; he could barely recognize his nocturnal decision in the morning. In his exposed position as a POLITICAL MONOPOLIST OF ALL DECISIONS, he was by no means prepared to react as another person or his own nature told him to. He preferred to assume the form of a Norwegian boulder which the Ice Age had already pushed into this position of responsibility, as it were. In fact, in an obviously hopeless situation (but he alone was allowed to speak to himself about it) he was generally unconcerned whether decisions were 'right' or 'wrong', for there is 'nothing right within what is wrong'. In a period when negative announcements flooded everything, decisions thus became a scarcity.

'I could see the human side of Hitler in that,' said Kurt Zeitzler, 'in the way he always reacted to devastating reports with denial. Human beings do that while soldiers are inhumanly forbidden to do so.' He was slightly ashamed, Zeitzler continued, to contribute to the many souvenirs about 'What was Hitler really like?' But he had to convey his impressions. In front of witnesses, Hitler always ACTED THE FÜHRER, and was accordingly strictly disciplined and 'rock hard'. In the stage background, however, in the dark of night, lit only by an intimate vellum-covered lamp, he by no means became sentimental or a human being; rather, he became unable to determine the boundary between himself and the other. He inadvertently shared with another person the knowledge he kept to himself. That, according to Zeitzler, was a question of tone.

Tensing of the Stomach Nerves, Visible in the Lip Activity of Speer and Hitler During an Arms Inspection

The mouth area of Armaments Minister Speer, as well as that of the Führer, displayed a tension which testified to the fact that no soup had been served since the early morning. The weapons inspection, in this case an improvement of the 7.5 cm tank gun, had been underway for hours. The regime was that of the experts, the people who could be proud of this new development. They were inconsiderate.

A small pot of pea soup or a chicken leg would have contributed more to the agreement of the minister and the Reich chancellor than firing 88 shots (counted afterwards), all of which hit the targets more accurately than expected based on the statistics from previous guns. Two adjutants, one from the air force and the other from the navy, hence not actually competent in this area, agreed that it would have been better for the overall handling of the war if the physical basis of those making decisions had been reinforced by a bite to eat, rather than simply wanting to show like engineers that one had improved in the last 14 months.

The top leadership of the Third Reich was showing a tendency towards gastric or bowel complaints. The war was lost, according to the medical doctor Karl Brandt, because of insufficient attention to the physical sensibilities of the leadership. One cannot make effective decisions at five in the morning without emptying one's bowels; this applied to Field Marshal von Rundstedt during the hours of the invasion. Nor could one— because the timing was determined by forces beyond one's control —take up the engineers' enthusiasm into one's soul and clothe it in words of encouragement if there was too long a time between breakfast and lunch.

—But then who controls the chances in war? Who determines what times are too long?

—Not any individual. No one who plans it. It is benevolent secretaries and planners on both sides of scheduling who dictate the times to the great men.

—But they could change the schedule at any time.

—If they had the time for it!

The Berchtesgaden Syndrome

Starting with his accession to office, but more vigorously after the death of Hindenburg and during the winter crisis of 1941, Reich Chancellor Adolf successively gathered the MONOPOLY ON STATE DECISIONS in his innermost circle. He was a BANKRUPT OF TIME. Yet the same person who made decisions also needed to eat, have a good night's sleep, shake hands, walk back and forth, go to the toilet. He also tended to indulge at length in trivial stories that he found relaxing. In the autumn of 1942 he gave the authority of command in the south of the eastern front, extending to the divisions and individual companies, to himself. Once he had thus taken over all jurisdictions, he travelled to his domicile in Berchtesgaden, where he could not be reached for questions or messages, for a few days of quiet. Since then, the concentration of all authority in a single person followed by their departure has been known in statecraft as the BERCHTESGADEN SYNDROME.

The Important Thing Was to Achieve Victory Night after Night

In 1910, a respected minister of the French Republic publicly believed to be a homosexual, surprisingly resigned from his post. At the age of 83, he had fallen in love with a locksmith's 19-year-old apprentice from Normandy and taken him into his household. He had resigned from his duties before any rumour could develop. That was considered honourable.

In a salon of the kind run by Madame Verdurin in the novel *In Search of Lost Time*, Marcel Proust was asked about the events. The minister had retained the rank of reserve colonel in a cavalry regiment while giving up all civilian offices. Was his attitude, Proust was asked, like that of an old imbecile moved by a St John's Fire, or more like that of Socrates, who publicly embraced the younger Alcibiades?

Marcel Proust realized only too well that the questioner was not interested in the answer, only the presentation of his cleverly posed question. Proust took a 'Prussian' approach. In the case of an underage mistress, for example, a 13-year-old from Normandy, but an angel who had confused all his senses and whom he could not stay away from, the minister's resignation would be the correct course of action—not least because he needed time to keep such a young creature in his possession and, if possible, prepare her for her future career. He could keep his officer's rank in such a case, on the other hand, because one had often seen commanders with underage girls at their side in military campaigns. The feelings for the 19-year-old worker, however, were—as far as age was concerned—less reprehensible but all the more 'impossible' in terms of social standing. They demanded absolute secrecy. They should not have been made public by the minister's resignation. At the same time, they made the military rank 'untenable' to a particular degree. The man could be challenged to a duel at any time, even if someone claimed no more than what the minister himself had admitted. His honour would always be tainted, and could only be washed clean by blood. Now, in this salon, Proust had dwarfed the scheming question of the *Figaro* editor, who knew about his homoerotic inclinations. The important thing was to achieve victory night after night.

After Victory

In our task force, lent by the secret service of the People's Republic of Poland to the People's Republic of Vietnam, we were disappointed when the impressive victory, the occupation of Saigon in the summer, was followed by a postwar period in which little happened. Reintegration of fighters into the civilian collectives, repair of damage to buildings and rice fields. We Poles had lost six of our people; our brother republic hundreds of thousands. And now the administrative team took control of things. We sent our explosives experts home. Svatoslav Lemke with only one hand, the other blown off. But we were expecting reinforcements in the form of six economists. The accounts of the People's Republic, still separated into North and South Vietnam, were prepared by the year's end.

Lehrter Bahnhof

The grounds of Berlin's Central Station are the image of a political situation; this was concluded by the journalist Pierre

Ledoux of *Le Monde*, who visited Berlin. One must mentally add the periphery of hotels, shopping streets and restaurants that usually surround a train station. The Central Station also lacks the function it was intended to have when it was planned, namely, the major connection between the north and the south and traffic between the west and the east: the routes to Stockholm, Berlin, Prague, Vienna, Budapest and Constantinople, according to Ledoux, were as underdeveloped as those to Peking, Moscow, Warsaw, Riga, Paris and Madrid.

To get from the politicians' apartment blocks to the Central Station, calling a taxi or a staff car is too much of a fuss, but the way on foot is tedious and long. The only neighbours of the Reichstag, the offices of the lawmakers and the Federal Chancellery are the old building of the Swiss Embassy, the belfry in the Tiergarten and the House of the World's Cultures. No provision was made for access to libraries, places for unforced meetings or ministries. The boulevard only begins on the other side of the Brandenburg Gate.

Grounds Entirely Abandoned by Demonstrations

Like boulder blocks, a long-distance train station, car silos, hotels and an airport complex stand there with no recognizable entrances, like a road system in the former landscape. This is third nature.

THE THIRD RUNWAY has been built without any demonstrations, the fourth is being planned. The local government is exploiting the lack of attention to the airport in recent years. The demonstrations against the western runway started from a forest; the fighters and the police forces found their places.

Meanwhile it had become difficult to find an equally suitable location from which demonstrations against the further expansion of this structure could begin—assuming there were any demonstrations. Public attention has drifted away in a depressive fashion.

Adam Smith and Ricardo speak of industrial society as second nature. There is a third nature which sets itself apart from this like a spaceship ready for take-off in the Rhine-Main Area; its reality lies in construction sketches, write-offs, future value or a ruin value, not in the objects and people that move about inside it. In third nature, a wanderer would not be able to follow the signs in the sky, which are concealed by fumes, nor the directions signs set up for him. He would have to slip into this network of buildings by vehicle, aeroplane or railway.

'The Outer Skin of Power'

Since taking office as a minister, he had no attention left for his body. What he ate, when he rested or how much oxygen the air he breathed contained was not subject to his decisions. He was pushed into a seat in a helicopter, completed courses of an official meal after arriving at the meeting-place, negotiated until midnight, and was then already expected by his flight crew, who wanted to fly him to another continent by morning. Who cared about his biological equilibrium? About the balanced condition of his cells? Any resistance against this excessive programme would have cost him time that he did not have.

And so he remained inattentive to the candida cultures in his intestines, which had soon also affected his food pipe and mouth. He only just noticed that his toes were inflamed and the skin in his crotch was reddening. The skin tickled. He took it for an allergy and sought to fight it by washing with soap. This does nothing to exert power against the world of parasites.

The foreign creatures settled inside him, following their own policy. Later, after doctors had put him in the picture, he had the impression that the fungal cells had gained influence like a lobby. He was to drink more beer, add a dessert to meals, create conditions on the inside that were agreeable to them. When he was tired, he gave in to this urging. Had they already occupied his brain? Settled in? The body overturned this programme, both that of the parasites and that of his professional demands. He reacted with a rash—not only under his clothes but also all over his face. Press photos were now virtually impossible. It was not the vote of the doctors that ended his political career but, rather, professional mistakes that he made. But essentially, it was the unexpected ugliness of his face which the body had used to defend itself.

In the Fields of Sustainability

One says of her that she possesses Westphalian energy. This refers to the strength of her ancestors, which clearly runs through her. In the past her siblings went along behind her. After their mother's death, she guaranteed her father an orderly household. Today she is a political authority.

This week, the responsibility for the following projects rests on her narrow shoulders: the German-Turkish University in Constantinople, a foundation university with funding pledges from the German government, needs to be confirmed by the

Turkish parliament, but, instead, this point has been taken off their agenda; the hard board lies in the fact that the matter has to be restarted before the chancellor meets with President Erdoğan and a possible dispute develops about another matter (German-Turkish secondary schools). Aside from that, she assumed responsibility in the supervisory body of the Oden-waldschule; the school must be taken back to its reformist origins and guided out of the terrible public attention it is currently experiencing. As president of the German Adult Education Association—and we are still talking about the same person—she is responsible for the present and future of adult education not only in Germany but also in Europe. In a time which changes so quickly that people find their prior school education inadequate by the time they reach the middle of their lives, a time in which ÉDUCATION PERMANENTE is thus called for, there must be an increasing effort with reduced budgetary means to find motivated teachers through publications, internal advertising, events and organization. In the 68th hour of her working week, this woman drives on motorways to a final meeting that could only be timetabled at this late hour. She uses the opportunity to explain to her companion the balances that are needed when the chancellor, with whom she had spoken on the phone just two hours previously, meets with the headstrong President Erdoğan in the Turkish capital. She suggests what she would do if she were on the Turkish side and had to assert the country's interests. Because that is what one has to imagine if one wants to decide how our side should respond.

Where does she get this alertness? This concentration of goodwill, portions of which she lends to third parties. This energy, her assistant reports, does not come from this world. Nor from the body or her individual soul alone. It is the thrust of families that still cultivated their own fields. They all have hopes pinned on them as far as the annual harvest is concerned, the sequence of generations. I don't know the names of my boss' ancestors. My own, says the assistant, were first called Habermeier, then Viertelmeier, later Sechzentelmeier, that is, their fields were divided during the Middle Ages.[4] Their hardship made them work harder. Some of them emigrated and participated in founding America. It is these dead that drive us forward. They are the ones we can trust, even if we don't know them personally.

In the Network of Favours

In the complicated exchange in the political society that determined cultural policy in 1950s Germany, change was paid back in the form of good deeds. Those who took part in them could count themselves among the decision-makers who, especially if they treated those deeds as a necessary but secondary issue, would not be passed over in larger matters. Until the 1960s, cultural policy was CONVERSATIONAL. Officials who did not command this technique from the OLD SOCIETY (a technique that had been consolidated further under the hammer blows of the Third Reich) were looked down on. Such a decision-maker could talk a lot, but no one listened to them. On the other hand, a high-ranking official who had mastered this technique, and who was thus accompanied as a matter of course by a pool of good favours or philanthropic results, was treated as a person whose status was above that of a mere official.

This constellation saved Wilfried Helm, who was sentenced to life imprisonment as a minor, from the emotional crippling that a young person cannot escape if they spend longer than 10–15 years in Bavarian prisons. As a child, leading his younger sister by the hand, he had headed west after the bombing of Dresden in February 1945. Soon he was the mascot of a US Army company. The position went to his head, he became a thief. He evaded investigation by fleeing to Brussels. After being apprehended there in the black-market milieu, US constables transported him in their vehicle to Nuremberg for sentencing. Despite wearing handcuffs, he shot the driver and front-seat passenger dead with a weapon that his wardens had left on the back seat.

Sentenced to death by a US military court, he owed his life to a group of lawyers who knew one another from the Nuremberg Trials. They sent a clemency appeal to the president of the USA. They pointed out that according to German law, minors could not be sentenced to death; herein lay the legal difference to the Third Reich. And so the sentence was commuted; the Bavarian justice system decided to give him a life sentence.

Referring to rules about jurisdiction that took the place of birth of the convict Helm's deceased parents as the point of departure, a network of decision-makers, connected through earlier practice, persuaded Dr Fritz Bauer, attorney general of the State of Hesse, to transfer the prisoner to Butzbach Prison. The retrial initiated by lawyers and activated networkers, based on German juvenile law, had a chance of success in Hesse. A pardon and remission of the remaining sentence required them to specify what profession the released offender would practise. Max Horkheimer, rector of Johann Wolfgang Goethe University,

Frankfurt, was persuaded to employ the FORMER UNDER-AGE MURDERER as his personal driver. In the system of favours, of the generally human approach that enclosed the circle of Hessian antifascists, Horkheimer could not turn down the request from his friends. At the same time, he was not sufficiently enlightened to rule out a repetition of the terrible deed. His mind told him that the young Helm, now 21, would not repeat what he had done in the heat of the moment during the confusion of his childhood. His feelings, however, registered danger. So this legendary scholar solved the problem by employing the young man, but no longer using the rectoral car. He was not inclined to excursions in any case. But thanks to Hessian scholarship system, the pardoned offender was able to take his A-levels, became a businessman, and now lives in a villa in Hamburg's Elbchaussee.

Still on Watch

The November wind hisses through the underpass at Münster Central Station. The trains race above it. The old woman is wrapped up in two coats, double shirts, a pullover. A little hot-air blower is warming her stall which is located in the middle of the underpass where there are shops.[5] Paperbacks and newspapers can be bought. Because of the direction of the hot air from the heater, her thighs are too hot and her neck, turned towards the station underpass, is too cold. But she does not get colds as often as she used to. The fine skin on the forehead and temples of the old woman. Filling out ready-made receipts causes her difficulties. But she can still read the small-printed price tags on the books. In front of her on the draughty table: *Playboy*. She sells two newspapers and up to seven books an hour.

It Was a Close Shave . . .

He was outraged. But he also knew what the next steps would be when he continued speaking. She was already carrying on with her verbal attacks on him. She would later pack her suitcases— once she was surrounded by her friends, her family, her advisors and her lover, who would all support her stance, she would be irretrievably lost.

So he controlled himself and reminded her of the bitter days of her sickness, in which the two of them had stuck together. Had they not overcome the bankruptcy of his business as a couple? The new beginning? Had they not got two children— now grown up—through all their schools, children who were now missing from the household, which had exacerbated the crisis? He reminded her of earlier deeds, just as Bonaparte had addressed his grenadiers before one of his last battles in the winter of 1814 and invoked past events in the irredeemable moment.

It was more the change in his tone of voice than the content of his words that ultimately resulted in the two going for a meal together. Was the intensity of their conflict, which was so recent, partly due to a low blood-sugar level? That no longer mattered. They were reconciled. In such crises there are no empirical values which are useful for the next time: it was a close shave, he told himself.

A Basic Political Model from the 1930s
Transformability of Function

Every day, the children from Halberstadt's better families were collected in the morning by Miss Runde, a professional child minder, and brought together to a different one of those children's homes; they were given playtime there. In the afternoon, the whole lot were dropped off at their homes. It was a relief for the parents.

At the Roehrs', the family of the abattoir manager's son, there was sausage soup for lunch. At the Klamroths' we played in the pavilion which was actually set up for indoor tennis matches but now served as a children's playground; there were sandwiches from the kitchen for lunch. The Spiegelsbergenweg was where all the villas stood that were confiscated later on, after Germany's defeat, first by the US officers, then the British and finally the Russians. At 42 Kaiserstrasse, our house, the nursery was too small for this bunch. The dining room and conservatory were made available. Because the playground changed daily, social hierarchies within the Halberstadt upper class were, as far as the children were concerned, dissolved. Nonetheless, the social boundary between the upper middle class and the upper class remained intact as far as the parents were concerned. Thus the Roehrs, Kluges and Liesenbergs could not have private dealings on equal terms with the Klamroths, even if they did encounter one another at public events.

Even today, the throng of production partners of the firm dctp mirrors the wandering collective of Miss Runde. Spiegel TV, Focus TV, the *Neue Zürcher Zeitung* (a newspaper that has existed for 225 years), BBC, the *Süddeutsche Zeitung* and the culture magazines are separated along class lines. And there is no headquarters. The partners do not go to different houses like Miss Runde's flock; but they do form a classless network of informative quality that defends itself against pure ratings.

Only a few years after Miss Runde's regime came to an end, Halberstadt's politico-civic system was destroyed. A boy like Harm Backer, son of the editor of the *Halberstädter Zeitung*, who, as a mere party member, would not have been received at the Klamroths', and was moulded into a National Socialist boy with cod-liver oil and weekly alpine sun, was a boss once he became a *Jugendschaftsführer* in Halberstadt's best youth unit.

The upper town formed Unit 9 of the *Jungbann* which extended to Wenigerode and Quedlinburg. It never assembled in its entirely, not even for big sporting events; this indicated the sheer number of its members. One occasionally saw the *Sturmbannführer* at a speech. One also knew that the *Sturmbann* doctor in Wenigerode was responsible for issuing medical certificates for exemption from service. As for the rest, one could only imagine the size of the total formation.

The lower town provided the members for Unit 2. Those were workers' boys. The unit was superior to the upper town boys (the offspring of doctors, teachers, lawyers, directors, artists) in muscle. In this sense, the town's youth was divided into two groups, just as the town itself had been divided into an upper and lower town for over a thousand years.

These progressive accumulations are not reflected in any modern media organization. Nor do they seem repeatable in their capacity to articulate oppositions and ways to bind people together.

Periods of Happiness Are 'Empty Pages of World History'

Stefan Aust, founder of the journalistic project *Die Woche*, which was long considered secret, points out in a series of illustrated articles that by the standards of the Third Reich's 12-year existence (eventfulness, starkness of oppositions, rises and falls, life stories), the 16 years of the Kohl government constitute a period in which little seems to have happened. In fact, the years between 1951 and 2010 could be viewed as a whole era of 50 years in which families were only torn apart to a limited degree and people were exterminated on a smaller scale. These times are UNHEROIC, he argues, and in that sense favourable for the proliferation of life stories. But they are not 'empty pages', as the Swabian philosopher claims in his formulation about world history.

What Is a Manager of the World Spirit?

G. W. F. Hegel refers to Caesar, Napoleon and Alexander of Macedon as MANAGERS OF THE WORLD SPIRIT. What does such management entail? asked the writer Arno Schmidt with reference to this formulation. Caesar became known as the founder of a term of office, for a road system and for a way to avoid further civil wars. Then he was killed before he could conclude his management. Napoleon, according to Schmidt, emulated Caesar's life, and his title of emperor followed on not from the medieval heightening of the German kingly title but directly from the classical tradition that comes from Caesar. One could say that Napoleon continued CAESAR as a play, but the third and fourth acts are missing. The term 'manager' is supposedly far more apt in the case of Alexander of Macedon. His activities are often misunderstood. He is considered a warlord and battle planner. But the battles of Issus and Gaugamela, Schmidt writes, were three years apart. These and the other battles, which usually only lasted a few hours, reveal the true core of Alexander's deeds: he was not a conqueror but a city-founder. In that sense, what Hegel calls the WORLD SPIRIT and is organized by management is here the network of places, the marriages brought about and the setting down of documents—including stone coffins and burial inscriptions that would not have existed without Alexander's orbit. His most important quality, however, was something very different from what one would call management: his generosity. The Persian kings, we are told, had locked up the world's treasures in their arsenals like captives in a prison. But he, the Macedonian, took out those treasures, arbitrarily distributed them as gifts among his people and in the world, thus using the method of the economist Maynard Keynes to create an economic miracle that lasted 300 years—the age of Hellenism. Even today, people still search in the Fergana Valley for cellars with stores, known as ALEXANDER'S PHARMACIES. But while the Russian archaeologists still sent written applications for the funding to extend their search, Schmidt continues, the traces of the *Res gestae Alexandri Macedonis* are to be found in entirely different TEXTS: in the horses of that valley, for example, which are descended from Greek horses. For such genes would never have arrived there, at the foot of the Pamir Mountains, had it not been for the management of that young rebel who stirred such enthusiasm.

FIGURE 8. Hegel

FIGURE 9. On the left Sarkozy, on the right Federal Chancellor Angela Merkel, in the middle Helge Schneider as a DRILLER OF HARD BOARDS. On the far right, looking away: Obama.

A HUMMING OF SOUL LAMPS:
JACOBINS FLY TO THE MOON IN A BALLOON

Daedalus was the master builder of the labyrinth. His employer, King Minos, later banished Daedalus to Sicily for unknown reasons. Even there, he still pursued him. Daedalus supposedly doused his persecutor with boiling water, killing him. Daedalus is considered the inventor of the plumbline, the saw, flying, glue and the drill.

The new Daedalus—Le nouveau Dédale—is the name of a text written by Jean-Jacques Rousseau in 1742. Rousseau had watched a demonstration of a balloon's flight. The airship sank in the Seine, having only travelled a short distance.

In his essay, Rousseau describes (corresponding to what he had seen) the impossibility of navigating the sea of air like a surface in the same way that seafarers navigate the oceans. Rather, he writes, objects moving through the atmosphere always plummet down sooner or later.

J.-J. ROUSSEAU
AVIATEUR

LE NOUVEAU DÉDALE

(1742)

Pour A. JULLIEN Libraire

A GENÈVE

1910

FIGURE 10. In the Battle of Fleurus on 8 Messidor of Year 2 (26 June 1794), the French Revolutionary Army gains a view of the enemy through the legendary ascent of a balloon.

View of the Tiananmen Square Massacre from the Revolutionary Museum

Manfred Seifert was a spy for the GDR from Department IX of the HVA. He accompanied comrade Krenz to China in the summer of 1989. The celebrations there marked the 40th anniversary of the founding of the People's Republic of China. Owing to his thorough training at the workers' and farmers' faculty at Halle University, the 200-year return of the Great French Revolution echoed loudly in his heart. In that moment, however, the comrade was in the rooms of the REVOLUTIONARY MUSEUM at Tiananmen Square.

The party had sent him to buy original manuscripts by Marx at an auction in England, and he had brought them along as a gift from the State Council to the Central Committee of the PRC. They were stored in the museum's safes. Now he looked through the large windows of the monumental building, together with other comrades, including French ones, and watched the events outside: the fleeing people, the impact of shots, the attempt to set up improvised barricades which were, however, no obstacle to the personnel carriers and tanks of the military forces.

The display cases behind the observers, which contained the incunabula from earlier revolutions, reflected the conflagration: in the eyes of Seifert, the trained observer, this created a disturbing picture. Certainly, he had nothing against hooligans being expelled from the square. But he had his doubts, which were clearly shared by the other comrades present, that these were hooligans. Admittedly, using the cardboard Statue of Liberty was a provocation, indeed an act of tomfoolery. But the movement itself, based on the impressions from the previous days, the wall newspapers, the conversations Seifert had had, did seem to possess revolutionary attributes. Only yesterday he had believed that the revolution was rearing its head once again. Party discipline did not prevent him from preserving his impressions inwardly. Where do the people end, where does hooliganism begin? Who decides the form taken by outrage?

Ralle-Balle

No petrol at the petrol stations, disturbances in the TGV system, grotesque delays at Charles de Gaulle Airport in Paris. These

were the consequences of the strikes in protest against the raising
of the retirement age to 62 years, a bill proposed by Sarkozy
that would be presented to the Senate this Wednesday. Stefan
Aust tried everything, but could not avoid getting from Paris to
Berlin with a severe delay. He was always good for a concentrated summary of his immediate impressions. This is what he
said:

—Great France reminds me of a second GDR.

—Why?

—A perfect repair service.

—But the GDR wasn't perfect.

—In its own way, France is perfect!

—Because it's based not on the October Revolution but the
Great French Revolution?

—It's not based on any revolution.

—On what then?

—It's unique. France is a condition, not a programme.

—What gives you that idea? Just because there's no petrol
at the petrol stations?

—Nowhere else in the world does a society adapt to a general strike as smoothly as in France. One calls that *bricolage*
(tinkering).

—According to Lévi-Strauss, *bricolage* corresponds to the
principle of evolution.

—If societies want to survive, that's how.

With a few words, Aust had already processed his initial annoyance. He seemed to sympathize with bizarre France. Was he grateful to the difficult transport conditions for giving him the thought he had just expressed? Stefan Aust did not have much time. All appointments had been postponed by the delay. This quick-travelling and even-quicker-thinking man held one souvenir especially dear: the word *ralle-balle*. He had never heard it before. 'Ruckus,' he said, was not the correct translation. He spent a long time looking for a better equivalent. Late at night he called me and asked whether I had found a translation myself. We left it at *ralle-balle*.[6] It was a matter, said Aust, of uninhibitedly expressing displeasure with one's own government. But this happened in the context of a 200-year routine (unlike with a ruckus or a weavers' rebellion). What sorts of things can be undertaken by the lowlands against haughty Paris, by workers against a parliamentary majority, by youth against age, by the suburbs against the centre? Those involved are not one people, one state or one society but, rather, a kaleidoscope of all those. Even so late at night, Aust was palpably preoccupied by his return journey which had been so vehemently disturbed by his experience in France.

Living Picture

On the day the women came to Versailles and irrevocably took the king to Paris, the palace was almost deserted by evening. Someone with a long beard was making an effort to chop the heads off two Gardes du Corps who had been killed at the great stairs. Some took this wretch for a famous robber from the south. It turned out that he was a model from the Painting Academy;

FIGURE 11. The Jacobins travelling by balloon to revolutionize the moon.

that day he was wearing the costume of a slave from ancient times. Never before had anyone witnessed this Nicolas—that was the model's name—acting violently. He was carried along by the mood of the day, he had wanted to carry out an original energetic deed. He said he had viewed a theatre scene or a picture corresponding to this beheading.

The two severed heads were taken away from the perpetrator and stored away. Later they were taken to Paris on pikes. One of these pikes was carried by a child.

Cheerful, Sad, Boisterous, Merry and Desolate: A Stream of People

The king was shaking all over when the queen stepped onto the balcony and showed herself to the people. He feared the worst. When it all ended well, he said to Lafayette: 'Can't you do something for my guards?' 'Give me a guardsman,' replied Lafayette, the god of the day. He leads the man onto the balcony, has him swear the oath and display the national cockade on his hat. The guardsman embraces him. There is a call from the crowd: 'Let the Gardes du Corps live!' The grenadiers of the National Guard of Paris, who obeyed Lafayette, had put on the caps of the Gardes du Corps for safety, and they gave them their own. As one could no longer identify them by their headwear, one could no longer shoot at the guards without the risk of hitting one's own people. The first exchange of uniforms in the history of civil wars was considered a successful invention.

At Mirabeau's suggestion, the National Assembly decided that it would be inseparable from the king during the current legislative period. If he fell, it would fall too. It is one o'clock at night. People have to leave.

Hundreds of lawmakers surround the king. An entire people wanders back to Paris. Louis XVI leaves the palace of Louis XIV, never to return. Everyone thought one could never go hungry if in the company of the king. 'We are bringing home the baker, the baker's wife and the baker's little boy' (meaning the Dauphin): that is what the marchers were singing in groups, varying the order. Jules Michelet describes it thus: cheerful, sad, boisterous, merry and desolate, a stream of people.

Required Time for Education Processes

In the summer of 1790, after his masters had abandoned their castle and lands, the private tutor Etienne Dreux walked from the Ardennes to Paris. Soon, with money he had borrowed from a bank in the Palais Royal, he founded a teaching business. The aim was to enable revolutionaries to learn the rudiments of Republicanism. Several schools of this kind came into being. The teachers knew no more about their teaching subject than the students.

These places were attractors that drew their power from knowledge. When the revolution became bloody, Dreux succeeded in disguising his businesses. After Thermidor he said to himself: 'Finally I can continue my work with full force and in public.'

Education takes effect in the long term. The first generation of young teachers who could support Dreux in his work were trained by 1802. At this point the school was already part of the underground again, as the police administration of Minister Fouché distrusted teaching in the form of independent association. Thus the products of free Republican schools are only finished when history no longer wants or needs them. There was no use for the Republicans until 1832; by then Dreux was an old man.

FIGURE 12. Playing card with the inscriptions 'sage' and 'Social Contract'.

Varying Educational Levels in the Provinces

At the federal celebrations in France in June and July 1790, whose energy is still palpable in the holiday on 14 July, it became apparent that there was a highly divergent educational level in the provinces, which now became *départements*. This had no effect on the shared elan flows beneath all the things that can be conveyed through teaching and rules. An incredible excitement was seeking expression.

In Dôle, the holy fire with which the PRIESTS OF THE REVOLUTION, visible by their caps, burn the incense on the altar of the fatherland, is drawn from the sun itself by the hand of a young girl using a burning lens. In Saint-Maurice (in Charente), the laws and decrees of the assembly in Paris—written material—are placed on the altar and subsequently burnt as a sacrifice. In Saint-Pierre (near Crépy), an Ark of the Covenant was confiscated from a Jewish community building, and the fire is carried to the altar in an iron vessel hanging from this cult object. In a neighbouring village, a map of the world is used as an altar cloth. The following objects are used as REVOLUTIONARY ORNAMENTS: a sword, a plough, a pair of scales, as well as two bullets. It is claimed that the bullets came from the Bastille.

Energy of the heart is in fashion. The signatures beneath the protocols written by the literate during the holidays consist of crosses, as illiteracy is predominant. At the altars, children of the fallen are adopted by the community and marriages are registered. There is lunch for everyone at the altar, later also around the maypole. The food is communal. People are drinking in Lons-le-Saulnier: to all people, even our enemies, whom we swear to love and to protect!

An Attempt at Legislation for about a Week

In the days after Louis XVI's death, the convention was in complete agreement: 'There are no more parties, only the unity of the nation.'

A credit of 900 million assignats was unanimously approved. In addition, the conscription of 300,000 men. The municipalities were given the right to confiscate things so that the material for clothing and equipment could be collected within eight days. That was the beginning of the militia army.

It was during this mood that the debate turned to the future of teaching in France. The century was, after all, that of the EDUCATION OF THE HUMAN RACE. In the constitutive National Assembly and the legislative assembly in Paris, however, there was barely a teacher to be found.

In the convention, each demand was outdone by the next. First there was the view, which seemed for a few days to belong to a minority, that education, the expansion of knowledge and one's political horizon, should be supported at all levels. One must come together! Adults meet in circles to study. They are accompanied by young people. We read the texts together! What texts? Not those of the priests! And that happens in the presence of the children. The representatives of the people imagined children flocking in from the fields at harvest time and volunteering for study groups. Nothing was decided for the time being.

Some groundwork had already been done: Talleyrand's ostentatious report ON TUITION as well as Condorcet's INVESTIGATION. The latter's plan of organization entailed four steps, from primary school to the institute. The National Assembly's committee for public tuition had been given copies of these.

Lanthemy, chief of cabinet in Roland's ministry, brought together the central ideas in a draft bill. After a free primary-school education, the hardworking child of poor parents can enter the class of 'students of the fatherland'. The teachers are chosen by family men from the municipality. Knowledge is the exercise of freedom.

The priest Durand de Maillane, a scholarly type of man, stood up from the benches of the right wing. He justified his vote in such a way that those on the left, the Jacobins, could only agree with him. He suggested: tuition should only take place in *one* group. It would be a violation of EQUALITY if the schools were divided into different classes and by achievement.

In a comprehensive school, pupils would be introduced to the fundamentals of morality. And the most beautiful tales from the history of peoples would be inscribed in their memory, he concluded his speech.

The swamp, the middle of the assembly which remained passive on the majority of questions, erupted in tumult at the question of tuition. It felt confronted with an irresolvable dilemma. Not to be resolved by legal means. Either one had to dethrone higher tuition, topple science, invent an 'unscholarly science' or introduce the most advanced knowledge into primary-school tuition. Children who were still learning to spell would then have to listen to explanations of infinitesimal calculus.

A *Fronde* of Girondists, opposing their own minister Roland in this matter, fought for the AUTONOMY OF KNOWLEDGE, regardless of how it entered the classroom. This contradicted the idea of the comprehensive school, but also that of regulation according to levels of knowledge. There had to be equality between the AVANT-GARDE OF KNOWLEDGE and the ENTHUSIASM OF LEARNING. Let us first clarify the SUBSTANCE, said these lawmakers: that which is supposed to be learnt. What is it more important to teach—morals or the law? Which are more significant—the skills of the present or the experiences of history? Must children know how to build a bridge, for example, from Bayonne over to Spain, or would it be more important to learn foreign languages? The debate fell apart in the subsequent weeks; it fell prey to the struggle against the Gironde. Never again until the end of the Great Revolution was tuition a central subject of political confrontation in the National Assembly.

On the Gradual Emptying of Revolutionary Ideas While Speaking

For the Enlightenment thinker Condorcet, the ABSOLUTE IDEA OF RIGHT forms the Revolution's centre of gravity. Even God is subject to this idea. If he violates right, he turns into a demon and loses his omnipotence.

Jules Michelet shows that Robespierre demands in his early writings the absolute rule of right, that is to say, its inviolability. Later, according to Michelet, this decisiveness withered away. Absolute right was replaced by MORALITY (a multitude of intentions). That was in turn supplanted by PUBLIC WELFARE. This requires compromises in the fatherland's moment of need; permissiveness and strictness, the two open ends of the world of compromise, divide the nation—even the assembly that represents it. Thus the substance which could have formed the content of the tuition was called into question.

The busts of Mirabeau and Helvetius, who were claimed to have demanded an education reform, were brought over from the pantheon, shown to the Assembly and shattered before the eyes of the lawmakers. 'The politics of action'.

The Abolition of Hereditary Nobility and Hereditary Shame

'On a hot June evening in 1790, the National Assembly managed to rekindle the rapture of 1789.' The noble movement initiated by the suggestion to transfer monuments of the old regime from their traditional places to a new location was used by a lawmaker from the South of France to demand the abolition of all aristocratic titles. The suggestion was supported by the majority—including Lafayette, Montmorency (a member of an especially long-standing family)—and only fought by Mary, a carpenter, as reported by Jules Michelet. At this meeting on 19 June 1790, the Assembly abolished hereditary titles. Some of those who had voted for it regretted their decision the next morning. The relinquishment of names confused the world; now Lafayette was 'Mr Mortier' and Mirabeau 'Mr Riquetti'.

The equalization of names followed a revolutionary but also atavistic logic: no more transfer of earnings to one's children. The same National Assembly augmented this logic with a further resolution: no transfer of guilt to the following generation if their parents had perished at the gallows.

EVERY PERSON SHOULD BE RESPONSIBLE FOR THEIR OWN DEEDS, BOTH GOOD AND BAD.

For, as Michelet recounts, two young people had been condemned to the gallows and executed for forging banknotes. Because of this incident, the Assembly decided that the families of the condemned should live in shame because of the execution. The decree was published. But there was still inequality, as the children of the respective hangmen remained in shame. Legislation is never complete.

The Observer's Position

To the calm observer Wilhelm von Humboldt, who was used to conditions in Rome and spent August 1789 in Paris, the excitement of his travelling companion Campe was an alien phenomenon. He wanted to apply the attribute 'strange' to the events he observed around himself, which struck him as a form of theatre. But not the word 'significant'. He was an egocentric spirit focused on the rhythm of his self-interest and his sensibilities, not one that could be suddenly ignited. Where did he see places of education? Where was a continuation of the process of Enlightenment, or of the encyclopedia? Where could one find a reception of Greek spirit that would found a polis? That is not how one sows the seed for a new century, he said, nor how one stores the harvest of the old. Nonetheless, he said to Campe, he did detect an 'ineluctability of the people's will'. He knew of no power that could conquer such an expression of will by military or police means. If anything could, then only the source of time itself or the diversion of this will. It remained unclear, however, how a people intended to ascertain the precise content of its will as revealed in such impetuousness, in ELAN. One could not, replied Campe, respond to such an imposingly 'moved people' with demands. Indeed, the events could generally not be understood from an observer's position but only from that of a participant. But the only position available to me is my own, Humboldt informed him.

An Arrangement in the Fourth Year of the Revolution

The Chevalier de Monges, impoverished and protected for the time being by a pseudonym, convinced his young wife, who had still viewed marriage with him as a social advancement only four years ago, to enter a money marriage with one of the successful speculators inhabiting the premises of the Palais Royal. From that position she would provide for him during this time of need. The new husband was called Émile Regnier. The three had arranged that the chevalier could still visit his former wife every Friday night. From the outside this looked like the *ius primae noctis* but was actually an inversion of those circumstances. With time, the young woman learnt to love both gentlemen, even if she had no high opinion of their characters. ONE DOES NOT LOVE VIRTUE, SHE SAID, BUT, RATHER, ONE'S DEAR HABITS.

Immanuel Kant's Soul-Sack

Hegel's expression 'Kant's soul-sack', which its inventor used polemically, is taken up more sympathetically by Oskar Negt. On the long walk to emancipation, Negt comments on Kant, improvised carrying objects like baskets, large bottles, tubes and sacks are indispensable. Thus in 1945, fleeing across the Curonian Spit, Negt added, when I was leading the procession of siblings as an 11-year-old, we transported jars of marmalade and flour, books and accounting records well sealed in sacks.

For Hegel, who followed a 'mania of mediation', Kant's 'natural characteristics of humans', which had supposedly originated in history and been carried along by it, were claims entirely lacking in dialectical derivation—and in that sense, a soul-sack rather than a system.

Immanuel Kant starts from three groups of human faculties of which he supposed that they form an adequate basis for natural law and faith in reason:

—the FACULTIES OF REASON establish the principles,
—the FACULTIES OF UNDERSTANDING develop the rules,
—the FACULTIES OF JUDGEMENT (as well as literary imagination) distinguish the particular and connect it to the general.

FIGURE 13. Immanuel Kant preparing mustard, drawing from 1801. The organ of smell: an especially reliable instrument of the faculty of judgement. Until his death in 1804, Immanuel Kant, who never left his home town of Königsberg, followed current events by reading newspapers and listening to reports from visitors. He also observed the history of France in this way for 15 years after 1789. He never joined the chorus of negative judgements about the Revolution, as Hegel did in his PHENOMENOLOGY OF SPIRIT. In the dispute of faculties, Kant refers to the EVOLUTION OF A CONSTITUTION OF NATURAL LAW, which will come into being even if blood is spilt (which Kant did not condone). According to his observations, the MORALITY of individual human beings does not improve; but the increase in LEGALITY was an event that he followed with empathy.

How does the one, Hegel asked, develop from the other? For Kant, it was enough that such characteristics were evidently present among people on a considerable scale. Wherein their alchemy lay—that was a question he chose not to answer. Finding the motivation whereby one could cause powers of reasoning to transform into principles was something he left to practice rather than theory. Or should one wait, he asked in return when presented with beginnings of the critique later published by Hegel, but already voiced in private, for a psychology to explain the basic powers of humans which they used practically anyway (and demonstrate in the laboratory of the Revolution)? EMANCIPATION CANNOT WAIT. Nor does it *want* to wait, Kant added in conversation with a visitor.

Grand Design at the Pyramids

In his correspondence with Louis XIV, G. W. Leibniz recommended the occupation of Egypt by France. With that position, a strong European power could await the decline of India and the Ottoman Empire and acquire an Alexandrian empire. At the time, writes Jules Michelet, France had such a strong fleet (with a presence in the Indian Ocean) that such a plan would not have been unrealistic. Roughly a hundred years later, Napoleon's expedition army did indeed occupy Egypt.

At NEW YEAR 1799–1800, thousands of French officers took part in celebrations in Cairo and Alexandria. The supreme commander attended both events. At this point there was a plan, marked by the turn of the century, to continue and establish the revolution that had more or less failed at home in Africa. What else could they do if the British fleet blocked the army at the Nile? They did not want to be an armed prison camp. They were young officers and troops. A third of the Frenchmen in this expedition were scholars. Cavalry divisions had advanced to Zanzibar and the Western Sahara for exploration.

The Death of General Kléber

General Kléber, from Eastern France, took over the supreme command after Bonaparte's departure from Egypt. On 20 March 1800, his troops took Heliopolis. June was quiet.

On the morning of 14 June, Kléber inspected a parade of the GREEK LEGION. After a meal he had taken at the quarters of his chief of general staff, Kléber went in the direction of his quarters, accompanied by the architect Protain. Then a young

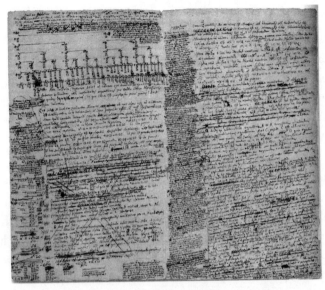

FIGURE 14. Double page with a note by G. W. Leibniz

FIGURE 15 (BELOW). The Citadel of Cairo. At the bottom, a French artillery piece is drawn by camels

Muslim approached him, seemingly wanting to hand him a piece of paper. When Kléber, a tall man, reached for the document, the assassin drew a knife and pierced the general's chest several times. The architect Protain struck the 24-year-old man in vain and was wounded himself.

After being brought back to the quarters of Darnas, the chief of general staff, Kléber died of his wounds. The assassin, a fundamentalist fanatic from Syria, was called Suleiman al-Halabi. A military court sentenced him to death along with three clerics (religious teachers at Al-Azhar University) who had encouraged him to commit the crime. The three clerics were beheaded, the heads placed on metal rods and displayed on one of the gates of Cairo. This took place directly before Suleiman's sentence was carried out. Suleiman was 'impaled': his body was skewered on a pole with a sharp tip in such a way that his intestines and peritoneum were run through. The delinquent endured his torment, it is reported, 'in a courageous, quiet fashion'. For the French executioners, that was more shameful than if he had screamed loudly. He remained in this position for four hours. Then he died after an officer, at his request, brought him something to drink. In the young man's amorphous and disturbed bodily mass, the liquid triggered a spasm that killed him.

A later appeal in a military court, initiated in France, subjected the barbaric execution to the criticism of a judge; but no one was punished. At the trial, the accused officers responded that the cruelty of the punishment corresponded to the oriental mentality; any other form of execution was not considered a punishment. The directness and cruelty of the attacks demanded a form of punishment that the officers would not have suggested for their own country.

FIGURE 16. The assassin pierced the general's chest several times.
On the left: the architect Protain.

The fundamentalist's corpse was left out in the summer air
for three days. The head surgeon, Larrey, then removed all bits
of flesh, parasites and microbes from the skeleton. When they
withdrew from Egypt, he ensured that the skeleton was taken
to France in a wooden box. The remains of the famous assassin
were exhibited at the Natural History Museum in the Jardin des
Plantes.

The Army Leadership Becomes Islamic

Kléber's successor, in keeping with length of service, was General
Menou. This general had converted to Islam and was married
to a young Muslim woman from Rosette. He had augmented
his first name, Jacques, with the name Abdallah. 'Excellent
administrator and economist, without any military talent.' After
the British troops landed on 8 March 1801, he positioned the

soldiers so unfavourably that he was defeated. Trapped in Alexandria, he was forced to capitulate on 2 September 1801.

—It has been reported that Menou plans to take control of the North African coast up to Tunis?

—That's right.

—The Armée d'Orient took on a life of its own?

—Fantastic plans. A march on Constantinople was also considered: one would then have reached Vienna by the spring of 1802.

Philosophy, Interest and Morality
as Ghost Lights of the Revolution

In revolutionary France, it could be considered a generally accepted assumption that the perception of self-interest was the foundation of morality—just as mortality conversely defined self-interest, namely, the ability to acknowledge or love oneself. Those were the results of a philosophical discourse that ran through the century and had become as entrenched through argument and counter-argument as the humming of the synapses in a human brain. Such a general attitude is based on repetition, response, echo and predetermined stimuli.

All three concepts—PHILOSOPHY, INTEREST and MORALITY—proved murderous in the course of the Revolution. They were abstract, with little rooting in practical experience that balances out everything according to probability. They became motives for the guillotine which ultimately killed the Revolution itself.

It was entirely different with the triad of RIGHT, DISTINC-
TION and AUTONOMY. The precise definition of *difference* is
the mother of objectivity. It creates 'situations', vessels of life.
Right ensures distance from the other, 'elbow room for everyone'. It makes society *liveable*. Autonomy, finally, corresponds
to *self-assurance*, which is the beginning of philosophy before it
becomes a stream of words. Could a republic founded on this
triad have defended itself against usurpers? Certainly. For it
would not have been a uniform republic, the kind a general
could take over. Rather, the result would have been a kingdom
without kings, belonging to all: freedom, *sans phrase*!

That friend of right, Abbé Sieyès, who belonged to the
Directory, was lured by Bonaparte, who proposed the formulation of the constitution for the Republic of Genoa to him during
his Italian campaign. Three constitutional tenets were central
for Sieyès: freedom, law and the indivisibility of the republic
(which meant the state's monopoly of power). Bonaparte
referred to this idol when, after 18 Brumaire, he declared that
there were only two principles of the constitution: (1) ACTION
and (2) SURPRISE. That was the road of violence.

Napoleon's Planned Visit to the Ruined City of Rome:
The Culmination of a Reign

In January 1813, in frosty Rome, the preparations were still
underway for Napoleon's expected triumphant return. Strictly
speaking it was not a 'return to Rome', as this was to be the
emperor's first visit to the ancient world capital; the word
'return' referred to the campaign in Russia. The Danish sculptor
Thorvaldsen was working with numerous staff on the relief in

FIGURE 17. Napoleon at the end of his march on India in the winter of 1812.

a Roman shade of matt red, which was meant to depict stages in the life of Alexander of Macedon. He could already see the emperor walking past at a brisk pace in front of the gigantic work—once it was completed and the emperor was free to come to Rome. The scaffolding for the planned parade lay stored in the depot.

Then came the news from the Beresina. The emperor's visit was postponed indefinitely. The intact administrations in Illyria and Italy still had no idea of the empire's collapse. No one could imagine that Thorvaldsen's relief, which took on its final form in those days, would never be viewed by Napoleon.

Sketch for a Film by Stanley Kubrick on Napoleon.
Planned Start of Filming: August 1969

Length of the film: 180 minutes. Length to produce per day: 1.3 minutes. Filming schedule: 150 days.

—Battles and marches: 30 days. Yugoslavia.

—Outdoor shooting: 40 days. Yugoslavia.

—Indoor shooting: 40 days. Italy.

—Lost to travel: 10 days.

Thirty thousand men. Troops for two dollars a head in Romania. Five dollars a head in Yugoslavia.

There was a New York company that produced printed uniforms made of DuPont fireproof, drip-dry paper fabric; its breaking strength 3,000 pounds. These paper uniforms cost between one and four dollars. Costumes made in London and Paris, on the other hand, cost 200 dollars.

FIGURE 18. From Kubrick's ring binder for the closing sequence.
Length: 12 minutes. Saint Helena. The mountain road above the harbour town
leads inside the Isle of Death, where Napoleon is being held in a country house.
In fact, brigands from the Caribbean tried to capture the imprisoned emperor.
They ascended via the steep mountain path (on the right in the picture), but did
not find the emperor's quarters. They were apprehended and eliminated by
British soldiers.

FIGURE 19. In exile, Napoleon did the reading for which he had not had time during his reign. On the right: one of the crates forwarded to him in exile.

FIGURE 20. The designer of worlds in the garden of the country estate, with English neighbourhood children.

Napoleon's Heraldic Animal

The young Bonaparte, who later made the bee his imperial insignia (he had chosen the symbol for himself from pharaonic sources during the Egyptian campaign), had a British biologist explain the habits and state system of these insects to him.

—Do they form societies, states, nations?

—They are factories.

—That produce honey, or provide cooling in the summer and medium warmth in the winter?

Just as he did later as emperor, the consul Bonaparte already tended to surprise his guests with his own knowledge. The time spent on this was lost to him as working time; he gained nothing from responses to things he already knew. On the other hand, such 'stimuli' hastened the guest's efforts. Thus Bonaparte's 'technique' also had an advantage. The Briton replied:

—They produce a queen. The queen rules over the offspring.

A big fat queen, Bonaparte exclaimed. It is, continued the Briton, as if we Englishmen had a figure 6 metres high that we called our king, and which produced thousands of soldiers or merchants every day. That's what I call a factory, the consul agreed.

—How does such a gigantic creature come about, a solitary race on which all the others depend?
  —Through a special diet for the larva that is chosen to become the queen later on.
  —Not through its bloodline?
  —It would seem not.
  —The workers, the whole colony of bees, paid into these fabrications of offspring and happiness with their efforts?
  —That is what makes the bee colony, the bee factory special.
  —Yes, a special body politic.

In those years, Bonaparte tended towards the exaggerated view that a regent, no matter what their lineage augured, could capture the affection of their subjects so intensely as to give rise to a giant creature which could produce fame, expansion of empire, radiance and 'happiness' like a factory, that is, at will. It was superior to the charisma of kings, which was only claimed to exist.

But at what moment would the potency of thousands of patriots enter the body of Napoleon and make him grow into something OUT OF THE ORDINARY, into the queen bee? The consul did not dare to ask his learned guest this question. He did not want to hear that such qualities can be 'inherited' by people. He was critical enough not to believe he would become the queen bee because of his family legacy.

FIGURE 21. As manager of the world spirit, in the year of his death.

A Patriot of Napoleon in the Village of Zilly

The French period from 1806 to 1813, during which the village of Zilly belonged to the district of Halle and thus the Kingdom of Westphalia, was assessed positively by Karl Pätz, the grandson of a farmer, in a document from 1921, the year of his death. Until the occupation of Central Germany by Napoleon's troops, Zilly's farmers were obliged to provide their labour, draught animals and harnesses, even if their own crops were spoilt by rain in the meantime. The French cancelled all these obligations.

Karl Pätz only knew these facts from the accounts of his father and grandfather, as well as through hearsay among the rest of his relatives. This set the reports of Prussian soldiers' behaviour all the more clearly apart from the liberating actions of the Corsican. These soldiers had taken up residence in Zilly during 1812/13. The women of Zilly wore skirts that reached the ground (they only got shorter from 1918 onwards) and equally long petticoats underneath, but no underwear. That was the custom. One evening they were waylaid by the Prussian infantrymen, who tied their skirts above their heads with ropes. In that state, for no military reason, they were led through the village with their lower bodies exposed. Cellars and larders were looted.

The nationalist teachers in Halberstadt's primary schools sought to convince the young Pätz that the period of French occupation was 'Germany's dark time'. The argumentative Pätz was born in 1839; what he had heard about the French period contradicted the teachers' statements. Pätz would not tolerate any insult to his ancestors. He did not believe that they had lied in their accounts.

Automaton of a Thousand Wishes: The Child Emperor

On the night of 30 April, the eve of May Day, a reduced circle of the faithful—the head physician of the district hospital, the head of the popular theatre, Dr Reich (for a time), and other bosses from Halberstadt—had got senselessly drunk as my father's guests. When three of these people obtained the keys to the larder from the housekeeper and stayed there, my father sent the whole group home. It was six in the morning. Not worth going to sleep.

Outside in the Bismarckplatz, the Combat Groups of the Working Class assembled at ten o'clock, as well as collectives from the food service and machine-building industries, the youth and the party. From his desk, my father had an excellent view of the events. He switched on the record player and listened to the second act of *Die Meistersinger von Nürnberg*. At the same time he studied part of the history of Napoleon's campaigns dealing with the Battle of Aspern-Essling. The battle had been lost because of a series of superficialities by the emperor at the start of the day for which he never forgave himself. A mill that had been thrown into the Danube by the Austrians drifted downstream and destroyed the bridge which Napoleon's reserve was supposed to cross. The emperor just managed to withdraw his army to Lobau Island which is separated from the banks by two branches of the Danube. Napoleon had the dam to the enemy-occupied riverbank destroyed. During the night, pioneers attempted to repair the bridge to their own riverbank. No one rested until five in the morning.

The emperor did what a Roman legion would have done, that is, to set up the small island for his numerous army: it was drained, latrines were built and tents made of branches were 'invented'. And indeed, it started raining soon afterwards. Was the emperor clairvoyant? He was now making the effort he should have made the previous morning.

Outside in the Bismarckplatz, the speeches had finished. The people's army was making music.

One part of the 'bourgeois' person is a strong individual character. I see my father's hands, doctor's hands. His sensitive feet in patent-leather shoes, procured from the west. He wears this covering for precious feet on his everyday visits to patients. People are meant to see: Western goods, that sets him apart. These are characteristics of the predominant society of the 1930s, which no longer exists here in the GDR. It can happen that my father pours a bottle of perfume on himself after his morning bath. Then the clothes over the fragrance. One the one hand, he does it as a joke. But on the other, it is so that he can at least pile on a single ATTRIBUTE OF SPECIALNESS.

A bourgeois person like that is a developed life form, geared towards 'making an infinite effort' in an area of their choosing. They belong to those who have already 'moved up the ladder'. They will not be able to make *more* of an effort than they already are. They cannot be upgraded as a person: they do not want to be an aristocrat and know they are not a prince, nor do they want to die as soldiers in foreign lands. My father is essentially well balanced.

And so he chose the ruler Napoleon as an idol: he came up from nowhere. Gradually, through achievements. Standing in for all of us, he shows CAESAREAN SPLENDOUR. The efforts of the speakers outside in the Bismarckplatz, talking about the internationalism of the working class, cannot compete with that. The emperor works wonders on the night of Aspern-Essling. My father leafs through the pages to the battles in France in the winter of 1814. There the emperor shows himself in a rejuvenated state (it is the end for him).

The emperor is an automaton. He is spurred by a thousand wishes of those who want a new world but will not create it themselves. The emperor must see to that! He is an automaton in human form.

The Marxist descriptions of the 'bourgeois type' are misleading. Such people are not fat, even if they appear corpulent and have bellies. The limbs, the essential forces are tensed and filled with human spirit. The character of the volunteer-corps fighter Puntila, as portrayed by Brecht, is closer to the truth.

Napoleon is a concentrate of this bourgeois type. The skin on his neck is sensitive. The young general's facial features are initially those of a youth, later those of a clever child. That is partly because the portraits were painted by Jacques-Louis David, the emperor's propaganda painter, secretary of the Committee of Public Safety, an intellectual counterfeiter. One can only get an idea of Napoleon's actual appearance from the accounts of visitors, and the emperor always knew how to manipulate their perceptions. He was considered drunk on his longing for glory.

In the night, the group of loyal friends who had taken up residence in the larder spent a long time revelling in a song with 17 verses. Each ended with the refrain:

> 'A fellow just as smooth as silk
> Such a shame he was a drunk.'

The Principle of Surprise

I received a pedal car for my birthday. One evening I broke it in the course of driving. Magda, our nanny, saw my unhappy face and advised me to place the damaged vehicle in a shed in the yard overnight. 'Perhaps it will get better if it sleeps.' The next morning the pedal car stood there, repaired. Probably Mr Laube, the husband of the caretaker (he had technical skills), had taken care of the car at Magda's request. Even today, I hope for such an overnight miracle whenever I postpone solving a problem. This is the PRINCIPLE OF SURPRISE that Napoleon described as the foundation of his constitution. Its counterpart in the US constitution is the human right to the 'pursuit of happiness'. It is less because of Napoleon's military victories than for his promise to repair the world that, in the production of tin soldiers, both his battles and his celebrations in the Tuileries are among the most popular themes.

Bonaparte's Life Lasted 18,878 Days

On his brief trip to Paris on Sunday, 23 June 1940, Hitler had commanded the immediate transfer of the coffin of the Duke of Reichstadt (Napoleon's son) from Vienna to the Dôme des Invalides in Paris. Legation Councillor Fritz Kanneguth, who was one of the group in Hitler's entourage viewing Napoleon's last resting place, was ordered by Hitler's calls to direct the transportation. By chance, Hitler had inspected Kanneguth's personal file; it mentioned his studies in history and art history. Thus the transportation of the precious deceased was entrusted to him. A certain self-satisfaction was involved: the Führer loved

FIGURE 22. The future of a great empire: Napoleon's son, King of Rome.

FIGURE 20. The nursery in the Tuileries, from Stanley Kubrick's ring binder.

to voice a sudden knowledge that shot into his head and then turn it into a command. He often considered how few such ideas, lightning-fast flashes of memory and the resulting directives, could fit into a single day of governance whereas his lifetime was constantly slipping away.

Kanneguth had caught the Führer's notice on the flight to Paris with the comment that Napoleon had the stature to create a new world but he exhausted his enormous power by preserving an old one.

Hitler definitely wanted to do things differently. No one should see him hesitate! Nor would he succumb to the temptation to marry a high noblewoman and spawn a prince with her.

So Kanneguth's appointment was caused by two things: Hitler's coincidental knowledge of his file, and his remark, which a legate councillor in the circle of the Reich chancellor was not actually entitled to make but which gave him the idea of comparing his life with Napoleon's.

Consultant for Kidnapping Cases in West Africa

I am a consultant for kidnapping cases. I am based in New York. I advise a firm of lawyers. This firm is in turn hired when, for example, employees of a bank or oil company in West Africa are kidnapped. How does one pay the ransoms? How does one establish who is really holding the hostage? Our job is to find that out and give advice.

Now seven employees have been kidnapped from their quarters in Arlit, a mining town for the Areva company, 850 kilometres northeast of Niger's capital, Niamey. The mining town is a high-security area. Three hundred police officers of the Republic of Niger offer protection. The fact that 30 armed men were able to carry out this kidnapping suggests they had helpers among the security forces. Being a consultant in this matter is a lucrative job; Areva is the largest manufacturer of uranium fuel elements. The second-largest uranium mine in the world is supposed to open in 2013. Chinese, Indian, Canadian and South African businesses are involved, with concessions. The construction work is in the hands of the Santoma firm. So it is not simply a matter of identifying the kidnappers and paying the ransoms but, rather, of planning how to find and destroy their nests.

Any mistake can only be made once; hence the great value of our collaboration. So far no demands have reached us regarding the KIDNAPPING OF THE SEVEN. The Areva security experts suspect the organization al-Qaeda in the Islamic Maghreb (AQIM) of carrying it out. My feeling, however, is that Tuareg are responsible. Areva's mining area cuts through the territory of the Tuareg. The groundwater tables, vital for the nomads, are 70 per cent silted up as a result of the mining. Pipelines would be needed to restore the water balance, and there are no plans to build any. The Tuareg Rebellion that began in 2007 was super-ficially calmed through a peace agreement in 2009.

A French aid worker was kidnapped in July along with 18 other people. In his case, France ventured a rescue operation. Because Paris cooperated with the authorities in Mauretania and information was exchanged, the operation failed. The hostage was murdered.

Last week, AQIM 'declared war' on France. They feel the need to send signals. One would have to be suspicious if they now boasted of kidnapping THE ARLIT SEVEN. By negotiating with AQIM, which is possible through Mauritania, one will lose time that is needed to establish contact with the Tuareg as long as the hostages are still alive. Communicating with these nomads is one of the most difficult assignments of my profession.

The Air Observer

Air Observer Mendès-France is a member of parliament and was elected in a district in Normandy. As a metropolitan person, a scribe of sorts, gaining a majority among the farming tribes of Normandy involves a certain dramatic ability. At the same time, it is already an art to bear it at all, whether in peacetime or wartime. The state of war affects Mendès-France in Beirut: surveillance flights along the Iraqi border, description of military presence with or without a purpose. Eight months after the outbreak of war, Mendès-France is transferred to Paris after repeated requests. As a member of parliament, he is received by the minister of aviation, André Laurent-Eynac. Nine o'clock, in his office.

He wishes to be deployed offensively against the immediate enemy, the Germans, as an air observer, Mendès-France demands. That can be arranged, the minister responds.

France does not have a chance. It is amazing—after so much was published about aerial strategy in the preceding years, it turns out they have none. The air observer, Member of Parliament Mendès-France, registers the stages of defeat with precision. One can see it more easily from the abstraction of the air: the nervousness of the ground crew, the confusion of attack orders. The engines and the screws in the wheelwork understand defeat better than the military staff.

Conflict at the Southern End of the World

In December 1941, a British minesweeper arrived at the Kerguelen Islands, a cold, rocky terrain near the Antarctic. Envoys from Free France set foot on the jetty of the French island. The governor of the outpost was obedient to the Vichy Regime. The envoys of freedom spoke and were immediately arrested. An attempt to occupy the minesweeper was thwarted by its crew.

The ship disconnected itself from the pier and left the fjord. That was two days before Christmas.

On Christmas Day, during the festivities, with the sounds of the fatherland's radio stations crackling out of their radios, the little troop, which consisted of weather specialists, logistics experts and a few soldiers, did not want to leave the visiting strangers in their cells any more. They fetched them to have a meal together and then an evening of drinking, and although the captives were locked up again at the end, the hostile opposition of the first moment, which rested only on their commands, could not be maintained. A few days before New Year's Eve, the envoys of Free France were already moving about the inhospitable terrain as freely as everyone else. They often sat together in their shacks. In those December weeks, the globe was subject to 'world war' conditions, as the western bloc was waging war against the Axis powers as a whole. That certainly did not mean, however, that the whole world was indeed in the grasp of war. War: a complicated, artificial (because always dependent on a rekindling of hostilities) web, a relationship that overtaxes its forces. It needs to be tended to, like a garden. War is only 'real at times'. The majority of individuals and areas on the planet are not affected by it.

Captives of Fate

The passage around Cape Horn was difficult for postal ships in the eighteenth century. That is why the news of the 1789 revolution only reached the South Pacific archipelago a year later. The frigate *Navgal* thus still represented the unchanged naval policy of the Ancien Régime when it inspected the bays of the Australian trading stations. Near Samoa, two of the ship's officers arrested the rebel Yves Génie who had been wanted for four years. He sat in a narrow room at the back of the ship. When the commander of the *Navgal*, the nobleman de Barres, learnt of the upheaval in the homeland, he summoned the prisoner to the captain's cabin.

De Barres: I have orders from the admiralty to return to Brest. I will hand over the ship to you, my prisoner, if you let me out at a Spanish port.

The revolutionary was unwilling to accept such a compromise. He thought he could give a passionate speech to the crew and take over the ship 'revolutionarily'. But you can't navigate it, replied the commander. I, on the other hand, can guide it to Hamburg or enter a British port.

The crew won't agree to that, the prisoner countered.

It transpired that they did not want to fight each other but nor could they decide anything with polished words. Not in that cabin. The mentalities of the two prisoners of fate were too different. One could only resolve the conflict between slyness and moralism PRACTICALLY.

'The Guard Dies but Does Not Surrender'

In the autumn of 1944, Philippe Pétain, head of state of the remainder of France that existed within the borders of the Vichy Regime, together with his top official from a detachment of the

German occupation and a shipment of furniture for moving house, but with military salutes, was taken away and brought to Hohenzollern Castle in Sigmaringen. A guard detail from the French army, heavily armed, kept watch at the castle gates. German citizens, including the ambassador Abetz, could only gain entry to the exterritorial site, which constitute the remainder of INDIVISIBLE FRANCE, with a special pass.

One could certainly not call Pétain a follower or heir of the Great French Revolution. In the constitution he had drawn up, he had given his deputy and possible successor the title of Dauphin. His regime was authoritarian. Nonetheless, around this opponent of the revolution whose emblems had found their way into the republic's flag, its principles—the centrality, singularity and legality of France—were present. A whole slew of jurists had accompanied the head of state upon his removal, and a train of legal scholars travelled after him. The insurgents of the so-called FREE FRANCE (the Londoners in the circle of Charles de Gaulle, which a very sizeable number of patriots had already joined) had seized most of the French colonies and, in the wake of the Allied forces, substantial parts of France. The islands of Guadeloupe and Martinique and the colony of Indochina (blockaded by the Japanese occupiers in a way similar to the central government, but equally indivisible) were still connected to the head of state in Sigmaringen. Heavy radio devices were operating from the top floor of the castle, directed overseas. One of the responsibilities of this government, barricaded within a narrow space, were over a million French prisoners of war and forced labourers on German Reich territory, as well as the 20,000 soldiers of the Charlemagne Division.

Like a seventeenth-century Catholic prince with his confessors, Pétain was advised by the jurists he had brought with him. Now of all times, pushed back to the status of a residual power, he could afford neither sacrifices nor any mistakes that would have diminished the authority of eternal France (*la France perpétuelle*). Eleven million square kilometres of naval territory belonged to the nation. Pétain could still have given Captain George Brouder, owner of a fishing fleet in Brest, a concession for the exploitation of such a maritime area. Never had as much LEGALITY been concentrated in such a small space as at Hohenzollern Castle.

Friedrich Sieburg as Pétain's Literary Accompanying Physician

Friedrich Sieburg accompanied the French head of state Pétain on his last exile like a 'political doctor' (as a comforter, confessor, advisor, entertainer and informant). The general was 'as if in a foreign country'. In fact, he did not belong in the time at all. Now he had been taken to Hohenzollern Castle, the castle of the Catholic line of that princely family, where the Prussian rulers had never resided. Time had been bought.

Roughly 2,000 staff at the castle and in the town: the regime of a minor princedom in the eighteenth century. The writer Louis-Ferdinand Céline had arrived in town—no substitute for a political leadership, but a witness at least. He took up residence at the Gasthof zum Löwen, room 11, which he used as a doctor's surgery. In the midst of this muddle, Friedrich Sieburg's calm voice. He certainly did not speak for the Foreign Office which had employed him. Rather, he purveyed the ancient Stoics' line of thought: how to maintain one's composure in a hopeless situation. That, not the comfort of a religion, was what the lonely marshal needed.

Pétain had made an effort (in 1916 and 1940, and later too). What good did it do him? He predicted that he would be shot like the deserters of 1917. It would make a difference whether he was executed shamefully by hanging or decently with a shot in the chest. It was into this mental wound that Friedrich Sieburg poured the elixirs of literary memory. This is one of the rare cases in which historical events and COMFORT THROUGH THE SPIRIT coincide. The 88-year-old statesman was a farmer. Sieburg used grotesque stories by Rabelais to entertain and distract him, and to prepare him for absolution, as it were. Sieburg's advice: to leave for Switzerland, and from there *voluntarily* present himself to the French Supreme Court while the world still assumed that he was safe in Swiss exile. A final attack, a *surprise*, if he showed himself at the French border. Sieburg had taken this gesture out of his literary safe; it was the very last degree of voluntariness that was still available to him, a political element with a weight of a few grams. The court decided to commute the death sentence that had been given to Pétain, instead banishing him to the Île d'Yeu for life. For they would not be able to sentence him to death, Sieburg had predicted, after he had emerged voluntarily from his quarters by the Swiss Lake Walen. 'Not caught, not hanged.'[7] A final triumph of literary experience amid the thorough defeat of the Third Reich.

FIGURE 24. The triumph of Prussian archaeology at the pyramids.

FIGURE 25 (BELOW). Bad Ems, 1919: French officers view the torn-down plaque commemorating the Ems Dispatch. Bismarck's unilaterally undertaken and publicized sharpening of the language in a message from the Prussian king about a conversation with the French envoy triggered the Franco-Prussian War of 1870.

A PICKPOCKET FINDS HIMSELF IN A MERGING GROUP: 'THAT DAY HE POSSESSED NOTHING BUT HIS ZEAL'

Outside, the frosty November sky over Hanover. Inside the opera house, on the rehearsal stages and the main stage, people are preparing the elements that will be put together by Peter Konwitschny for a passage in Luigi Nono's SCENA IN MUSICA: 'Al gran sole carico d'amore'—IN THE BRIGHT SUNSHINE HEAVY WITH LOVE. The director has asked sociologist Oskar Negt to come. In the audience space of the Large House, he is warming himself with Nono's music which reminds him of Bellini.

The passage in Nono's opera that is being worked on deals with the Russian Revolution of 1905. It is about a mother and her son Pavel, a socialist agitator. He has to be hidden from the police. The REVOLUTION OF 1905 did not produce any regime and barely descended into violence. Oskar Negt and Peter Konwitschny agree (and they feel that Nono's music confirms this) that the pull of this brief revolution produced a longing for awakening and social renewal that continues to this day (as if from a vacuum).

FIGURE 26. 'A Train in the Night of the World'.

A Russian Reading Hall in Heidelberg
During the Revolution of 1905

Having returned from his trip to St Louis, Max Weber is fascinated by the news from Russia. It describes a rapidly spreading revolutionary movement affecting the cities and some of the countryside. Within a month, Weber learns how to read Russian newspapers. His judgement is based on encounters with young, intelligent émigrés who constantly meet in the reading hall which is equipped with newspapers.

Twice he makes plans to travel to Russia. But just as the émigrés from the reading group stay in Heidelberg, he also restricts himself to grasping the tremendous movement IN HIS THOUGHTS. He is editor of the periodical *Archiv für Sozialwissenschaft und Sozialpolitik* [Archive for Social Science and Social Policy]. The texts he writes have to be published there. The process is time-consuming in relation to the events; they overtake the written word. Vyacheslav K. von Plehve, the tsar's evidently hated interior minister, is assassinated. Suddenly the revolutionary movement is over. Weber's basic deliberations have still not been published.

His analysis is oriented towards the long term. He follows on from his study on the HISTORY OF AGRARIAN REFORM IN ANCIENT ROME. The farmers' hunger for land strikes him as the motor of the revolutionary process. In this sense, he writes, Russia (not the USA) is the 'land of unlimited possibilities' for the German Reich. In the weeks when news of the upheavals was reaching Heidelberg daily, Weber felt that the things he was writing down were coherent. Now that the historical moment has disappeared, he finds his notes incoherent. The thought of a chance for Germany strikes him as *greedy*.

What Is a 'Merging Group'? /
Rosa Luxemburg and the Revolution of 1905

The 'merging group' is the element of all revolutions. Humans join forces. Before they even know it, they move from their previous lives to a new kind of condition in which their qualities are combined unintentionally: below their willpower, under the impression of unrest that has seized the city, and because of their keen awareness and vigour. Rural populations supply further people. They join the ranks. The 'new revolutionary human being' (an initially unstable element) does not consist of *persons*, of the old humans themselves but, rather, comes about *between* them, from the gaps that separate people from one another in everyday life.

In Kiev, a pickpocket found himself in a merging group moving towards the central train station. Its members wanted to occupy the station. Tsarist guards sought to hold up the crowd. The pickpocket was tempted by the opportunity but he forgot about his trade. He became one of the scouts exploring the path for the train of protestors, which led through side streets to the square in front of the central station. The boy did not steal anything for several hours. In the evening he had to go hungry. That day he possessed nothing but his zeal.

A lawyer whose time had always been precious to him (lawyers are service providers) had stumbled into the same group. He proceeded through the city with the rebellious horde, involuntarily (and while subjectively disapproving of such illegal riotous gatherings) reinforcing the power of the attack on the police barricades by walking along with the crowd. He moved through the city until the evening hours.

Rosa Luxemburg, who had come from Berlin after hearing the news that the revolution had broken out, tried—having arrived late—to reconstruct the experience of the first days of the revolution. She collected accounts. The reports all agreed on the fact that at the moment of upheaval, messages, ideas and impulses to act had spread among the people more rapidly than could be achieved by telegraphy or means of transport. It seemed to her, she wrote in her articles for the *Leipziger Volkszeitung* with a certain pathos, as if a SINGLE LIFE FORM, A REVOLUTIONARY COLLECTIVE WORKER was in action. A few days later this was no more than a memory. The 'giant' of which Rosa Luxemburg had written seemed to have crumbled in that time.

Unlike a human child, wrote Rosa Luxemburg, which is born as a tiny bundle and grows into an adult, the revolution is born as a giant body, as a NEW SOCIETY, and it needs time to transform back into the individual human beings of which it consists. For her, the decisive question which preoccupied her to the end of her life was this: How can one keep the GIANT BABY THAT IS REVOLUTION alive through the first weeks, and then especially the first centuries; how can one nourish and bed it? There was no known way to save such a MERGER under the conditions of everyday production or family privacy in the long term. No revolution could thrive in a wrong life. NO RIGHT LIFE WITHOUT REVOLUTION.

FIGURE 27. Max Weber (second from right) in 1916, serving in the
First World War as administrator of a military hospital.

In the Gridlock of Time

At Whitsun 1917 and once more in October, a ghost parliament
of young people and rejuvenated elders gathered at Lauenstein
Castle at the invitation of the publisher Eugen Diederichs, following on the emphatic youth gathering on the Hoher Meissner
in 1913. But now, in the midst of war, the concern was to
make decisions about the future of the Reich and of Europe.
The participants included Ernst Toller, Friedrich Meinecke,
Theodor Heuss. Max Weber captivated these young people with
his interventions.

'Drilling with passion.' Passion is not characteristic of institutional activities. It existed for a few years in the Prussian administration after the defeat by Napoleon in Jena and Auerstedt. None of that was repeated after 1914. The slow passing of months in war paralysed the powers of souls in the Reich. The exciting proclamations are always those of the others: those in Russia, those in China.

What evening classes are there to train the human of the twentieth century? Political people who combine passion and sound judgement must not be laymen. The current emperor, a number of governors in Prussia and a few South German head officials will look like laymen when the new youth RISES UP in profound objectivity (rationality) and a highly strung capacity for horizons (passion). Around him, as he later said, appealing types. Max Weber went so far as to speak of the berserkers, their ecstatic readiness for battle, whose fearlessness in the face of death had to be crossed with the ability to organize an office, just as Moltke set up his office in his tent at the Battle of Königgrätz. Weber did not have much success among the young people with his idea that one needs education, and hence needs to study. They were in a motive gridlock. They wanted to INTERVENE, not study.

'The Human Becomes a Thing'

The spirit of capitalism is a spiritual concentrate, Weber continued, distilled within a space of 400 years out of FEAR OF DEATH, FAITH (as an answer to hardship and terror) and the TENSION OF THE ENTIRE SOUL: a fluid 'that suddenly becomes crystalline in an entire people and turns humans into things'.

Max Weber baffled the young people and his rivals at Lauenstein Castle with such utterances. The idea of *profession* is a similar concentrate, said Weber: the notion that my work connects me to all other people in the world, and must therefore be guarded like the food supplies in the larder. That is the truth! A third attractor is power. It accumulates the trust that grows anew in families with each generation. AS IN A MILLION CHARCOAL BURNERS' HUTS, A SOCIETY GETS ITS

FIGURE 28. Max Weber (second from right, standing). Below (second from right, sitting) the writer Ernst Toller, later a revolutionary in Bavaria. Fourth from left: Theodor Heuss.

EMBERS FROM THE DOMAIN OF FAMILIES. This is the basis for the connection between FAMILY and POWER. Power is therefore imagined as a human being, and when the PHYSICAL BODY OF THE RULER is later beheaded, the personalism of all individual members of society increases: everyone is a king. But the monarch becomes silly, says Max Weber to applause, like our autocrat Wilhelm II.

Journey to Kalinovka

One takes the night train from Moscow to Kursk. From there two hours west by car on gravel roads and sand tracks to Dmitryevka. From there south to Khomutovka. There one goes southwest to Kalinovka.

At the height of his power as secretary general of the CPSU, Khrushchev was surrounded by pandering advisors and assistants. In the spring of 1960, through a remark made by their leader, they learnt of his teacher Lydia Shevchenko. They investigated and arranged for the old woman to be brought to Moscow, where she gave a presentation at the Pan-Russian Educators' Congress. She reported that Kalinovka was a 'dreadfully boring village'. As far as she knew, Khrushchev (as a pupil and on visits to his home town) had expressed an *aversion* to the farming class which was trapped in its hopeless situation. One should at least strive to become a miner in the Donbass. Farmers were not proletarians. Because of these statements, the woman was quickly taken away. Khrushchev visited her; it transpired that he had gone to Kalinovka twice a year in the past decade. He held the aging rebel in his arms for a long time.

FIGURE 29. Lydia Shevchenko, primary-school teacher of Nikita Khrushchev, who attended the school in Kalinovka in 1905 at the age of 11. The young atheist and rebellious teacher discovered the boy's intelligence. She planted the spirit of 1905 in his mind.

Max Weber Compares the Roman Agrarian Reform to the Russian 'Thirst for Land of 1905'

According to Max Weber, it was not the quick ideas, the formulable slogans of the city-dwellers who appointed themselves as spokespeople of the Russian Revolution of 1905, which were the decisive tendency (and one whose effects would continue after the collapse of the revolution) but, rather, the THIRST FOR LAND, the impetuous willpower of those who worked the soil, pent up for centuries. He did not say 'farmers', because he sought to establish a theoretical connection to the dogged efforts of the Roman agrarian reform. That had dragged on for 400 years (a sub-revolution of the AGRICULTURAL REVOLUTION, which comes from Babylon). One could not call the people who had driven this development ahead over generations farmers. They called themselves *coloni*. One of them was the Emperor Diocletian.

Weber felt he saw a continuous movement in the agrarian history of Rome, comparable to a subterranean river that gave the empire its secret strength. The central aspect was the ability to demarcate land and cultivate it through division of labour. The true growth ensued in the mind, which was a SECOND-ORDER FIELD. POLITIES GROW ON SUCH SOIL. The interior of humans: 'like a well-raked garden'.

As Weber says, this 'Roman element' can be found neither in the German Peasants' Wars nor in the Russia of 1905. But it was equally invisible in the city of Rome in the year of its foundation, 753 BCE. Weber estimated that in 50 to 100 years, the impulses of 1905 could give rise to a 'republic of the East', led by a new type of person. Not property and work but, rather, the adaption of the soil to the already existing delicacy of the brain, the MELIORIZATION OF THE INTELLECTUAL SOIL, was the object of this process. This new intelligence, prepared for 'drilling through hard boards', was capable of taking over the ADMINISTRATION OF THE WORLD.

A Research Team in Akademgorok

From 1984 to 1987, 12 academics who had been assigned by Andropov and later advised Gorbachev conducted research in Akademgorok, Novosibirsk. They were investigating the question of whether the obvious progress in great Russia (which contrasted with equally obvious deficits of motivation and politicization) had a special root that was particular to Russia.

For then it would be possible to reverse the slogan 'socialism in one country', the cause of so many regressions and sacrifices, and envisage something useful to the world. The unfolding of productive powers, the researchers believed, presupposes an echo from the world, if need be in the form of markets.

It could be, the researchers said, that a 'centre of emotions' would form in a different way—presumably inaccessible to the governing bodies. The existence of the MIR in the firmament, the surprising fact that naval power had almost been attained under Admiral Goshkov—the researchers considered the latter unproductive, but amazing as an achievement—the explosion of the education system, the engineering system and not least glasnost were outgrowths that had to have a root. IN THIS RESPECT, THESE 12 RESEARCHERS BELIEVED THAT PERESTROIKA, AND ALREADY THE TRIAL PHASE OF DE-STALINIZATION UNDER KHRUSHCHEV, WERE A FOLLOW-UP TO THE IMPULSES OF 1905, NOT A CON-TINUATION OF THE PUTSCHIST ACTION OF 1917. 'Deep under the snow' was the heading of a joint publication by the 12, who, after the collapse of the empire, were scattered in the USA among Berkeley, Stanford, Harvard and Yale, and no longer worked together there.

The Unevenness of All Progress in Russia

All developments in Russia are uneven, remarks Leonid Andropov, a sixth-degree nephew of the secretary general (and cites Alexander Pushkin to support his claim). Andropov is an economist from the school of Nikolai Kondratiev. Thus fishing in Russia since Lomonossov, he explains, who was a fisherman's boy and a researcher, was developed in the Barents Sea but completely underdeveloped on the Pacific coast. Russia has the strongest icebreakers in the world, but no practical type of fishing boat. Since Peter the Great, things have not progressed beyond the Dutch plans for the building of small boats. Some large-scale constructions, on the other hand, come too late. In the 1940s, for example, in wartime, there was a sizeable population of whales within reach of Russian ports. Then, in the 1960s, the Soviet Union built the *Sovetskaya Rossiya*, a whaler the size of an aircraft carrier. To make it affordable, the barely profitable whaling industry was artificially pushed (with the help of manipulated figures). In the meantime, whale populations had shrunk worldwide; it was not worthwhile to use a large ship. The *Sovetskaya Rossiya* was decommissioned and is now used as a floating abattoir for Australian sheep. The necessity of supplying the home crew in Antipodean waters eats up any economic advantages, and the statistics have to be falsified once

FIGURE 30. Leonid Andropov   FIGURE 31. Nikolai Kondratiev

again. Thus successes that are unconnected to other things, says Leonid Andropov, paralyse the country's economy.

A Prophet Is Killed

The Russian economist Nikolai Kondratiev, a Marxist but also a 'theorist beyond that', developed the THEORY OF LONG-WAVE CYCLES OF ECONOMIC DEVELOPMENT. Each of these long waves, which have existed since the start of the Industrial Revolution, encompasses between 51 and 59 years.

1787–1843 / 1843–1898 / 1898–1949 / 1949–2008

A cycle, according to Kondratiev, can be divided into spring, summer, autumn and winter. In the winter of capitalist development, depression and stagnation reign. That may be what we are experiencing now. The most dynamic point lies in the 'spring' and the 'summer of capital'. The late autumn of the respect cycle is marked by excessive dynamism and speculation bubbles, as if the life forces of money were massing together in the last moment before the cold comes. Kondratiev's observations did not correspond to the law of the falling rate of profit, which dictates that the downfall of capitalism, not its long-term wave movements, dominates the future. Kondratiev was imprisoned by Stalin and sentenced to death on 17 September 1938. He was already shot on the day of the verdict.

Four Last Notes by Kondratiev

In January 1939, a little book of notes by Kondratiev was published posthumously in Paris—a message in a bottle. To paraphrase his words:

- There is no golden age of capital.
- Most organizations in which people can collectively defend themselves do not have their own production structure. In an emergency they can be blackmailed.
- We must search for organizations of solidarity that have their own production structure. They do exist. In these, people can not only defend themselves but also (without directly attacking a system) posit autonomous alternatives instead. Heterotopia, not utopia.
- Autonomy is subject to the law of gravity. Here, Kondratiev argues, it transpires that the cardboard cut-outs of kleptocracy do not ultimately exert such a strong attraction on people. There is stronger gravitation in human self-confidence.

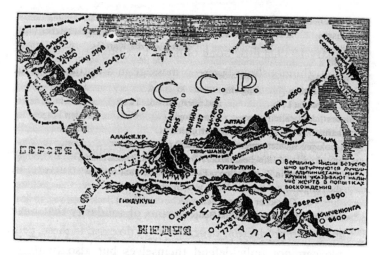

FIGURE 32. Among Russia's treasures are the mountain peaks. Climbing them is the highest virtue of a comrade—although, as Khrushchev mentions, 'Our country people do not naturally have strong climbing ambitions.' By this he meant that they were sluggish, and did not spontaneously strive to move upwards in the party either.

Discovery of a Forgotten Exhibition from 1937

It was not so easy in 1987, when all Soviet citizens were looking towards perestroika—which, after all, means looking at the present and the future—a commemorative exhibition for the 70th anniversary of the October Revolution (1917–1987). Vladimir J. Schlomberg, a confidant of Gorbachev, had taken over this assignment. In the course of their research, his people stumbled on an unregistered machine hall near Moscow. Here, packed in crates and placed on large racks, were the exhibits from an exhibition that had fallen through in 1937 when its organizers fell prey to the wave of persecution and were murdered.

The billboards, the coloured replicas of climbable mountain peaks, the life-sized figures of legendary mountaineering heroes, all of them revolutionary comrades, belonged to the organization Obshchestvo proletarskogo turizma i ekskursii (OPTE). One of the heroes and curators, comrade Krylenko, a high-ranking functionary in the People's Commissariat for Justice, had arranged with his last authority for the exhibition he had initiated to be packed up and stored in the warehouse (he had even ensured that the hall's name was deleted from the inventory sheets). He was arrested the next day and shot a few days later.

FIGURE 33. Inaccessible mountain peak adorned with USSR flag.

FIGURE 34. Special issue stamp: agricultural worker with Trotsky's facial features sowing grain. Aeroplanes rise from the soil and fly towards the sun.

Climbing the Highest Mountains in the Soviet Union

Gorky formulated the motto 'ever higher and higher' for the aspirant Soviet who overcomes the forces of nature. This happened through Soviet aeroplanes, through the tractor-production figures in the statistics, and through MOUNTAINEERING. For some time, LENIN PEAK in the Pamir Mountains was considered the highest. Then a different peak in the Pamir proved to be higher, with a height of 7,495 metres; it was given the name STALIN PEAK. After Khrushchev's secret speech that dethroned Stalin, it was renamed COMMUNISM PEAK. By 1937, the mountaineering Komsomol members had climbed a dozen mountains in the Altay and Pamir ranges and given them socialist names.

In July 1937 the first wave of arrests hit the Soviet alpinist associations. The professional mountaineers had been in contact with mountaineers in other countries, for example, with members of Austrian *Schutzbund* members (comrades who had escaped the reactionary overthrow of 1934) and refugees from the Spanish Civil War. That made them subject to ubiquitous suspicion.

Vitali Abalakov, Hans Sauberer, Peter Zaričnjak and, finally, Krylenko fell victim to the accusations. The alpinist mass organizations, as well as the alpiniads of 1935 and 1936, were led by important politicians.

FIGURE 35. Only two ideas became material forces because they seized the masses, Schomberg asserts: electrification and aviation. In that sense, the Soyus Orbiter was a continuation of the double-decker of 1923. The exhibition *Russia 1917–1987* was an attraction.

FIGURE 36. 'We were on Mount Elbrus. Now we will climb Mount Kazbek. After that we will climb Stalin Peak.'

Are Glasnost and Perestroika a Departure to the Future, and If So, from Whose Soil?

Walter Seidel belonged to the team accompanying the German federal president Richard von Weizsäcker on his 1987 trip to meet Mikhail Gorbachev and the Russian head of state Andrei Gromyko, who was responsible according to protocol. He came from the circle of the Institute of World Economy in Kiel and was fascinated by the upheavals taking place in the Soviet Union under the names 'perestroika' and 'glasnost'. Seidel obtained his information not from newspapers but from dossiers available to the institute in English and Japanese. Seidel was young, and he sensed that the questions of this time awaited quick and profound answers like those which he—he was freshly trained for the purpose—possessed. He enjoyed answering difficult questions.

The meeting with the consultants of the Central Committee in Moscow, whom Seidel had termed responsible and competent, took place in a new building that had been constructed 14 years previously on architectural plans from the 1920s: as quarters for the central authority of the Communist Party, precisely at a time when its decline already seemed imminent. The new accommodation in a built-up space was meant to stir up movement in the 'diseased social vessels' once again. The long-dead cool-headed planners of 1923 had designed the buildings in the manner of a grand hotel. Before and immediately after the Russian Revolution of 1917, revolutionary meetings usually took place in hotels. The planner of 1923, whom the architects of 1973 had followed faithfully, had proceeded from this memory. In reality, only that period before the seizure of power (with a brief echo effect during the time afterwards) had been *political*.

Seidel's papers were checked at the hotel counter. As if it were a real hotel, the keys were hanging on the wall behind the porter who held a high rank in the secret service. The party bureaucrats, who were responsible for the overall political assessment that had accompanied the measures actually taken in the managing decision-making centres, sat in narrow, tube-like rooms—the kind that come about if one empties a generous hotel room meant for previous guests, and then uses shelves and partitions to turn one room into two. This was a compromise between historical splendour and economy, and had already been built into the ground plans of the Swiss and Parisian hotels which served as a model for the design of the command building.

The head of department who was in charge of 'new economic strategies' struck Seidel as sluggish and uninformed.

The man attempted to be polite to the foreigner, partly to be rid of him again quickly. Why was he living in this tube? What interested him? What was he planning to undertake once he had dealt with Seidel? For Seidel, all the details of this party headquarters felt like parts of a decoy, a kind of camouflage to distract from the fact that the genuinely relevant decisions were taking place elsewhere *despite* this political control. THE POLITICAL SUBJECT HAD EXITED THE HOTEL BUILDING WITHOUT LEAVING AN ADDRESS.

There was no plan to install a drinks machine in the building. The revolutionaries before 1917 hadn't needed that sort of thing either, as they frequented cafes in the neighbourhood. Those cafes, however, were not included in the plans that were developed in the maintenance sector, independently of the POWER OF THE PARTY.

An analysis of the Russian Revolution, which seemed to return for a moment with glasnost and perestroika, yielded the following image for Seidel: large scientific institutes and economic combines, with fixed positions and benefits assigned to them, functioned like LARGE COUNTRY ESTATES. They produce pensions. They form the ground, a ground of second nature. Thus institutes, businesses and organizations covered entire landscapes and coexisted with forests, rivers, localities and the complete flat territory of Russia, which is degraded to a merely supplementary reality, a parallel economic zone. Government, institutes and combines—as well as the military structure, with the associated country estates and supply units—are subject to 'decided reform', something resembling a land reform in the fifth dimension.

'Great Russia raised its spirit
Then courage swelled
Then sparks flew'

—So in that sense, perestroika was a peasant revolution? A takeover of estates by their serfs?

—No, by the bosses themselves and their deputies.

—Was there no redistribution?

—No redistribution of the social ground but, rather, a dissolution of that ground—for it consists of second nature, not of soil, water and weather, rather, of pension plans, directives as well as habits. A perestroika politician had to be a jurist.

—This is where the economic angle comes in: Could one apply Schumpeter's concept of CREATIVE DESTRUCTION?

—Just as capital historically replaces traditional arable farming. But there's no capital to be seen.

—Capital is the exuberance, the momentum that comes about in people's heads?

—This is where the industrialization of consciousness should begin. An education offensive!

—You think a socialist society can live on information and texts?

—Somehow survive, if the institutes and organizations still feed it.

—And we won't be brought back down to reality? From second nature to the muddy paths of the *rasputitsa*?

—Never. The real ground has long since been built over. The villages of 1905 no longer exist. The inhabitants have inexorably become Muscovites.

In the notes Seidel took to Vienna, the information was correlated to observations from the writings of Adam Smith. Assuming the processes in Great Russia were not interrupted suddenly and violently, a second path to the information society of the future would come into being here.

FIGURE 37. Khrushchev and his wife Nina Petrovna.

FIGURE 38. Khrushchev in San Francisco. Did his policies anticipate perestroika? Was he a follower of the Revolution of 1905? A Stalinist? Or a bit of everything?

Plan for a Cooperative Network

The deputy head of the GDR's banking system—who, according to the organizational habits of the Eastern Bloc, was thus the political head—whom Hilmar Kopper later came to trust, developed the following approach in order to save the substance of the GDR's former ship-building industry: the production of a fishing fleet for the fishing combines in the White Sea around Mumansk and Archangelsk on credit. In exchange for delivering fish according to a 10-year plan. The ice-cooled goods, brought by rail in express trains, would be processed and canned in businesses on the Baltic coast, especially in Rostock. Export to the west—protected by a guard of Frankfurt designers who would be introduced to an Eastern production's way of thinking by means of adult-education courses. The target group of consumers was probably beyond the Rhine, said the banking expert, where there was less prejudice about Eastern quality. The approach was conceived in subjective-objective terms, that is, it related to people, machinery, prey from the sea, route networks and mentalities. Through skill and personal contacts, it sought to overcome not only the constraints imposed by the Treuhand, interventions by West German fishing chains, incomprehension among the crews, translation difficulties between German, Russian and French, but also the different language etiquette of the Eastern national economy compared to the Western mercantile jargon. He ruled over a NETWORK OF CONNECTIONS BETWEEN SKILLED PEOPLE that would have surpassed any black-market network of 1946. A thousand projects like the one suggested here, claimed this deputy head, whose services were later accepted by a major German bank, could have sustained the self-confidence and industry in East German states like a well-planted garden.

The Equilibrium in the Political-Emotional System of the German Democratic Republic

In the debit and credit of the political-emotional balance—that is, not only the economic one—PRODUCTION IN THE BUSINESSES constituted an inertia (in the positive sense) that started anew every Monday, in which everyone came together along with the massive volume of PERSISTENCE IN PRIVATE HOUSEHOLDS (the laboriousness of working on relationships): an EQUILIBRIUM CREDIT. No society will collapse as long as it is anchored by these weights.

On the other side of this credit (and various special items from successful politics) was a debit: the exhaustion of loyalty that had accumulated over 40 years, a mass of debt. Even as little time off as 10 days, which the French Revolution implemented in the month of September, would have caused the POLITICAL BALANCE to collapse, for production would have halted and private households would have done things their own way. The spiritually restrained seven days between Christmas Eve and New Year's Day did not topple those in power. But a holiday month like August 1989 can already cause an imbalance that shakes the republic and forms the kind of a predetermined breaking point of which the state's security agencies have always warned.

The Big Wheel at Chernobyl

The same organizational power that kept all sections of the USSR going was responsible for the annual preparations for LABOUR DAY, 1 May, as well as the porous planning (carelessness, technical concentrates and disruption of responsibilities) that led to the ACCIDENT IN BLOCK 4 at Chernobyl on 26 April 1986. The town had already been evacuated. But the leisure facilities for the 1 May celebrations, no longer noticed by anyone, were still set up. Towering above them was a striking big wheel that stayed there for another two years because no one dared take down the contaminated device. It stood there rigidly, waiting for the rust in the coming winter. The mute witnesses to a memorial day and the scenic ruin, covered by invisible lava, of the technological district: TWO POLITICALLY OPPOSING SIGNS OF HUMAN LABOUR.

The Concept of Alienation Was Unknown to the Ideologue

In the third year of perestroika, around the time when German federal president Weizsäcker visited Moscow, the political personalities of the Kremlin were behaving especially accessibly. If one joined the crowd surrounding Alexander Jakovlev, who was in charge of ideology at the Politbureau, one could question him. Although every minute he used up in this way held up the Soviet Union's process of change, he showed no impatience. His speeches were of a general nature. Economics interested him as a question of looking after the urban population in winter.

He was not familiar with the word ALIENATION. Confused, he picked up the English word for it, which seemed to fit the facts that were familiar to him. One needs time to learn new things, he said. Conservatives like Ligachov, he added with an ironic expression (he succeeded in contorting his facial features in a hearty, confidence-inspiring way), had an entire bank account's worth of time at their disposal; they had also read Marx better than he had. He was always in a hurry and could not reread things. If nothing happens, he said, the defender wins. The persistent conservatives in the administration can wait, but we can't. That sounded sceptical.

He had fought against the Germans in Leningrad. Now, on the occasion of the visit, he was meeting a German federal president who would have stood opposite him on the occupying side, a member of an elite regiment. But because they did not advance quickly enough and had lost time in northern Russia, the Germans had been defeated. The attack on Berlin was only the completion. The politician considered number two in the hierarchy seemed tired. It remained unclear to what extent he compared the group that was driving perestroika's mode of attack—that is, themselves—with infantry regiment no. 9, which failed on one of the Baltic Islands or before Leningrad because it came too late. Many things struck Jakovlev as meaningless.

The motives of the defenders, he said, were the better ones before Leningrad. Could one say something similar about Ligachyov, who defended the positions of the apparatus and the agricultural sections? No, answered Jakovlev.

The chandeliers in the Katharinensaal were based on those that had illuminated the tsar's receptions, and for a very short time those of the infiltrator Napoleon, with candles in those days. They were carefully engineered electric products from the

1930s, custom-made for the party leadership. Now the guests are called to the gala dinner. A fixed seating plan is inappropriate for political conversation, as one never manages to seat those people next to one another who have something to talk about. The allocation of seats is hierarchical. In Germany, however, the head official is responsible, and in the USSR it is the deputy head official. They are never seated next to each other. In addition, each of the two dinner guests would require a translator, bilingual, sitting at the ready on a little stool behind them. In addition, a second interpreter who would be translating not the language but the historical meanings of the words, their context. The food should not consist of five courses. Hot soup is enough, because it relaxes people. After that, people would have an opportunity for political conversation, but the unsuitable seating plan will prevent that from occurring. All of this—reviving classical concepts and transforming a state dinner into a forum—is among the tasks of perestroika.

'Brain Radius'

The focus of Leonid Vasilyev's department was psychophysical brain radiation. For short moments one could produce a humming of soul lamps in the rooms of the institute. For the materialistically trained, however, it was possible to understand this as 'physical radiation'.

—When lying next to a person one loves, especially in the morning hours, when the bodily powers are awakening, anyone can experience the flow of these forces.

—Isn't it simply warm?

—Not at all.

—And it's not mental?

—It's inspiring. But actually it's the 'noise of the senses', like the sounds of two cities, or the streams of light produced by a city with a river running through it: both sides of the city act on each other with their masses of light.

The Biocosmists declared people under socialism, that is to say, United People, a kind of physiological city. Just as the city stacks people in multistorey houses, and these indeed rise into the third dimension (viewed from the flatness of the fields) in airships and aeroplanes, and in astral cities high above the clouds, so too the elemental properties of humans in socialist societies are stacked up. They form a twofold industry: in the factories and in their relationships with one another as a SOCIAL FACTORY.

It is well known that Lenin rejected any form of belief in spirits in his text *Materialism and Empirio-criticism* (directed against Alexander Bogdanov). Now, no Biocosmist ever spoke of spirits; they are all consistent materialists. But they are materialists in the spirit of the saints and bishops of late antiquity. This is a Russian prerogative. If a body of a dead person shows no traces of putrefaction when the sarcophagus is opened, this is proof of their holiness. The Revolution, however, is concerned with fulfilling this PROMISE OF IMMORTALITY, which was wrongfully made by Christian propagandists, under the actual conditions of knowledge, labour and the socialization of our republic.

—You mean immortality and resurrection of the dead metaphorically, for example, as a museum project? Or as an embalming project?

—Not at all.

At times, 46 departments at the Academy of Sciences in different Russian towns were working on the revolutionary project of the 'New Humanity', that is, the RESURRECTION OF THE DEAD, the rejuvenation and ultimate immortality of the living, equal rights for the unborn.

—The political must subject itself to the criticism of the unborn?

—What else?

Characteristics of a Female Citizen on Travels

'Where Is the Face of a Bourgeois Soul Located?'

On her travels in the Soviet Union, the daughter of the millionaire, United States ambassador to Germany and confidant of Roosevelt, Dodd, suffered greatly due to the conditions in the toilet of the small steamer on which the tourists were going down the Volga. The installations were made of cast iron and crudely painted. Their surfaces were so rough that any foreign body, any dirt stuck to them for years. This millionaire's daughter did not want to sit down on such a thing with her Western bottom. Instead she squatted above it, her muscles tense with the effort, seeking to avoid contact with the cast iron and the paint.

Shortly before Astrakhan she made the acquaintance of a young man, a Soviet secret agent, who later described her thus:

'I encountered a bourgeois lady. These bourgeois ladies clean their anuses, on which they sit just as we do on ours, more scrupulously than their faces. The latter is exposed to the air and the weather and cleans itself, as it were. Occasionally the bourgeois ladies support the skin of their faces with a hint of cream. At the same time, such a bourgeois lady takes little rolls of soft paper (unsuitable for writing on) with her. There are no notes written on these little rolls (I checked thoroughly); their purpose is to clean the anus after the activity itself and then be carelessly thrown away. The supply of such little rolls is "sacred" to the person under observation, the bourgeois lady. She became very upset when her power to dispose over these little rolls (through a manipulation of ours, a test) seemed lost for a few hours. I subsequently "found" the "papers", to her relief, without her ever learning why we had removed them.

'The bottom is especially sensitive among bourgeois ladies. Evidently this young woman was never struck on her bottom with a rod. She responds to stroking of this anti-face, her most important skin organ, with affection. Also sensitive on the shoulders, the neck, behind the ears. The lips, on the other hand, which we Soviets use to accompany contact, have a more defensive function.

'She demanded absolute confidentiality regarding everything we exchanged in the short space of a few days. This applied most of all to the staff of the US Embassy, whom we soon met in Astrakhan. I was not able to ascertain any anti-Soviet activities or secret knowledge (aside from the personal

customs and erotic habits of a bourgeois lady). Signed A. M.
Shvirin, Major.'

REINHARD JIRGL
Heterotopia

After the collapse of the state socialist systems in Europe at the
start of the 1990s, the seals of various archives thus far inaccessible to us historians were also broken: from the party archives
and Secret Command Documents to the Vatican. A completely
new field of activities for the science of history to explore; a
dawn with a thousand paper suns! For the states, regimes and
world empires rise and fall, but the files remain.

One of my students, the hungrily ambitious, diligent Cornelia Schmitt,[8] began her PhD thesis at that time, entitled 'On
the Change in the Political Relations between the Victorious
Powers of the Second World War from 1945 to 1989'—a stan-
dard topic at the time. The necessary research activities led her,
among other places, to the party archive of the SED in Berlin
(in the former Wilhelm-Pieck-Strasse, now Torstrasse). And
there she discovered a slim filing folder; there was no marking
except for the registry number, and it was deposited in the category 'Discard'. The folder contained a summarizing description
of the political situation in the spring of 1961, as well as a loose
collection of partly handwritten and partly typed texts with different paper formats. The latter had evidently been categorized
as useless, and had later even passed over for shredding.

As she read this at first glance odd collection of notes, written in very strange German, what unfolded was the report of a

secret scout among the Soviet delegation during the conference between the secretary general of the CPSU, Nikita Khrushchev, and the US committee headed by President John F. Kennedy in Vienna in June 1961. This conference had been initiated by the Soviet Union; the object of negotiations at the highest state level was the status of East Berlin. The question at hand was whether the Soviet government should be allowed to sign a separate peace treaty with the GDR, in contravention of the previous Four Power Agreement. Vienna had been chosen as the location for negotiations because of Austria's neutrality as a state (the Americans would not have accepted holding the conference in any other European country).

No representatives of the GDR were admitted to the negotiations, however. Hence their fearful question: Would the Soviet side be able to convince the Americans to agree to a separate peace treaty with the GDR government? For then the GDR state leadership would have sovereign control over the access routes to all of Berlin. The experience of the blockade of West Berlin in 1948 had, despite its failure, demonstrated one thing: how quickly the Western powers 'cave in'!: after the ultimatum on Berlin issued by Khrushchev to the Western Allies on 27 November 1958, demanding the one-sided cancellation of the Four Powers Agreement for Berlin and all of Germany by the Soviet government, which was intended to convert West Berlin into an *independent political entity* and bring about the withdrawal of the Western Allied forces from the city, this would therefore have led to a revision of conditions after the blockade of 1948. Right at the start of 1959, the committee of the (West German) task force in Washington reacted to this with the following idea:

Would it be possible to resettle the entire population of West Berlin in the Lunenburg Heath via the access roads into and out of Berlin? Thus, from the safe location on the Heath, the necessary reservoir of workers to rebuild the Ruhr region would also be available. If, however, the GDR henceforth had sovereign control of the roads to and from Berlin, such resettlements of an entire city's population would no longer be feasible; a new blockade would promise greater success for the Soviet-supported GDR government.

Two fundamentally different negotiating partners meet in Vienna: Khrushchev, known and feared for his unpredictable mood swings, faces a US president with little political experience at an international level whose position is further weakened by the failed operation in the Bay of Pigs off the coast of Cuba a few weeks earlier. The overall situation between the two world powers is uncertain anyway: there are Soviet submarines along the US coast and other military facilities, especially tactical missiles, in Cuba. In Turkey, Jupiter missiles aimed at the Caucasus and southern Russia. The instability of this wider situation corresponds to the instability of Khrushchev's temper. In the eyes of Khrushchev—whom the Soviet delegates only ever call 'The Boss'—the Soviet successes in space travel strengthen their position; almost at the same time as the American failure off Cuba, Yuri Gagarin orbited the earth as the first person in space. A debacle on one side, a triumph on the other—will this asymmetry induce the Americans to intervene here and now?

Independently of all the Soviet Union's technological successes, Khrushchev urgently needed political successes of his own! The negotiations over East Berlin would serve this purpose for him.—Thus the (absent) GDR leadership was left to worry about the course and events of this Vienna conference, and: What price would the Soviet side subsequently make the GDR state pay if it was successful in the negotiations?—

Mentally anticipating the worst possible evil helps one to face them and, should it come to pass, to take off its edge at the right moment. And so the GDR state leadership decided to secretly plant a spy among the Soviet delegation in Vienna. It would have been completely impossible to sneak in a German informant of their own. Consequently they took the great risk of attempting to recruit one of the Soviet delegates for their purposes in order thus to access information earlier than normal, and better information than that later filtered by 'Big Brother'. And the GDR Secret Service (Department of Eastern Reconnaissance, a department that was not officially allowed to exist, as one sister people does not spy on another—but this Secret Service department was in fact very active to the end) landed the coup at the very last minute: the GDR Secret Service was able to recruit a lieutenant-colonel in the Red Army whose (real?) name was Yuri Antonovich Alegyev, who was participating in the Vienna negotiations as an interpreter, because it had found his weak point: in 1945, as a young officer, Alegyev (born in Leningrad in 1924) participated in the Red Army's storming of Berlin. Later, during the occupation, he met a young German woman in bombed-out Berlin; a son resulted. This erotic traffic accident with resulting child remained undiscovered by the Red Army authorities (Soviet military courts usually reacted to such *violations* of the strict ban on fraternization with the death sentence), but since being recalled to Leningrad and returning to his wife and two children, this man felt a rash of guilt about the abandoned German woman and his illegitimate son (encapsulated in the recurring image of a thin flower dress and the remembered odour of the foreign young woman's body). Sentimentality and a persistently lingering guilty conscience provided the Achilles heel in the armour of duty: it was here that the GDR Secret Service thrust its spear. Lieutenant-Colonel Alegyev became a scout for the East against the East; beneath his uniform a secret sensory machine with a dual motor.

For further research towards her thesis, the student Cornelia Schmitt travelled to Moscow to look for additional references to this scouting case in the CPSU archive. Thanks to my long-standing acquaintance with the archive's director, Ludmilla Teshenkova, my student received all necessary documents of authorization.—Before her departure she had left me, her mentor, the following notes by the aforementioned Yuri Antonovich Alegyev for perusal.

In the=government train. En route since 1 week ago from Moscow to Vienna with detours: Kiev—Warsaw—Prague—: the-Tsar wants to show himself to his 'allies'. At every stop: delegations of workers at the station, marching bands, flowers & red swashing banners promising eternalfriendshipwiththepeoplesofthesovietunion—sweet little children on The Boss' arms, everyone turned towards the-cameras laughing. Just the way The Boss loves it. (?What reception is awaiting us in neutral Vienna—).

Standing around The Boss, gathered in the lounge car, upholstered class, the horde of 12 staff members. The remaining full 3 dozen employees in the remoter compartments, installed in the kitchen and medical area. We're not included in the-conversations=of the-innercircle with The Boss. We hang around. Playing table tennis, dominoes, even chess is impossible during the-ride because of the bad condition of the rail routes—the balls miss the table, the players the ball, dominoes and figures slide 'n' roll across the board in forbidden moves. All that's left is card-games and obedient lackey-tittle-tattle : impish chitchat from every flunky's longing to have a share in the state & the commanding heights.—Off-duty time is time for shithouse-slogans & intrigues.

Dual function of the-employees, the equation of power : (correspondent / interpreter / cook / doctor) + Chekist = everyone their own spy.—Among the-interpreters I (the disobedient one) am in the entourage too.

Stuffy smell of sweat from everyone sitting around, coming from the seats of their trousers and rising from shoes & jackets, old smell joined all the time by new, with a thick coat of sickly sweet men's per-fume slapped on. The glandular emissions of the-chosen in the competition of subservience : whoever can go the-longest without changes his clothes must be The !Most imp-ortant . . . . (The fibres of the armchair cushions, the heavy curtain materials, the silk wall coverings & the lamp tassels soaked in plumes of old tobacco smoke.)

In this 1 week: !strict alcohol ban from The Boss for=him-self=&=everyone. (The bottles circulate in the rear compart-ments at night &: the-minders who want to be invited to drink with them, otherwise report-to-The-Boss the nextmorning. But an invitation doesn't rule out being reported; reporters have to report, that's their profession, & later the-reported are: *removed* . . . . .)

(Writing these notes is a problem : *A Decent Comrade* !*only writes for the-party*. Someone who writes for no reason arouses Miss Trust . . . . . Impossible to take notes synchronously. Have to trust my senses, the secretly stolen images in my eyes, trust the echoes of eavesdroppings in my ears, my taste as the memory of my tongue, the vibrations& the pressure of the soles of my feet, which touch the floor here=in-the-train, this piece of home, during theride through ½ of Eastern Europe & the pressure of my hands, with all the words still to be written in my capillaries. (Around-me the skinless dogs . . . . . .) Writing only possible during the lunch breaks, better still at night, under the lonely little drop of lamp that smears its dulloily yellow light across the paper above the head end of my bunk. Complaints about the guy in the bunk-below snoring and about myfault from the other end of thiswar. I'm an old rust patch on the sword&shield-of-the-party. Time for me to pay. / My writing hand trembles during the rattling night ride—)—

(Since I started writing by-secret=order, I feel as if I'd grown another pair of eyes. They watch my old eyes, sending signals into my brain that I turn into Other Words. For the new ones, everything is without reservations without credit : new 'n' free.) Only ever a few hours of flickered sleep—

—!*Comrade Alegyev*: comrade !*Chairman is expecting you*.—Just after 6 a.m.: The boss loves the-early-hours for staff meetings because at-this=time his energy & decisiveness are the greatest (:The Boss is getting old, now he's only horny in the morning). Staggering sleepily along the narrow corridor behind the orderly towards The Boss' lounge compartment. The orderly officer in his square suit jacket: curious to see somebody one only knows in=uniform in unfamiliar ink-blue civvies for a change. Body, movements, the way of speaking: all=of=us enshrined in the coffins of diplomacy.

At the end of the corridor the big samovar=for=the=staff, next to it like a grey thick cloud the *deshurnaya*, sitting 'n' ever-dozing. Her tousled hair sloppily done, grown old&mute from everything seen & heard during life=long service in the-ante-rooms; here=on-board the one-ly woman.

All the windows in the train are closed, only to be opened on-the-orders of The Boss with a special key from the-orderly; all curtains are likewise kept shut day&night—*For-health-reasons*. (Sometimes lies say more than truth & the-superiors are always very afraid of love . . . . .-from-the-people) | Entrance through the delicate lounge door, matt white glass with engraved plant ornaments on the panel—: theair in the lounges & com-partments hot-humid, a musty vapour, dull round & heavy.

The eternal evening light in=here is shines bright yellow from the small chandeliers on the lounge-car ceiling, swinging gently during the ride & the crystal ornaments quietly tinkling—the morning light shimmering behind the heavy dark-brown fringe curtains. In the thick-gluey air block in the lounge suite, spoken words seem to stay around longer than usual. Anton Porfirovich Chelyakin has just spoken, a brutish individual with bushy eyebrows & a booming voice. The long, coarse hair of his moustache clouds his thick-lipped mouth, growing around the corners of his mouth into the thicket of cheek 'n' chin hair which sprout downwards inside his collar like bristly-wiry felt. His close-set eyes burn black under the low hairline of his fore-head. (An Austrian swearword: *Tschûsch* . . . .)

He's the main speaker when I enter, his breath, by the block, spits mockery :—*Those-Yanks only understand a* !*fait=accompli—that means: a sound kick in the* !*balls.* And:—!*buttermilk boy.* Crassly rude and obscene defamations & unmistakably aimed at Kennedy as the end of a presumably long rant; stays stuck in the heavyair. Bursts of laughter from the mouths of the-Twelve gathered round The Boss at the longtable, reverberating in oil-flat waves—. The Boss-himself secretly feels flattered by his employee's outburst (I know that look of almost childlike joy on his face); swearing everyone to his offensive line seems to be working. The Boss calls that: discussion. And that means: The Boss states his opinion. After that people from the round of twelve take turns with variations on this opinion. The Boss then summarizes these in a further opinion which is once again covered up with deliberations. After that The Boss declares His=opinion; results, dependent on The Boss' momentary mood, are approved by raising a hand—dissenters are barked into=line by Chelyakin—& are thus frozen into *resolutions.* In addition, The Boss now has a chance to take his superior temperament for a walk, self=restrained on a leash, and remarks with patronizing clemency that we shouldn't have any trouble with these amateurs from the Bay of Pigs & !losers in space,—& spreads himself out across the lounge table—.

This remark by The Boss also ended the opulent breakfast. Since entering I've been standing in front of a long table, scattered with half-eaten white bread butter dishes red-shimmering salmon leftovers started ham jam pots pieces of puff pastry—breadcrumbs scattered like light pebbles, greasy knife blades, fork prongs, spoons sticking out of tea glasses (layers of sugar on the bottom). Unclean table, choked words—The Boss loves these kinds of *work meetings* that proliferate from debauchery. Lost in thought, his fat fingers play almost tenderly with cups, plates, glasses, cutlery—group tightly around the stout King Sugar Bowl—; but I also recall fits of rage, & with a motion of his arm he could cry out and sweep all porcelain-followers in his proximity from the table (only the sugar bowl, that fat white table idol, was always left unscathed.)—Now, The Boss' plump body veritably swims through between the crockery clashing loudly 'n' the reverberation of Chelyakin's brutish outburst, an elemental action, & willingly pours itself into His prepared form.

The Boss now seems to draw courage for=himself from brutishnesses like Chelyakin's unhewn verbal debris, far more than from the gilt-edged warning sermons of the political ass-thete Ivan Petrovich Yedurov (who, sitting almost at the left end of the table, always contorts his face in pain at outbursts like these. He knew Lenin; soon, owing to age, he'll probably be *removed*). Over-a-long-time I despised Ivan Petrovich as much as Chelyakin, albeit for opposite reasons. Yedurov (whom I secretly took for a worm of God, bending up towards heaven to pray) often gushes about *man's treasure chest of humanity* as well as the *Inner Light that can guide people on their woeful way through thedarkness in the political catacombs, as long as they, people, trust their=light deeply.*—(:Such talk would almost have sent me to Chelyakin.)—But since this journey, I have become inwardly closer to Yedurov. After one of The Boss' temperamental outbursts, Yedurov, who was sitting next to me, pointed briefly to Chelyakin and murmured unexpectedly openly:—*The-day is not far off when thesetwo)=beautiful-souls*

will get on even better, & !that will be the-hour of my end.—
(:Why !this statement to ?me: ?Can one already make out the
see-cret dissenter in my ?eyes. But I value people with no illusions about the-future, and shared disgusts bonds too.)—Meanwhile, from His form, The Boss is fashioning the armour for His
Arrogance for the-negotiations in Vienna . . . . .

And His gaze now falls on me, as if he had only just noticed
my presence. When The Boss tells me that the total of 6 interpreters are divided into 2 teams & I'm the 2nd in the 1st group
to translate & this order can be repeated if necessary, so that
each of us only has to perform simultaneous translation for a
relatively short time—as well as that, He makes me the leader
of the translation teams, being the longest-serving member—the
colour of His eyes changes from dove-grey to a watery blue.
This separation, The Boss notes, is for !health reasons. As He
speaks, the fat fingers of His right hand bunch the used, clinking
cutlery next to Him, the blades and fork prongs point at me.

Then his eyes look right-through-me, somewhere undeter-
mined.—No speaking or sounds, except for the noise of rattling
iron from the driving train.—In front of the side wall of heavily
covered compartment windows (glowing early June sun outside,
visible in slim strips through slits in the cloth) thetable & the-
Twelve, motionless in ink-blue suits, frozen in their agitated
poses, at the centre of the table The Boss, Self=absorbed, not
returning my formal farewell. As if Da Vinci had painted them—

Despite the train's speed: time locked up inthetrain, onelong
eternal evening, suffocating . . . . .

2 June 1961: Arrived at Vienna Central Station in the
morning. For the 1st time in days&nights the droning wails of

the wind ebb away, still the phantomvibration in= thehead-
&hands from the swerving wheel-punching train ride. Halt
now,—but our iron block of time keeps racing on roaring on
in=myhead—

All members of the delegation step out into the carriage cor-
ridors, grouping together like paratroopers about to jump out
over enemy territory. We, the-entourage, await The Boss.

With his fat-naped skull heavily bowed, it seems as if
The Boss' stiff grey brushed felt hat had taken on immense
proportions—had slid down to the neck and shoulders. The hat
must be heavy, meaning That's what's bending the coat-wrapped
figure of The Boss over into the posture of an attacking bull.
!Onto the platform. It's the morning.

Bright liquid daylight burning in my eyes; squinting; the
wind's freshness in the station air infused with water vapour &
bitter soot—, stepping out of the iron tube—gusts grip = throw
coat bottoms roughly into each other & tangle the hair on some
insufficiently quickly covered heads into air vines—

The feeling of freshness only in the 1st moment. Soon, even
at this early hour, the closeness starts: high humidity, hardly any
wind, already over 20° Celsius.

On the platform: greeted by the Austrian president Adolf
Schärf. Elongated skull, sparse grey hair, a ministerial figure. A
soigné gentleman (certain=ladies would say), the paternal and
soft features of a 70-year-old, his pleasant mouth is capable of
conciliatory but firm words. An aura of chancellery, a
metropolist out of politeness. Thus an extremely velvety reception for our delegation, over-hearty pleasantries (seemed a bit
ironic to me : still a ?silent triumph because of 1955: vodka

diplomacy for the treaty, Schärf was involved, had co-authored it & beat us-Russians with our own weapons). For the reception, no delegation of workers no adorable children no band or banners, The Boss is missing the familiar=setting;—instead diplomats, the state's dignitaries, honourables : strictly according-to-protocol. The carpet in front of the train leads to the station hall—a bright red band (—the carpet has a small fold directly in front of the escalator).

Krushchev's annoyance about Kennedy only arriving by air the next day; the differences in the speed and form of travel lead to differences in the degree of urgent, reinforced decisiveness.— The Boss presumably fears that his built-up eagerness could trickle away in the loose sand of wasted hours . . . . .

Thus he insists on beginning the negotiations !immediately after the American president's arrival (it's still morning, static heavyair, 19° C, rising fast—: Kennedy isn't used to the continental climate here; he needs time to acclimatize, desiring refuge in the synthetic cool of air conditioning). The Boss sees through the tactics of the-Americans & declines all polite offers to create 'a relaxing atmosfear in-advance'. He senses that his chance lies in haste and thestuffyair.

1st negotiations on the morning of 3 June 1961, a Saturday, at the US Embassy, the former Austro-Hungarian Oriental Academy; its purpose was to improve relations with the Middle East & the Balkan.

The ceremonial motorcade of the-state's digni-taries (:!*how many kinds of -tary there are*: *secre- mone- volun- sani- tribu-no- digni-tary*) : one behind the other in four spacious, calmly rocking Chaika limousines (one for The Boss; three for his 12 closest staff members)—black high-polish metal with a silver teeth-baring cooler grille, moving along like a caravan under a milky sky. While driving up to the US Embassy, Boltzmanngasse 16, the imperiously distorted anamorphotic image of the multi-storey Baroque building that was once the Royal Oriental Academy appeared in the shiny mirrors of the state car-riages— its likeness cast by one advancing limousine-across-the-next like a gauze veil with woven-in ornaments, stucco work, pillars, architraves—formerly strict tracery for the speeches of rulers,— the darkly highlighted distorted reflections in the metal-car-riages lend the petrified power something very ironic.

For the other members of the Soviet delegation—a good three dozen—the embassy has provided a total of eight Volgas, 5 passengers per car, each sticking to/the/other. I squeeze into one of the vehicles, sink into the dark upholstery, feel thebody-heat of my neighbour.

The original plan is to have a-re-ception with refreshments. But The Boss is looking nervously at the clock, not wanting to let the morning (!Thetime of his Highest Energy) pass unused. The beefsteak will take !toolong;—The Boss orders the-start of the negotiations, taking his=escorts aside from the-others; we stay behind in the canteen, wait, are served sandwiches & coffee ('hot brown water').

Spacious & full of nooks and crannies, this room in the embassy basement, the floor is covered in stone tiles, walls & ceiling painted a light colour, maybe there Used To Be a ware-house or storeroom here, Nowadays it's the canteen for the embassy staff (the soothing coolness of the stones accompanied by the cold smell of food and cobwebs). Sacro-sounding silence=here, carried by heavy stone pillars, now&again a cough a mumbled banality (:the premises could be bugged). Next to me a colleague, leaping up from his chair when=called=from-the-door, interrupting his tedious prattle & twisting his pale grimace into a look of importance:—!*The call of=!duty*.

The Boss seemed to have changed the order of his interpreters; 2 of my colleagues were already back from the conference hall and I had not been called yet. The flat gazes of the-returnees were meant to look knowing, their mouths pursed into silence.

Short break in the negotiations; outside in the lobby. Air static, 26° C outside; only a few degrees less in=here. Sharp faces spill out of the conference rooms, broad people, severe gazes, mouths determined=mute. / And !immediately-ordered end of the break: back into the conference hall, the-figures slurped in by the narrow-mouthed high portal, into the Baalian haze of politics.

!My 20-minute work rhythm : lined up along the middle of the table stand a squad of leptosome Coca-Cola bottles, decorated like party girls posing in skimpy black dresses. : In parallel the second halfway line: the big carafes plumply smooth & watery-light—black | white, the chess figures before the endgame.—The parallel fronts are broken up by large round plates set at regular intervals on place mats, covered with biscuits from a 'best selection'. Likewise well-filled little baskets of fruit, apples pineapples bananas oranges grapes, their colours well coordinated,—alternately protruding into each side like glacises.

During the debates. Adopting the structure of the table decoration, the alternation in the addresses of the negotiation leaders : Khrushchev begins. His speech is the drumming of word-hooves over dry, firm steppe soil, relenting in-nothing, riding down the-opponent into thedust—. (His fat hands working the air as if moulding tough masses into sculptures of rapid overpowering. Time is running out, The Boss' energy reserves are dwindling, the morning has almost passed and is tending towards noon; the roll of fat at the nape of his neck is moist with sweat, the white hairs around his tonsure stick damply to the rosy skin of his head. The always-overtight hat brim has imprinted itself on the egg-shaped round skull as a reddish-shimmering notch, the tropic-of-obstinacy. | Kennedy awaits the-attack, ducks inwardly, runs his fingers slowly through his full, blow-dried hair a few times, lowers his eyelids, wants to give the impression of tiredness. Occasionally smiles in a forced=ironic manner, frowns; his look underlines the intention to find an expression of accommodation and: demanding-respect; while sitting, his upper body & face stretch into the vertical dimension. Waiting for the end of the drumming from the other side.

The Boss' heavy torso pushes forward, he throws his tight-collar-tied neck back&forth, seems about to rob his staff of their energy (they remain wordless, not daring to interrupt); with his last power, The Boss throws his head upright with his already-pale face, now elongates his broad face, narrowing it further by opening his mouth wide & drawing in his cheeks. His skin folds, stroked in the perpendicular, lend his face rigour & order,—a teacher seeking to spoil his student's appetite for escapades in-advance. / Kennedy now senses that the time for his=appearance has come. Suppresses the ambivalent gleam in his eyes. Pulls=himself=together.

Then: gather the words in-his-mouth until they freeze &
turn to ice—. He speaks thin-lippedly with a crooked mouth
while his right wrist dangles limply from the armchair rest; he
speaks about Berlin with slow, drawn-out diction. Scatters
well=considered, friendly remarks about Soviet policy in thiscity.
Because Berlin is essentially a lawless place, the Allied bombings
in thewar & the-capture of Berlin by the Soviet army did not
bring thiscity to heel. (My seat is behind The Boss on the right,
I whisper my translations into his outer ear, white-grey bristles
are sticking out of it. The ear keeps still.)

Khrushchev is not in the-mood for friendliness. He visibly
doesn't give a damn about the-compliments from the American.
While Kennedy is speaking, Khrushchev interrupts him; in a
loudvoice he demands *chai* with sugar & white bread. There's
plenty of the latter in the form of sandwiches, but the-Americans
don't have a samovar for the *chai*; the device now has to be
brought over from the Soviet Embassy almost 6 kilometres
away. Which happens—by courier, & allthetrafficlights on the
street corners are switched to=green (The Boss relishes his
Triumph.) Time passes——

Meanwhile, Khrushchev picks all the filling out of the sandwiches offered to him, also removing, disgustedly, the butter,
onion rings, lettuce & cream,—all he wants is the naked white
bread. (The Americans=opposite follow his every action silently
& suspiciously, as if this deconstruction of the sandwiches
threatened to put them at a disadvantage in the-negotiations.
Kennedy's even features twist into waves of displeasure: he
certainly wishes for calm & circumspection, polite smoothness
in-dealings with other people; desires moods extra-vagances,

openly paraded, probably strike him as impertinent, tiresome. The sight of this Russian brute makes him inwardly=evasive, as if he feared physical contact with him=overthere, this oldboor, who probably gives off a sour=glassy smell of oldmeat when he sweats . . . . .) The US president promptly lights a cigarette, smokes and blows sheets of smoke towards the Soviet side of the table; he pushes his front evenfurther back, as if he wanted to cloak his retreat in mist.

Then the samovar arrives—the chai is served. Additional hot flushes emanate from the silver-shimmering vessel. Kennedy, nervously fanning himself with a piece of paper, resumes his speech (his voice crusty, full of restrained anger and tormented by the oppressive humidity=in=the=room.)—Chewing broadly and slowly (while appearing to listen to Kennedy's words), Khrushchev adds sugar cubes to his chai, pokes about in the increasingly porous cube portentously slowly & scrupulously, studies the sugary streaks and observes its dissolution in the golden yellow brew—then stirs up the sugar sediment again with his teaspoon, stares seemingly absently into the glass—. Clearly he has installed his inner activeness through the hot tea.

Kennedy moves evenfurther into the defensive. One must be unafraid, he emphasizes, to call things as they are: Berlin is a factor of disturbance for American:Soviet relations. (And dabs the 1st sweat from his brow.) / Now all he needed to say was: ?!What does Berlin, this worm-eaten apple of discord that We took a bite out of 'n' don't like the taste of, have to do with your ass. We're dealing with otherthings . . . . . here (:& everyone=here would have understood !What the American president meant). But he doesn't say It, keeps quiet, a few words before going over the edge into stupidity. / (:Translate everything one can't hear.) / Khrushchev dribbles a sugary drop from his teaspoon onto the tablecloth. Wipes over it with his jacket sleeve. (He'd certainly like nothing-better than to sweep all the dishes off the table or: throw it at the-American's chest. (I secretly glance at Chelyakin; his face is like an excess pressure gauge with the needle in middle position.)) / Kennedy has found a stodgy=warm tone with a hint of scraping to it, like a spoon stirring the bottom of a pot of simmering sauce.

The Boss (starting up from his apparent lethargy): —*Let's speak !frankly to each:other. In=the=war we were allies, the-postwar made us enemies. We have to !break this off. No possible way out. !You, Mr President, never got to know Berlin properly. Only acquired your=part of thiscity through negotiations, We got ours through battle-&-victory. I don't recall 1 single American soldier falling in Berlin: but thousands-of=Ours.*—Now the voice of The Boss sounds genuine 'n' undisguised, his *thousands-of=Ours* sounds like the coda of a hymn. And clenches his fists too, then brings them down on the table.

Meanwhile a few nimble hands, Russians, have swiftly seized and taken=over the plate with chocolate biscuits like a shock troop; the-Americans are only mildly on the offensive— Kennedy doesn't want to bring-anything-to-a-head; not looking for confrontation, wants to conduct his negotiations on the defensive—, they only take some of the crunchy oat biscuits. Kennedy's compo-sure (as if playing chess by the rules of poker) versus Khrushchev's erratic suicide chess. | Berlin, the white queen: !check. And the figures=on-the-board are the flesh&blood of socialism, to be beaten only by The Sword. End of the 1ˢᵗ day of negotiations. Standing up, pushing of chairs, decampment in delegations,—outside still pre-storm humidity, pushing one's breath down.

Final glance into the conference hall: the biscuit plates plundered, but Nobody touched the fruit baskets on the table, as if the fruit were poisoned or made of porcelain. Emptied out & knocked over on the once-white tablecloth: the glass ballerina, 1 Coke bottle. :?Who'll make the-1ˢᵗ-move . . . . .

2ⁿᵈ day of negotiations: Sunday 4 June 1961, in the morning (The Boss insisted on this time). No wind, steamy and humid (though no sign of a storm coming); as if yesterday mid-day had stood still at 26° C, glassily smeared sky. At the Soviet Embassy: Viennese neo-Renaissance, former palace of the Duke of Nassau; broad facade, open balcony with balustrade; interior furnished with granite & marble. Rising from the glass dome in the attic the flagpole with flag attached, a needle with blood-red cloth directly piercing the heart of the sky—(:!*If the mast is too high it attracts lightning.* / Rightnexttoit the Russian Orthodox cathedral of St Nicholas. (:*We'll never get rid of the-priests*—)

The-Americans advance with a fleet of 30 black, well air-conditioned state limousines, the little flag with the star-spangled banner on the wing of every single car. Catapulting of pennalism: ?*Who's got the-biggest*—into the diplomatic realm : & all the secret disgrace for those at the bottom.

Today it's my turn as the 1ˢᵗ interpreter of the morning.

Everyone is sitting around the long table in the middle of the room, heavy-with-heat, tobacco swathes like marble veins in the air block. Moving their heads into different positions, search for angles towards=themselves, towards-the-others, towards the furniture. Deep folds in some faces.

Kennedy's eyelids fluttering, he tries to pull them up & tie them in place. The skin of his cheeks smooth with no sweat, curves on either side of his mouth, but his lips soft, the ends of white upper&lower rows of teeth flashing.—*O-ccasionally*— (he begins with an emphatically cold voice, his lips rounded at the full-sounding O as if for a kiss, puckered like a chicken's arse.)—*O-ccasionally one changes one's clothes. You too are fully clothed, if I may say so. You will see, I don't disagree with you on anypoint. We, our two countries, have often been at-variance; now we're in-conflict from head to toe, so to speak.*— (As he speaks, he runs his right hand through his full head of hair again).

(!Don't translate everything *exactly* as one hears *it*.)

—*What you're showing me, Mr President, doesn't look to me like a newfashion: this suit you want to hang on my shoulders is already pretty greasy, the trouser legs are too short and they're bulging at the knees.*—The Boss' face is suddenly over-tense, as if his skin were too thin, but thehead, inflated into an egg shape & brightred, seem to have grown too large for so little skin. His hands with their short, thick fingers rest on the table-cloth, far away from him, his cuffs moist with sweat. His two large front teeth pinch his lower lip while the rest of the mouth cuts upwards into the flesh of his cheeks on both sides; the wrinkles are pulled up to the tear sacs: a grimace of tribulation & spite. Casting a long glance, he looks at his interlocutor. He could only view the latter's remarks as a trap : with the stodgy-warm voice and blow-dried hairstyle. (The bad-faith strategy of the-defensive: lure the-enemy far enough onto your land until the-enemy gets lost in it. Removal of the enemy through self-distraction . . . . . Theland then gobbles up the chunks of the-enemy just as theswamp devours whatever falls into it.) / The only response from The Boss:—*Hm. Hm.*—And then in a rusty tone:—*Enough of sartorial matters. Let us leave that to the tailors. I would like us to take a !break now.*—Stand up, move chairs, clearing of throats here&there. Go-to-the-door, end of my 20-minute=work. (The Boss loosens his tie, opens his top button, the neck fat roll makes use of its unexpected freedom and spills over the edge of his collar, a reddish sausage.)

End of the 2nd & last day of negotiations. Nobody made the 1st move, one-word didn't lead to another. Kennedy's flight to Europe, the aeroplane as a projectile in transitory time. His invisible baggage (the fiasco in the Bay of Pigs) can be lost by maintaining steady High Velocity. Thedisgrace wiped over by fleeing at an increased speed. : Smashes against our iron block of time, oneweek's train journey through ½ of Eastern Europe. Air-time : iron-time. (I, an intermediary for the-absent = my secret employers in East-Berlin, who have no idea about time or political reserves in the sensory. For Us, the-German-party-communists have always been most useful as idiots.)

At Schönbrunn Palace for dinner. Invited by the Austrian Chancellor Alfons Gorbach (newly-in- office since April; early 60s, pyknic physique, bureaucratic demeanour). Selected representatives of the-press in attendance, stay discreetly in the background. Not much flashing of cameras. Hardly any table talk, despite the Austrian's attempts to mediate. Kennedy only eats a few mouthfuls of the prime boiled beef, nips the wine. In the culture-of-frigidity, the-pose is already thewhole. Everything =around-Kennedy exudes the aura of the-girlish.—Khrushchev has eaten up everything on his plate. He says he can feel a cold coming on, and a man with a cold should eat=well. To conclude, he blows his nose into an enormous white cloth that he extracts awkwardly from his trouser pocket. The soft flesh of his hands pushes thecloth firmly=against his face, which disappears completely behind thecloth. As if he wanted to imprint thecloth on his countenance. (He doesn't want to be put on-the-cross, he just wants to go home.)

Nonetheless, a great surprise after the dinner when the hour is already late: The Boss asks Kennedy to come to his suite. He wants to be alone with him, without security personnel without advisors; only I, as the longest-serving interpreter, am to go with him. He brushes aside objections, whispered by some of those accompanying him, to this idea which has apparently come from a momentary whim of The Boss, He even stamps his foot like a stubborn child insisting on getting its way. (Whispers tremble through the American delegation in brief waves) : then Kennedy's compliance. The two men walk alongside each other, Kennedy very much pushed upright with long steps—swinging from the hips & elbows as if on his way to a tennis match. The stocky body of The Boss tries out the same posture, gets stuck in a round-backed stance. Followed by an American interpreter & myself. Silence between all of them, our steps brush over carpets as soft as moss—.

Entry into the suite of The Boss, a spacious ensemble of Baroque furniture & heavy with carpets. The Boss is in a sentimental mood, seems slightly self-destructive, not drunk, but he talks a lot. Before the start of a cold it's probably the upsurge of endorphins that's making him behave in such a clumsy=boorish way. Face eyes already lampy & glow. (:!Don't translate everything one needs to hear:)—*My country is !mysoul, Mr President, 'n' I drag mysoul behind me like a St Bernard. That is my shadow.*—The Boss is silent for a moment, takes a crooked, skulking glance at his counterpart from-below. The American keeps quiet, waits for the translation.

In the meantime, a sudden change in The Boss' expression. His gaze slides off the wall, moves across the thick carpet and down to his shoes. Now = in this situation he presumably feels thearmour of his confidence, which he fashioned during the week's train ride, crumbling in its porous, corroded state & covered in a rusty scab . . . . . as if heavy projectiles had hit him & sunk him to the bottom of the sea like a battleship—shots fired right in his chest. Strength leaves him, evaporates—and before me I see a different person from the one I've known for Idon't-knowhowmanyyears. Now he brings his eyes back, fastens his-gaze to the American's lapel, pulls his head in between his shoulders so that it looks as if it's stuck in a vice.

Then he resumes his chatter:—*If we=two were here alone, Mr President, I am convinced we would !long have reached an agreement. But*—(he moves a little closer to the American, confidingly, as if he wanted to whisper something to him)—*we are not alone. We=all have our shadow, Mr President. ?Do you know how one !gets rid of one's shadow : one doesn't run away from it, one kicks the shadow !right-!in-themiddle, then one's !rid of it, one's little own=shadow . . . . .* (On The Boss' brow 'n' neck sluggish slimy droplets of sweat.)—*I don't have money to waste on whores & the homeless , Mr President. Didn't buy myhouse to set it on fire and then go into theforest a free man. I once read that somewhere. Now I know it was written for=!me.*

—*You are a greatman.*—The American replies, visibly confused but very much with reverence, in a throaty voice. Then The Boss spreads his short, fat arms, the cushion-like hands slide far out of the ink-blue jacket sleeves towards the American, and tries to embrace Kennedy,—stumbles, turns on his smooth heels, loses his balance—, lurches against the wall: and crushes a large Baroque mirror with his broad-round shoulder blades—: shrill-ugly cracksplintering like thin skeletons shattering, then dagger&lance-shaped shards, lumps of glass, mirror powder burst out of the surface with an evil=dangerous glittering, spreading across The Boss' jacket and the soft carpet with a silvery shimmering of ice crystals. / As if awaking from terrible dreams, The Boss stares at the dull black surface that appears behind the broken mirror glass; without looking at anyone He calls out into the high-ceilinged room:—!*That's what's behind it: a hole in the world. Everything falls inside=there, everything. Our grave has already been dug, Mr President; yours & mine. One can't get started too early on breaking themirrors & looking behind them.*—Kennedy bends down, picks up a mirror shard, holds it out to The Boss in his well-formed, moneycured 'n' dry hand.— *You'll ?let me keep this, won't you. As a memento of our !extraordinary meeting.*—Khrushchev doesn't reply, stands there like a block, still. Kennedy holds the shard in his right hand, making it impossible to shake hands when-parting. The shards from the broken mirror crunch beneath the shoes of the exiting president & his interpreter, their steps springing as if walking over rubber.

The next morning in the reception hall in front of a wall panelled with dark shining wood: Khrushchev sitting next to Kennedy, his coarse right hand on Kennedy's thigh, each showing the cameras his own=individual smiling-face. : !This picture will remain, a chemically frozen little eternity, the-pin-up of politics, waiting for theday of fire . . . . .

The Boss is clever 80 hours before the conference & 120 hours afterwards; no sign of cleverness during the-conference. His stupidity is great in small matters.

Here the account of Yuri Antonovich Alegyev breaks off.

On the last sheet of paper in the folder, written with an ink pencil at the top left, (in Russian) just two words:

!*Achieve independence.*

We will never know whether this was meant as advice for his employers in the GDR, as a maxim for himself, or as the essence of what he realized during that conference between Khrushchev and Kennedy.

Weeks later, after her departure, I received a letter from Moscow from the student Cornelia Schmitt. She wrote that her inquiries in Moscow at the CPSU archive had not yielded any notable results, except for the fact that she learnt the current whereabouts of that same Yuri Antonovich Alegyev. She named a provincial town in the middle of Siberia. The man, she wrote, had 'fallen out of favour' in 1964 together with his superior and other staff; he was deported to Siberia and placed in charge of the local party archive in that little town until his retirement.

Now he lived alone, a recluse, long forgotten. That was where she wanted to travel now. Her return, the student added, would still take a while . . . —I sensed at the time that she would not come back. The words Seneca once wrote always come true: '*The forgotten are ever the happiest.*' And there is more than enough space for the happiest in this world.

FIGURE 39. John F. Kennedy and Nikita Khrushchev in Vienna.

THE FURNACES OF HISTORY:
TOPPLING OF THE TYRANTS

In 2010, a conference was held at Stanford University with the title 'Convergences of Order and Chaos in the Opposition of Enlightenment and Modernity in the Twentieth Century'. The hothead Slavoj Žižek contributed the paper 'The Furnaces of History'. His starting point was the Kienthal Circle (1916) and the irreversible revolutionary elan of the Spartacus Group (1919) triggered by the outbreak of the First World War. He was interested in the movement of FUTURISM which stood in stark opposition to it and also operated in the fascist milieu. If one looks at the structure, Žižek argued—that is, the expressive forces themselves, as opposed to a political evaluation after the fact—one could recognize the following:

- *Enlightenment and modernity stand in opposition to each other.*
- *The initiatives of Futurism are individualistic.*
- *The constructions of the proletarian movement, that is, mass, ornament (for example, parades) and industry, are artificial.*
- *The political alchemists of the twentieth century use small ovens, not furnaces.*

In his deliberations, Žižek relied on a text by the Tübingen historian Fernando Esposito: Mythical Modernity: Aviation, Fascism and the Longing for Order in Germany and Italy. *There the metaphor of flying is considered the root of futurist modernity. The shameful confinement to the earth's surface during the trench warfare of 1917 can only be endured in the image of flight and* homo volans.

FIGURE 40. An aviator.

FIGURE 41. Futurists.

FIGURE 42. The new Italy: war of aggression on Ethiopia.

Accelerated Time

In the years after 1938, people in Halberstadt too were affected by the ACCELERATION OF TIME which many considered 'political'. It was not only the result of a faster sequence of appointments, invitations to parties, an increased amount of special news announcements, marches and twists of current events.

My mother tried to 'train' her sluggish bowels which still followed the rhythm of the old time. Every day, she took a large spoonful of a milky-white laxative for breakfast. My father tried to stimulate his digestion, to adapt to the accelerated time, with several glasses of Gilka, a Berlinese-Hungarian caraway liqueur. He could barely find the quiet to pile earth on the plants in the rock garden.

Both parents always had the feeling of missing something. When the troops advanced on Athens in 1941, which (according to her own view) was no business of my mother's, she was so animated that one Monday morning she cancelled the tennis lesson in the lower town to make sure she was in time to try on her new dress at Marga Töpfer's in Breiter Weg.

In Retrospect

Even before the first Nuremberg Rally, as a city official, I was responsible for the flower discounts for the rally grounds. They mustn't be colourful. They have to complement the decorative flags and the smart uniforms of the participants. They must be arranged in such a way that they cannot be trampled by their boots.

When I inspected the still-intact rally grounds for the last time on 30 April 1945, groups of GIs who had just arrived were hanging around there. Hyacinths, columbines, tulips, narcissuses and the flowerbeds with forget-me-nots had already bloomed. My service ended that day.

As a gardener, my function at the major political events was one of service but unmissable, in the sense that the flowers are the continuation of my person in another guise. Although no one would suspect from looking at me that I bear the responsibility for this beautiful frame. I found it extremely hard to characterize my contribution to current events to the denazification committee. I never wore the party uniform, I always dressed as a gardener with an apron . . .

A King Called 'Real'

In his book CONSTITUTIONAL THEORY, Carl Schmitt examines elections from the French Revolution to the twentieth century. He remarks that with their choices, the voters always CONFIRM what immediately preceding events have led them to consider a REALITY.

Thus in 1793 the voters in France lost the king, whom one does not elect but finds already there, and subsequently embraced the INDIVISIBLE REPUBLIC. Much as school pupils make an effort in an examination, they attempt to interpret the result they see before them. They place their cross to the best of their knowledge and belief. Thus they seal Louis Napoleon's coup in 1848 in the elections, just as they recognize Bonaparte's seizure of power as an event and later confirm it with their votes. They do not establish what they wish for, Carl Schmitt continues, they merely show that they have correctly identified the POWER OF THE FACTUAL. They choose what strikes them as real, and consider counter-candidacies presumptuous.

There was no path leading to a boycott of the elections for the German National Assembly in 1919, which the political left had demanded. It was obvious that such elections would take place, that the outline of the constitution that led the country into war would be used to lead the Reich out of the war again—indeed, this war had evidently collapsed of its own accord, such that it was no longer possible to lead the way out of it, only to CARRY ON. Then it was no wonder that the March 1933 elections gave the National Socialists an improved (albeit not yet supreme) position, for one could hear on the radio and see by the flags hanging out onto the street, but most of all from the persecution of their opponents, that the party was in power and would not let go of it so easily.

By 1954, there had been a succession of 143 presidents in France (this was noted by Carl Schmitt in the second edition of his constitutional theory). These changes rarely took place following elections; either they occurred during a legislative period, or a violent change was confirmed through an election. It was different with the sequence of changing governments in Great Britain. There, the prime minister was first of all toppled within an inner circle, and only then did elections take place. Democracy is practised via acclamation, said the demo-sceptic Schmitt with reference to texts by Thucydides. A people are capable of toppling something they consider unreal. Otherwise, they tend towards affirmation (that is, towards 'homage').

Schmitt states that aside from a few short periods in Athens or Florence, he knows of no genuine people's rule. The institutional movements of a 'will of the people' are always pre-ceded by a 'rehearsal of action' in closed circles (lobbies, elites, conspiracies, councils). If need be, those are parties.

If democracy constitutes the relatively best form of state, as claimed in the Anglo-Saxon world, it is because it is anchored in the state's limited intervention. Politics does not revolve around the question of whom one trusts but, rather, of whom one believes to be abusing the political less than another person.

The reverse is true of the connection to reality. In this regard, an election is about trust that there is even such a thing as reality. Whatever seems unreal leads to despair or a storm. The Corsican, Schmitt writes, experienced this close to Madrid when he appeared as a monster that was inexplicable to the Spanish: accompanied by armed men, but preaching civil rights and liberties. None of this was perceived by the country's inhab-itants as SPANISH-REAL. Reality needs 1,000 years, according to the conservative Schmitt, to establish a world in people's minds.

An Especially Successful Training for Police Dogs

No one trains like the police dog breeder Trägemann, of Club MS in Mainz. The best dog material has been reaching the force since his first success in 1942, when he won the Police Dog Show in Charkow. Trägemann's metal-seeking dogs are a special breed. Strictly speaking, they are not a breed. Rather, Trägemann trains this type of Alsatian to find metal, for example, the male Babsi. 'He seems to like metal.' The dog sniffs out metal pieces of evidence such as bombs, fragments of explosive devices or hidden weapons; its training does have the drawback, however, that it swallows screws, plastic tubes and metal bolts it finds. One has to check it with a metal detector and either use a vomitive to make it give up its prey or operate on it, for example, if it has swallowed a spark plug acting as evidence. Trägemann says: 'I can trigger these conditional reflexes (naturally, I read the literature), or instil them firmly in the dog's character beforehand, but I can't control how strongly they are instilled.'

There is no demand for this type of dog on the market. Police stations are put off by the cost of metal detectors, and also fear indiscretions that would have the animal welfare groups after them if they had to operate on such a dog. 'We can't afford a canine vet and a surgical department either,' says Trägemann, 'just to deploy this type of police dog.'

Heidegger Expects to Be Appointed Director of the Führer's Accompanying Teaching Unit

From all of the *Gaue* (German provincial towns), German philosophers came rushing to Leipzig in the November rain for the German Philosophers' Convention. In Berlin, the Führer boarded the special train that would take him to Berchtesgaden. The locomotive of the Führer's train usually changed at Leipzig Central Station. Schmundt, the Wehrmacht adjutant, had intended for Hitler to meet Martin Heidegger. A series of extremely small events cut short Hitler's stay in Leipzig and prevented the encounter which insiders had imagined would strengthen the forces that were necessary for a SECOND NATIONAL SOCIALIST REVOLUTION. Thus the West missed the one, the last chance for philosophy to enter an 'immediate space of presentation and procuring for power in the Reich'.

NZZ.[9] What is 'Führer's Accompanying Teaching Unit' supposed to mean? There has never been a group like that.

PARTY MEMBER (PM) RICHTER.[10] It was necessary to set it up.

NZZ. Did Hitler know of his good fortune? Had he demanded such a group?

PM RICHTER. He had said that he wanted to keep learning anew. He had said that both in public and to close confidants.

NZZ. And now he was to be given a teacher?

PM RICHTER. Not by that name. The Führer is not a pupil.

NZZ. A philosophical scholar?

PM RICHTER. It was not so much about philosophy. It was about thinking.

NZZ. Couldn't Hitler think?

PM RICHTER. Any person can think if they are not afraid to.

NZZ. Some say that the Führer is superstitious?

PM RICHTER. Perhaps. That is part of thinking. A staff member for intellectual nourishment, so to speak. That was the idea.

NZZ. Like a head chef?

PM RICHTER. Something like that.

NZZ. Why didn't it happen?

PM RICHTER. The locomotive change didn't happen at Leipzig Central Station but, rather, in Wurzen, near Leipzig. So there was only a brief stop in Leipzig.

NZZ. This is all assuming that the Führer actually intended to install a Führer's Accompanying Teaching Unit . . .

PM RICHTER. That is assumed.

NZZ. A staff of prince educators?

PM RICHTER. The powerful have always had that sort of thing.

NZZ. How would Heidegger have been able to speak to the Führer? In the language of his publications?

PM RICHTER. Certainly not in the terminology that characterizes Heidegger's writings. The Führer has little time. Nor does he have an inclination to listen. A Führer's Accompanying Teaching Unit is not constantly in Hitler's proximity. The Führer's Accompanying Physician, that's an office in Berlin. The Führer's Accompanying Unit is the security regiment of 'Greater Germany' which provides the personal protection on trips taken by the Führer. In that sense, the Führer's Accompanying Teaching Unit is concerned with coordinating the education system in the Reich. The unit reports directly to the Führer and passes on instructions from the Führer to the relevant authorities. It supervises thinking and writing in the Reich. It is not, on the other hand, concerned with teaching Hitler, instructing him or giving him reading suggestions.

NZZ. So 'Director of the Führer's Accompanying Teaching Unit' is a title?

PM RICHTER. And a signal.

NZZ. Was Heidegger preparing himself for it?

PM RICHTER. Certainly.

NZZ. How?

PM RICHTER. Only with questions, really. Well-prepared, attuning questions showing that the Führer could place his trust in such an introduction to the SECRET CONCATENATIONS OF THE CENTURY that might initially seem unfamiliar to him, a philosophical guide, not academic in style, with a little

Schelling, Leibniz, Nietzsche, each time without mentioning the name.

NZZ. What budget was to be used to finance the unit?

PM RICHTER. The surcharges for special stamps of the Reich Postal Service. The stamps with the motif of the Brown Band horse races at Riem, for example, have a surcharge of 142 pfennigs per stamp on top of the nominal value of 44 pfennigs. With the amount that gets printed, that yields a tidy sum.

NZZ. How did Heidegger view the fact that nothing happened?

PM RICHTER. As a disaster. He was a persona non grata after 30 June anyway. Every talented young National Socialist writer could use him for practice. He was pounced on.

NZZ. But for a historic moment, attaching a master to the Führer was more than an idea.

PM RICHTER. Yes, a self-assured master of thinking.

NZZ. One can hardly think where that might have led!

PM RICHTER. As far as thinking can go!

As a Simple National Socialist

In late 1933, National Socialists who were dissatisfied with the so-called revolution after January 1933 were already expecting a COMPLETION OF THE MOVEMENT. Some of them sought a consolidation, others spoke of the necessity of a 'night of long knives'. Martin Heidegger belonged to the group that considered this degree of ABSOLUTISM and REVOLUTIONARY TURN imperfect. He would not have used the world 'left'; given Heidegger's contacts, later political chroniclers would have spoken of a 'left National Socialist'. When the ideologue Rosenberg spoke of the end of the Hegelian era in an article, he responded with the exclamation: 'Only now is Hegel truly alive!'

Then, in the summer of 1934, the murders of 30 June brought the so-called left-wing course (but also several other political movements) to a violent end. After that point, nothing indicating personal devotion could be found in Heidegger's statements on Hitler and the National Socialist movement. He remained a 'simple National Socialist', so to speak.

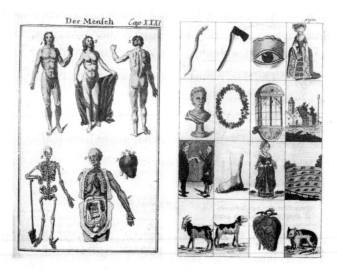

FIGURE 43. Pictures for children from the Age of Enlightenment.

FIGURE 44. Ancient ruins. Model for the Reich Ruins Law: state buildings of the German Reich are, regardless of expense, to be constructed in such a way that they will be awe-inspiring for observers in 5,000 years.

FIGURE 45. National-political tuition in 1935.

Furnaces of the Soul: Max Weber's Doubts about the 'Superman Type'

In the introductory statements to the 'Transcendental Doctrine of Method' in the *Critique of Pure Reason*, Immanuel Kant writes about THOUGHT AS HOUSE BUILDING:

> If we look upon the sum total of all knowledge of pure and speculative reason as an edifice of which we possess at least the idea within ourselves [. . .] we found that although we had thought of a tower that would reach to the sky, our supply of materials would only stretch to a dwelling-house, sufficiently spacious for all our business on the level of experience, and high enough [. . .]. Thus the original bold undertaking could not but fail for want of materials, not to mention the

confusion of tongues which inevitably divided the labourers in their views of the building, and scattered them all over the world [. . .] we have been warned [. . .] yet cannot altogether give up the erection of a solid dwelling, so we have to make the plan for a building in proportion to the material which is given to us, and which is sufficient for all our needs. [. . .] We shall have here to treat of a **discipline**, a **canon**, an **architectonic** [. . .] of pure reason [. . .].[11]

Max Weber took this text by Kant as a starting point in some notes for a lecture from 1917, proceeding to the following thought: the tower of which the Holy Scripture speaks was made of clay, reinforced along the sides with straw mats, and later crumbled (or dissolved). But 3,000 years after its destruction, around 1600 CE, it was recreated inside of humans and, as the CAPACITY FOR MULTI-LAYERED THOUGHT, is the chance for modern society.

Modern human beings, according to Max Weber, have withdrawn their glowing faith into their hearts, where they can melt them down into everyday work discipline: into industrial diligence. This is especially true of the Protestant character. It is overrepresented in the industrial belts of Scotland, middle England, the Netherlands and the Prussian Ruhr region. This is augmented by the 'tower in us' as an organizing force: that of 'stackable fields'. He thus speaks, like the French sociologist Durkheim, of 'fields of the soul', but also of 'workshops of the soul'.

He had not, however, observed any subjective elements signalizing an internalization of industry and heavy machinery. In that sense there are no FURNACES OF THE SOUL. He doubted that there would ever be a *superman*. It was more likely that barbarians would work the HEAVY MACHINERY . . .

Here the manuscript breaks off.

How Does the Modern Political Character Come About?

Betty Bielefeld, a student of the Marxist Fredric Jameson at Columbia University, argued the case in her doctoral thesis that all SOCIAL FORMATIONS 'requiring a degree of spontaneous preliminary work from the producers (that is, the workers)', namely, the commercial cities, capitalism, agriculture and the construction of machine tools, transform into SUBJECTIVE CHARACTER TRAITS (skills), and thus progress, in one of the subsequent generations. The conversion of the outside world into the inner world, however, has a different time scale. The characters of agriculture, for example, only moved inwards after 2,000 years; it was a long way from the rangers, gatherers and nomads to the Roman poet and lawmaker Ennius. The cities, on the other hand, were rapid in their development. In ancient Greece, the polis was established in a mere three generations.

It could be ruled out, by contrast—and this is the subject of the extremely long tabular appendix to Bielefeld's thesis— that factory work, and likewise all kinds of forced labour or slavery, produced a CRYSTAL IN THE SUBJECT, that is to say, a force. Without the coercion from the outside, the associated outside world was cast aside like a dress. Here Betty Bielefeld contradicted assertions by Soviet Marxists who expected a NEW HUMAN BEING HARDENED IN INDUSTRY. Their deliberations on the return of earlier social formations in the subjects, in turn, would—she politely brought this to the attention of her teacher Fredric Jameson—have placed them under SUSPICION OF IDEALISM among the Marxists of the 1920s.

Betty's ancestors had come from Wuppertal. They were considered stubborn Westphalians. And so Bielefeld resisted all objections and stood by her propositions. She could not please anyone—not the orthodox Marxists, nor the free economists of Chicago who denied that the experiences of work processes had any aftereffects within the human psyche. But she was convinced: THIS INTERIOR IS A SMITHY. But none of the tools one knows from the outside world are of any use in it.

That winter, the farmstead near Harvard where she was writing was surrounded by a dense snow cover. For two weeks one could not reach any of the neighbouring properties either by sledge, because the snow was too soft and too high, or by bicycle.

Sohn-Rethel

He spent his old age in Bremen, cared for lovingly by young women in a shared flat. As a young man, the son of rich parents, he had infiltrated the National Association of German Industry as a kind of academic spy. Here the news from the empire came unfiltered through the dossiers of files and the correspondences. The bookkeeping, conduits and control rooms of a modern society.

Whether Sohn-Rethel was a Marxist was a matter of dispute among his rivals in the protest movement and in the circles of the Institute of Social Research in Frankfurt. He had read a great deal. Some things he knew from hearsay. He knows Marx through people who have genuinely read the texts and whom he trusts, Max Horkheimer judged. Thus a particular theoretical grid had embedded itself in his mind.

PRODUCTION, Marx tells is, is 'the overarching'. Hence people's impatience, according to Sohn-Rethel, when DISTRIBUTION and CONSUMPTION—the slow markets—cannot keep up with the inventiveness of the engineers and machines. A Central European production of the 1930s cannot wait until it benefits from need and buying power; production blazes the way, if need be by force. Sohn-Rethel describes this as the PRINCIPLE OF THE FORCED-EXCHANGE SOCIETY. If the exchange only comes about tentatively, DISTRIBUTION occurs by force. Sohn-Rethel had the furnaces of the Ruhr region in mind as an image of this STRUCTURE OF EMISSION. One could go past these facilities at night on the express train, see them glowing in the distance. Or, for a daytime view, one could drive by car for over an hour along the pipe systems and slim metal chimneys of the chemical industry at Halle and Leuna. From an aeroplane, Sohn-Rethel related, a group of decision-makers resolved to build factories in the lowlands near Wolfsburg and Salzgitter. One can still see cornfields down there.

Sohn-Rethel was the only theorist who was familiar with the thought patterns of Karl Marx and Karl Korsch and also had the chance to accumulate actual inside knowledge of the industry.

The Arithmetic of Power

Following the abrupt death of Armaments Minister Todt, some of the country's various power brokers tried to appropriate parts of his political legacy. The weakest of them, Minister for Economic Affairs Funk, had agreed with Leeb and Witzell of the Wehrmacht Procurement Office to make Field Marshal Erhard Milch chairman of the central committee that would decide on the new responsibilities of the national arms industry. One could not have replaced the words 'make chairman' with 'elect as chairman'. No one is elected at the centre of the Reich. There are telephone calls between confidants. One of the conspirators suggests a name in a preparatory meeting. This prepares the ground on which a powerful man can say: I will take over as chairman. Precautions have to be taken so that no one else will intervene; otherwise the powerful man would not do it. He loses severely if it comes out that someone else can stop him.

A preliminary vote in the Industrial Council took place on 11 February. General Director Albert Vögler, the industry's opinion leader, was won over by the conspirators.

The next day, the central committee assembled in the large conference hall at the Ministry of Aviation. Present: Vögler, Wilhelm Zangen, director of the National Association of German Industry, as the head of the Army Ordnance Office; General Leeb, then Admiral General Witzel and General Thomas from the Wehrmacht High Command. Chairman: Milch. Funk on his right, Speer on his left. As soon as Todt's immediate successor, the new Armaments Minister Speer, had become aware of the conspiracy intended to plunder his inheritance, he had gone to see Hitler and made sure of his support. Now, at the meeting, he followed the staging of the plot. Vögler, director general of the steelworks, outlined the standing and quality of the man who would henceforth preside over a committee that united all authorities—those of the armaments minister, the air force, the navy, the army, industry and civil manufacture. This was followed by contributions from Leeb and Witzell, who 'essentially' agreed. Unplanned interjections from others confuse the scene. It is clear, however, that the president of this assembly, Erhard Milch, is the only candidate for the OVERALL CHAIRMAN-SHIP of a central committee.

Speer reports: At that moment I whispered to Milch. I told him: This session will be continued in the cabinet room. The Führer will speak about my duties. Milch understood quickly and comprehensively. Naturally, there had been no ministerial meeting in the so-called cabinet room—which had been set up in the new building of the Reich Chancellory, but where no ministerial meeting took place during the entire war—this time either. Speer's message meant that he had conferred with Hitler and it was no longer possible for Milch to declare 'I will follow this committee's suggestion and take over as chairman'. Thus the experienced Field Marshal wittily turned down the candidacy. All responsibilities remained scattered until the end of the war, as this was the only way for Speer to retain Todt's responsibilities.

'Politics Means Precisely Determining the Enemy with Whom I Want to Make Peace'

As Ian Kershaw writes, Hitler had unified all political powers in a single person in December 1941. Thus, in the subsequent time, there had been nominal political discussion but little in the way of political decision-making. After Hitler's death, on 30 April 1945, the 'hoarded political will' was returned to the people. Unlike in 1918, however, it was practised not by individuals (who were scattered to a degree, fleeing from the war and entering a war strike) but within the existing organizations and fellowships. The aim was 'precisely determining the enemy to whom I want to surrender'.

Convoys advanced powerfully in a general westerly direction. Via Swedish contacts, the Reichsführer-SS sought an opportunity to negotiate with the Allied headquarters. Hitler had killed himself at 3.30 p.m. The new Reich Chancellor Joseph Goebbels (he had barely ruled for a day) attempted to contact the Soviet Supreme Command in Berlin. Would it be possible to resume the status quo ante of May 1941? Following a herd of horses, Field Marshals von Manstein and von Bock made their way towards Schleswig-Holstein. They wanted to reach a particular manor.

With five vehicles, driving side by side, a tank unit rolled in close formation through the streets of Slovakia and into Czech territory. The troop wanted to reach Salzburg. The two central convoys, which were using the road, kept getting ahead and had to arrange stops so that the vehicles driving through the fields could catch up. Their political conviction was that that they could only run down the barricades of the insurgent Czechs if spread out as far as possible.

The precision in determining the enemy was hampered by errors and illusions. Defeat caught them all unawares. Even the department FOREIGN ARMIES EAST, spread between different bases in the southern area, had no documents detailing which Allied commanders would accept eastern troops entering their territory and which would be more likely to deny entry. Thus a division of the Waffen-SS was delivered to the Russians by a US commander; only 100 kilometres away, a different division of the Waffen-SS was taken into the Allied prison camp.

Politics at the Last Moment

None of the warring parties made any attempt to use the suffering of the Dutch people in the last days of the Second World War as a weapon. Only the previous year, that would have been a possible instrument of war on other fronts, both in British and German eyes, to put the enemy on the spot through the hardship of the civilian population. The lack of any prospect of success had chastened the members of the Axis. A joint conference took place on the afternoon of 30 April 1945. The participants: Lieutenant General Smith from Eisenhower's staff, Major General Suslaparov as a Russian observer and Prince Bernhard of the Netherlands. On the German side, Reich Commissioner Seyss-Inquart. By evening, the conference had proved a complete success. The Germans were still excellent organizers. Like students facing an otherwise imminent punishment, they performed.

To provide the Dutch populace with food, the record documents the following measures: DELIVERY BY AIR: the Germans gave the Allied supply aircraft 10 dropping zones, usable between 7 a.m. and 3 p.m. daily. 'During these hours, the Allied aircraft will enjoy full immunity.' DELIVERY BY SEA: Allied food ships could call at Rotterdam. The Germans would meet each ship and escort it into port. DELIVERY BY LAND: the Germans would make a road available.

The Primacy of Art over Hardship

A student of Heidegger was conscripted to the City Cleaning Authority in the Reich capital towards the end of the war. As late as 30 April 1945, the day of Hitler's death (though no one knew this at the time), the crew under his command left the depot in the north of town and worked its way to Wilmersdorf with their clearing and cleaning machines. From one of the street corners they cleansed of debris, they could see Red Army soldiers taking on a barricade a few blocks away.

FIGURE 46. Ezra Pound, trapped.

'Nor can who has passed a month in the death cells
believe in capital punishment
No man who has passed a month in the death cells
Believes in cages for beasts'

Ezra Pound, 'Canto LXXXIII', 530

FIGURE 47. Ezra Pound with his mother.

'I could have done without such jests [. . .].
And now it's stopped the green blood.'

Ezra Pound

FIGURE 48. Fascists being shot by partisans while looking at Lake Como.

FIGURE 49. On the left Theo Pirzer, leader of the
guard unit that was protecting the Duce and was
meant to bring him to Valtellina.

A Once-Powerful Man Breaks Through the Thin Surface of Institutional Reality at a Particular Time and Is Subsequently Declared an Outlaw

FIGURE 50. Alfredo Ildefonso Schuster, the powerful archbishop of Milan, with whom Mussolini sought protection.

Rainy day. A Monday morning in Milan. The cardinal receives the president of the Fascist Republic of Salò in his palace. Biscuits. A sweet wine. Meanwhile, the cardinal's secretary negotiates in the ante-chamber with three representatives of the revolutionary committee, a representative of the left, a lawyer of the city administration and the representative of the Christian Social Party. The threat of a general strike and an armed uprising weighs on the city. The announcement of this creates a hectic atmosphere at the radio station and the offices of the security agencies. In the city itself, the usual busyness. In such hours, reality is not spread evenly throughout the city.

At the moment, the cardinal is still making polite conversation with the stranded potentate. He points to the moment in Napoleon's life when he abdicated. The guard were still watching over the emperor. Had he stood by his abdication at that point (like you, dear Mussolini, when you were a captive on the Gran Sasso), his descendants would still be the rulers of Elba today. Like the Grimaldis in Monaco. The cardinal was a polite taunter. He thanked the dictator for the fact that the negotiations, whose outcome the church guaranteed, would prevent civil war in the city.

Subsequently, the chief negotiators of the new power were led in. They kissed the cardinal's hand. Mussolini's defence minister Graziani appeared hastily. All parties involved sat down at a table.

For a time, the negotiations were making progress. General Cadorna, the son of the legendary field marshal in the First World War, a representative of the Christian Social Party—hence a piece of 'authorized history'—conceded that while the fascist militia should not be spared, the family members of the militiamen should be left in peace. Then everything else can be sorted out, Mussolini replied. At that moment, Marshal Graziani brought the news (screaming) that the German Supreme Command had just surrendered to the Allies. Does that make these negotiations superfluous? Confused, Mussolini breaks off the conference.

As he exits the building, he is still intending to return later. In fact, at that point, he breaks through the thin ground of institutional reality and finds himself in limbo between STILL ALIVE and ALREADY DEAD.

He sits with his entourage at a hotel in Como. Then he sets off on the ill-fated journey that will lead to his demise.

It is a time in which everything has been decided, yet there are still long waits to endure. Now he could read the books he always wanted to read. He has none with him.

FIGURE 51. The girl on Mussolini's right is Elena Curti, believed to be his illegitimate daughter. She has hurried to the scene to save her father. She cycles through the lines of partisans to Como, where she has a troop of Fascist militiamen bring her to her father in an armoured car.

FIGURE 52 (BELOW). Armoured car of the Black Militia in which Mussolini was hiding when the partisans arrested him near the Swiss border.

FIGURE 53. Bottleneck where the partisans' barricade held up Mussolini's convoy. The armoured car (illustration used here) was capable of fending off the insurgents but not of turning around on the road.

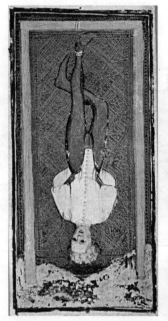

FIGURE 54. The 'HANGED MAN' is one of the 22 Tarot cards known as the 'Major Arcana'. It is the card of 'infamy', of the person who 'has been made inglorious'. The punishment originated in Florence during the Renaissance. It does not punish the man but dishonours the image of the man. Hence the punishment did not have to be inflicted on the actual traitor or murderer but could also be administered in effigie through the depiction of a body hung by chains attached to the feet.

FIGURE 55. Displaying of the bodies of Mussolini and his mistress at 12 p.m. on 29 April 1945 in the Piazza Loreto, Milan. The woman's clothes are fastened to her body with string; beyond exhibiting her as the companion of the INFAMOUS ONE, her executioners did not want to subject her to additional shame.

FIGURE 56. The two companions. They lay in this position for some time in a Milan side street owing to a gap in the organization. The one was previously very powerful, the other never. They were buried in the evening hours of 30 April in an unused part of the municipal cemetery. A total of 13 unmarked wooden coffins were used; only two contained the actual bodies. It was thought that if someone later attempted to exhume the coffins and remove bones from them, it would be impossible to identify them.

That's What Happens If You Were a Superman

He was still guarded by two women (Petacci, Curzio) and a Waffen-SS unit. In Valtellina there were supposedly a thousand fighters waiting for him. At the same time: millions were cursing the tyrant. He did not lack intelligence; he realized it was the end of the line for him.

In the 20 years he had ruled Italy—his power centre was Milan and the area where people vote for the Lega Nord today, so he was a metropolitan—there were moments in which his appearances had value: good moments in a scripted reality. At the time, eyewitnesses and biographers considered him the manifestation of Nietzsche's 'superman'. He saw storehouses of power before him when the British prime minister Chamberlain visited him at Christmas in 1938, assuring him support in the management of European conflicts.

Bursts of applause, joint willpower, the discarded and retrieved wishes of so many GENERATIONS, a collection of old material from the heads and hearts of a million people: this is what the superman feeds off. The precarious INTELLEC-TUAL SUBSTANCE did not survive a passage to Ethiopia.

The man who, here at the hotel in Dongo, attempted to persuade his German minder Theo Pirzer to carry out a final coup, no longer had anything in common with the person he had been in 1938 except his skin and bones. He requested that Pirzer, as a final act, drive the 30 kilometres to the Swiss border station with a motorized unit of the Waffen-SS. They should arrest the Italian border officials who had arrested the two ministers Mussolini had sent to probe a crossing to Switzerland, and bring his men back to him. Because, as Machiavelli notes, the measure of a prince's authority since Caesar has been that he is able to bring his men back safely from an assignment! Mussolini's words were muddled.

The distance his soul had (certainly not innocently) already travelled out of the prison of his body was 12 centimetres; this was confirmed by the doctor of the Prefect of Como, who had stood in for the ruler's personal physician and knew texts by Plutarch.

FIGURE 57. Street in Valtellina, empty in the morning. The sun casts swathes. Mussolini was expected here for the final battle.

GROUND ADHESION BY THE STOMACH

When one looks at the rocks in which oil is located, says the exploration geologist Wilhelm Dominik, one cannot see with the naked eye what they contain. They behave like a sponge, but all one sees is rock. It is only the immense pressure exerted from all sides on the deposits deep under the sediments that pushes the liquid, and with it the oil, to the surface. The mixture of gas, water and oil produces the fountain that catches fire so quickly.

It is similar with the political, according to Obama's new advisor (from the University of Chicago, like the previous one). One cannot see it in crowds, as if it were microscopically concealed in a porous rock, and it suddenly erupts. One should not believe, the new advisor closed, that a conservative business like News Corp. TV or Tea Party organizers in the Republican Party were capable of manipulatively creating a POLITICAL ERUPTION. That applied across the board, said the man from Chicago. He had studied it in the European and Chinese contexts. All the manipulators could do was 'tickle the deposits' with their drills. The 'geology of the political' reacted autonomously and uncontrollably. It was at home in the individual souls, not in the 'concept of the masses' which was a construction of the intellect.

The Parliament of Spirits in the Human Brain

Behind the forehead, with the strongest activity in the middle between the eyes and the back of the head, lies the domicile of the ZOON POLITIKON, the political animal. Its element, the neuron, is astoundingly simple and, as the brain scientist Prof. Dr Eric Kandel says, 'Essentially stupid.' It has three elementary reactions that it constantly repeats. Only in the movement caused by the billions of neurons amongst one another, that is to say, BETWEEN them, does SAPIENTIA ensue. Here, for example, lies the overwhelming power of the PRINCIPLE OF RIGHT: the majority of connections in the brain feel displeasure at a breach of the law. In social evolution, Kandel states, more people with this disposition have remained than those without it. A sense of justice seems to be a subspecies of equilibrium. It is located in the ear, says Kandel.

In the active people who carry this brain inside them, says Kandel, expanding his argument by making chalk sketches on the blackboard of the lecture hall, it is *the other way around* in a certain sense. The individual and their brain are excessively complex, indeed untameable as MANIFOLD ENTITIES, and— counter to appearances—barely receptive to commands. The community maintained by such individuals, on the other hand, is strangely primitive and seems 'essentially stupid'. And it lacks robustness, something the neuron can certainly be said to have.

A Behaviour of High Intensity

Eberhard Knödler-Bunte relates a peculiar incident. A young woman was discovered in the chimney of the house that belonged to her lover; she had starved to death. She had tried to enter the house via the chimney. Prior to that her lover, a local doctor, had expelled her from the house. He wanted to end their relationship. The young woman had not accepted that. The doctor, indifferent to all the rejected woman's words and gestures, had barricaded the house and gone away, which the woman did not know.

But the young woman was not willing to give up her attachment without an additional face-to-face talk, perhaps also an embrace or an attempt to bring about a surprising twist of fate (he would slip off her clothes and everything would be fine again!). She had climbed onto the roof and down the chimney, to a point where she could neither go any further down nor clamber up to the small section of sky which she had probably just perceived as a square blueness above her.

Residents, bothered by a smell that intensified over weeks, alerted the authorities who discovered the dead woman in the chimney. The fire service, inexperienced in recovering such a find, had some difficulty extracting the body. The doctor was still away.

It long remained a contentious issue who should cover the cost of the 'rescue operation' which had after all yielded nothing but a mutilated, dismembered corpse. However hard the fire fighters had pulled on it, the stuck body could not be brought out in one piece. The only thing that was whole was the intensity with which the young woman had pursued her goal to reach her lover directly one more time. None of the locals would have expected such energy from the delicate, somewhat petite woman.

The Founding of a Republic Because of an Accident
at a Depth of 750 Metres

A mining accident in the Atacama Desert with numerous casualties and the unexpected discovery of 33 buried miners drew
qualified researchers from all over the world who were knowl-
edgeable about rescue, emergency survival, sudden learning processes, education and the stabilization of human societies—in
short, about the human race. This was Frieda Grafe's formulation in the *Süddeutsche Zeitung* after the positive result of the
rescue operation which she had followed on film and whose
noisy publicity had covered up the original perception of the
beginning, when everything still seemed uncertain.

As soon as the casualties were discovered, the capable mining minister of the Republic of Chile, Laurence Golborne, had
instructed his country's embassies to spread the news and call
for help. Agencies reported from the Chilean capital and the site
of the accident. At a depth of 500 metres, a landslide had buried
the central part of the mine. An exploratory drilling got through
to the miners who had escaped to a protective space 750 metres
underground. For over 400 years, there have been stories relating to accidents in mines, for example, in Sweden. In civilized
countries, the following sentiment has become ingrained: miners
who are believed dead turn up while lost miners are dug up
decades later and, because of the chemical conditions in the
layers of earth, they appear as young as they were when death
took them away.

The experts who arrived in Santiago and at the scene of the
accident in the desert had to be accommodated. They were not
used to sleeping in tents. Nor were they ready to lie down and

sleep; they were excited. Not least because they met well-chosen people there; many of them had previously only known one another from books.

This much was clear: the buried miners had to brace themselves for a forced stay of up to 120 days in their burrow. How can one make such a temporal abstraction tangible? How does one organize a human society in such a place, deep underground? With people who had so far, as the newly arrived Viennese ethnologist Dr Helmut Reinl put it, had never founded a republic. Now they were supposed to form a human group in a closed place. It is virtually certain, added the evolutionary biologist Prof. Dr Leimar from the University of Stockholm, that there will be crises. But it had transpired that conditions were not confined. The captives had space in the mine network up to the collapsed zone above them.

Was there anyone among them whom they all trusted? To survive, a group needs a leader. Were the earliest human societies not based on a clan of equals? And later one of the strong usurped rule? asked a jurist who belonged to the group of experts. The reverse is true, replied the ethnologists: First the clan has a chief, then he is replaced. They debated in a hotel in Santiago. It's like this, added an anthropologist from Stanford: One person is trusted by the others, or is the strongest, then others conspire to topple him. After the dethroning (or murder), they quarrel over the inheritance. These events often (not always) result in a little more equality. This remained a matter of contention in the debate. The next meeting of the academics —they were too restless to group around a table, instead conferring while walking around and huddled together in front of the computers—took place in the rooms of the radio-astronomic facilities located on the mountain peaks above the Atacama.

After the exploratory drilling that had enabled the discovery of the buried miners, the people above managed to push down a supply tube. It was used to send down liquids, enquiries and food concentrate in very narrow containers. Scribbled replies to the questions went up, then a phone line was installed. It was hot down there. It transpired that the man everyone trusted now was not the worker who, according to the mining engineers, had called the shots before the accident—everyone familiar with the crew had named him as the most likely leader—but, rather, someone unknown who had not even belonged to the main crew before, only the crew of a neighbouring drift. The organizational management above ground adjusted to this change of circumstances. Advice from a great distance: from the STAR CITY near Moscow, where people were locked in tight spaces and tested in preparation for the 700-day flight to Mars. How, as a head organizer, does one deal from the outside with a small group of people who are supposed to tolerate one another in a tight capsule? How can one ration hope so that they do not despair but remain focused for long periods? There was a difference between claustrophobia-inducing situations and the experiential mode of a Robinson Crusoe, who was also the founder of a new society in his day but was not equally isolated. He presided over an entire island full of animals, savages landed on the beach, and the sea—the connection to POSSIBILITY IN AND FOR ITSELF—stimulated his imagination. Things were certainly different in the emptiness of outer space and the density of the earth's interior.

Did the buried miners need a change? Did they need entertainment? Were there any measures that could be taken to prevent the undoubtedly imminent crisis? The workers down there were to practise, both athletically and mentally. Actually, the victims could have used a seminar. The experience of 6,000 years of social evolution had to be re-adjusted in their characters. And it was of little use if the experts who had this experience reflected on such adaptation among themselves; it had to be smuggled into the heads of the miners, and from there into their behaviour.

One concern for the doctors in the rescue team was that none of the 33 workers become ill in the drift. This required an absolutely strict separation between the places for eating and relieving themselves. The workers had an important task in the rescue scenario. It was good for them to know about it, because it motivated them. It was important not to exaggerate the task and the HELP TO HELP ONESELF in order to avoid reducing their hope. One had to promise them a reward that was suitable as the goal of their rescue (which was, in a sense, their gift to *us*). For the giant drill used to drill the escape shaft would, in the final phase, pour gravel masses weighing roughly 4,000 tonnes down into the drift. The workers had to clear this rubble away into the other drifts. That demanded physical fitness.

In the last days of the rescue operation, it was initially assumed, the drill would only advance 5 metres per day because of the danger to the miners. Now, at the start of the drilling, the distance sometimes reached 20 metres. That demanded long waits. We must keep the workers' minds busy, said the tunnel-building specialist and economist Carlo Lamberti. It was not enough to fill them with the hope of being rescued. Rather, it was vital to stay firmly on the winning path of motives by permitting non-essential wishes. That was discussed with them. They responded that they would like a 'real' meal. Not the NASA fare in tubes. That showed us, said Professor Leimar, that they could shovel the thought of the dangers awaiting them at the end of the drilling operation out of their minds just as effectively as they were supposed to shovel out the gravel that filled the drift at the end. We sent them, in narrow, thin cylinders—the only kind of container that could be transported through the supply tube—pasta with mincemeat. In the days before the tube was available to send them provisions, the trapped miners had rationed and shared out the food and drink that was available at the time of the accident. Once a day, everyone received a few grams of tuna and a tablespoon of liquid; they had two of those. The experts worried that these conditions, which could return if the tube broke down, demanded a discipline that was rare in ordinary life and was unlikely to be kept up continuously.

The experts had gathered information from NASA, who had experience with accidents in space. Is there a basic structure of fraternity in humans? How should we know? replied the NASA scientists who had no experience with groups of more than six people trapped in a space capsule. Hardship alone, they stated, was not enough to arouse fraternity; hardship could also lead people to massacre one another. There did, however, seem to be reserves from the early days of the human race that caused them to turn to each other first in case of danger. But if this interaction is too narrow or hopeless, the group explodes.

We experienced, said the chief of local organization, who reported to the minister of building, how the drilling with Strata 950 (originally a valve shaft drill for depths of up to 20 metres, now modified) was delayed because a demolition hammer for the machine had to be flown in from Germany but the transport plane broke down.

President Pineira had instructed the minister of mining to study another 10 rescue variations with the goal of limiting the time of the operation to two months. What a surprise for the victims, what positive news for the global public if help came more quickly! One of the worries for the Chilean organizers was that even if the buried miners did not lose their nerves, the interest of the public and subsequently the rescuers might wane as time passed. The country's president therefore believed that one should not wait until the Advent season.

The question of costs set off a political debate that was very fruitful for the government: they were to be borne entirely by the mine owners. The implementation of such plans, and possibly also an international reinforcement of mine security, required long-term public attention. How does one organize that? The rescue team at the damaged borehole could not make any such contributions. Who on the world's various continents would depict the situation of these people, trapped in darkness at a depth of 750 metres for several months? The investor who ran the mine had declared bankruptcy. He wants to avoid the subsequent costs, such as compensation for the families of the miners who died in the accident, as well as wages for those awaiting rescue (being trapped counts as working time), but most of all the cost of the rescue measures. The firm has the status of a limited company.

Not up to the Crime

A lady in Brussels let an 11-year-old (she could see that he was an immature, physically strong boy, but she knew neither his exact age nor his name) carry her shopping bag. She found his offer to take the bag off her 'well-behaved' and 'polite'. She was sure that the bag-carrier could not have known she was transporting 11,000 francs in the shopping bag. She was an untroubled soul. After getting home, she noticed that the little bag containing the money had been stolen. The boy was long gone, rewarded with a 2-franc coin. She contacted the police. She had wanted to get the money out of the country and deposit it in Luxemburg. It was not easy to explain to the authorities why she had been carrying such a large sum while shopping.

Around 5 p.m. the same day, two male minors appeared in a discount shop for electronic devices and demanded a Natel camcorder, intending to pay with a 1,000-franc note. The woman serving them used a pretext to leave the counter and reported the incident at the police station. When she returned, the two youths were gone. They had grown suspicious.

In an arcade in the old town, not far from discount shops, patrolling police officers, accompanied by the shopkeeper, found the two boys. A search of their pockets yielded further 1,000-franc notes. It was suspicious enough that the two had left behind the device and the money they had already paid at the shop. Innocent people don't do that sort of thing.

The 11-year-old and his playmate could not be arrested. The fact that the latter had one of the notes in his trouser pocket was not enough to make him an 'accessory', as a minor could not commit a 'crime' in legal terms, and thus no one could be an accessory if they were equally young. This was an 'impossible attempt'. The boy had concocted a plan that he was not up to carrying out. He had evidently been watching the Brusselite lady as she left the bank.

There was unlikely to be any prosecution. Everyone was relieved that the boys got off lightly. It was enough to warn the parents and inform the child welfare services. Such files were like a mine that would detonate if the boy committed an offence later on. Then the earlier act would be part of the overall picture.

At the System Limit

'A system has no sense of the things
that lie outside the system.'
Niklas Luhmann

An affluent businessman who had acquired a property in Berlin during the real estate boom of the 1990s was called upon to prove his identity, in order to open a caretaker's account with a major bank where he was not yet a customer. This was in keeping with the terms of the Money Laundering Act. For that, he had to visit the branch of the same major bank in a large West German city with his passport and in the company of his wife (who was the co-owner of the property and also had her passport with her). There he waited in line at the bank counter, keeping an appropriate distance. When it was his turn to be served, all that happened initially was that the woman at the counter contacted the Berlin branch of that major bank and discovering that it only opened later (like many businesses in the capital). The man was asked to wait.

The businessman was not used to spending a substantial part of his Monday morning waiting.

The couple went for an espresso nearby. When they returned to the bank, the situation could still not be resolved. The passports were retained.

This is an example of the line separating a system, in this case a major bank, from the rest of the world. As a customer of one's own bank, that is to say, inside the system, the influential businessman with little time to spare would have been accommodated. He would not have wasted any time. As he was dealing with a different bank as an outsider (coming from the street), however, and complained in agitated language on top of that, it was hard to overcome the outer barrier. It was impossible, he told his wife, for a wanderer—who appears in a song by Franz Schubert, after all—to wander through town, enter a bank branch and make some decision there—for example, about a treasure he has with him. Banks are not trying to draw in people the way they used to.

As he had complained, and a representative had to be called over from the central office, which was in a different part of town, to register this protest, it took until lunchtime to complete the identification. The annoyance the businessman felt was harmful to his vascular walls.

The Institution Outlasts Its Members

Whenever I filmed the podium of a party leadership, with their heads above the tables and their name tags—including the party convention in Hamburg during the German Autumn of 1977—I had to think how many of those sitting there would soon be dead. I had a mental image of the line of party chairmen that had led the Social Democratic Party since 1900, whose photographs were exhibited in the entrance hall for the party convention. The institution of the party outlasts its members. In Hamburg, my cameraman, Günther Hörmann, focused for a long time on the face of the board member Wilhelm Dröscher. It struck him as tired. Something in the expression on that face captivated the cameraman. Two days later we received the news that Dröscher had died.

Crisis Without Speaking Time

Rainy during parts of the day. In 1928, the Reichstag faction of the SPD only had a quarter of an hour to make its decision. The result would be brought to the cabinet meeting via courier. Rudolf Wissell (SPD), Reich minister for economic affairs, used up a precious four minutes of their speaking time, with responses from Interior Minister Severing (SPD) and Hermann Müller-Lichtenberg (SPD), members of the General Federation of German Trade Unions. They used up the rest of the speaking time.

The issue was a 0.25 per cent increase in the contribution to unemployment insurance. Seventy million Reichsmark. If a patron had provided this sum (or a pension fund), the resignation of the last parliament-supported cabinet of the Weimar Republic under Reich Chancellor Hermann Müller, which became necessary after the SPD faction rejected the proposal, could have been prevented. It would have made the transition to the presidential cabinets unnecessary and Hitler's accession to power unlikely. We know this now, after the fact.[12]

What everyone who was privy to the organization saw (and that meant everyone in the SPD Reichstag faction) was the necessity of giving the group dynamic enough time that morning. The dispute would have reached a climax after 20 minutes of speaking time. After a three-minute break to gaze into the abyss, the experts would have found a compromise after another 40 minutes of talking back and forth. Presumably it would have consisted in delaying the 0.25 per cent increase until the following year, and passing a resolution to HALVE the contribution increase before then.

The Worker at the Bundestag

In the course of the student protest movement that lasted from 1967 to 1969, which invoked the authority of the working class, a political group succeeded in getting a worker from Recklinghausen voted into the Bundestag. The group, increasingly with the participation of editors from a major broadcasting company, had dedicated itself to the election campaign for a whole year.

The young worker Alfons Küppers, now a representative of the people, experienced all phases of the Ruhr region's industrial decline, then the incorporation of the East German territories, followed by the industrial sell-out over there. He was re-elected time and again because the basis of his electability, namely, the public opinion of 1969 developed by his group of supporters, kept growing like a garden. The owner of the garden, the member of parliament, clearly not bribed by anyone, remained dedicated to his constituency.

Today, after 11 election campaigns, Küppers feels trapped in the nets of the society of communication which is considered post-industrial. Where are the chimneys? Where can one see the tight teamwork in the production of metal spirals? Where would Küppers' skills, which had lain dormant during his mandate, be needed now? To what extent was he still a 'worker'?

Large concerns certainly do still exist in the Ruhr region, in Swabia and in Lower Saxony. They are barely present in Berlin. He was 25 at his first election, now this 'young Turk' of the SPD faction is 66 years old. Life stories are like windows in a house with numerous inhabitants.

How a Corrupt Law Comes About

The Bundestag MP Joachim Raffert, from Lower Saxony, was press merger officer for his party, the SPD. One day the *Frankfurter Allgemeine* published the information that he received a payment of 3,000 Deutschmark on the first day of each month from the publisher Bauer, a press company he was given the task of taming. Having meanwhile advanced to parliamentary undersecretary and become a member of the parliamentary faction's executive, the politician, he saw no choice but to resign from 44 of his 166 offices. He was not recommended for the next parliamentary election.

In the politics of film in the years after 1967, this UNFAITHFUL CUSTODIAN, together with his comrade, the Bundestag MP Ulrich Lohmar, was our most determined enemy. We said 'enemy', not 'opponent', because we believed he was corrupt but could not prove it. We brought it up openly on television by saying 'We consider you corrupt in the sense of Willy Brandt's statement about "intellectual corruption".' That did not give us any advantage in the political struggle. Bundestag MPs—from all parties—protect one another.

The danger did not come from the Confederation of the Film Industry's lobby, nor MP Martin from the CDU who championed their cause and propagated the so-called Martin Plan to save the commercial film business but, rather, from these STANDARD-BEARERS OF THE SLUSH CARTEL with their good SPD connections. We filmmakers were naive. We thought we could block a law arranged by the lobby without any organization, purely through the success of our films.

From 1962 to 1966, we prepared, shot and premiered our films. In the meantime, the Confederation of the Film Industry had, unburdened by the effort of producing films itself, orchestrated a law for the film sector. Under this law, a charge—a 'film penny'—was to be levied for every cinema ticket. This affected the American film distributors first; they provided the majority of films. In fact, the film fee strengthened their position from the time of the American occupation which entailed privileges like exporting the takings in exchange for a 5 per cent retention tax. What seemed to interest the lobbyists most, however, was the competing threshold for newcomers set by the law. The film penny, amounting to tens of millions, was paid out to commercial productions with a certain level of box-office takings. Most products of the NEW GERMAN FILM fell through the cracks. As this support, like inflation concentrated on a single sector, raised the prices for pay, copying and promotion, younger filmmakers had to face a competing threshold of roughly 200,000 Deutschmark per film; that was how much one needed to start from zero among the competition. This was the market adjustment scheme with which the Italian president Andreotti had wiped out the Italian CINEMA NUOVO in 1952.

Our protests achieved nothing. We boycotted the 'slush cartel' for seven years, and did not occupy the two seats in the Federal Film Board to which we were entitled by law. In the structure of legislation, no unauthorized arguments can gain admission. Herbert Ehrenberg, the powerful vice-chairman of the parliamentary faction and member of the SPD's federal executive board, received us; I think he found us likeable. He had no intention of picking a fight with MPs Raffert and Lohmar. We visited the young politicians on the 16th floor of the skyscraper Langer Eugen: Norbert Gansel, Heide Simonis, Björn Engholm. They were willing to act, but not powerful. It was only after Raffert's fall that Peter Glotz (SPD) and Burkhard Hirsch (FDP) began to work on a revision of the law.

Collateral Damage from a Natural Event

On the way back from Tampa to their headquarters in Afghanistan, General McChrystal and his staff were held up in Paris. Even he, the commander-in-chief of the troops on the roof of the world, was obliged to obey the flying ban that had been imposed by the European aviation authorities because of an ash cloud spewed forth by an Icelandic volcano. Thus the staff and the general spent a few days at a Parisian hotel. An embedded journalist from *Rolling Stone* magazine had joined the group. He was meant to report for the target group of the magazine which is trusted by young people. The staff officers, who felt as if they were in a peculiar limbo (not with the garrison, not in the area of operations), spoke in a relatively disinhibited manner.

The sum total of quotations, published in *Rolling Stone*, made if necessary for the US president to ask the general to resign from his post.

What can we conclude from this? asks Seymour Higgins, a political scientist at Stanford University, in his seminar 'Power and Public Opinion'. One can't put a military elite on standby, one of the participants responded. That already had disastrous consequences during Hannibal's stay in Capua. Other participants stressed that an American president had to sacrifice someone from time to time, otherwise the armed force would become a Praetorian Guard that no longer obeyed the political elite. The ash cloud gave President Obama a chance to make a mark. Yet another participant, however, pointed out the POWER OF NATURE. From time to time, she said, it showed its omnipresence by playing with the power of presidents and generals. It behaved like an artiste, and the collateral damage it caused even surpassed war which is usually something that gains, not costs, generals jobs.

Collateral Damages of Charisma

On the humid summer day when Napoleon crossed the border river Nemen—he had been waiting on horseback on a hill near the riverbank since morning, following the work of the pioneers who were preparing the bridge—a Polish non-commissioned officer tried to attract the leader's attention by unnecessarily sending his troop of riders rushing into the floodwaters of the river. He lost 40 cavalrymen. The bodies floated downstream. That was due to the charisma that the emperor, whether he liked it or not, exuded after so many heroic deeds in the last years, and which confused the minds of subordinates like a form of intoxication. When he saw the damage done, Napoleon began simply to ride away. He summoned the Polish officer and reprimanded him. Word of this got around.

Now there was a danger that no one would do daring deeds any more. The Pole's senseless act would have been a model example of audacity, after all. The army's crossing of the river had not made them faster. One needs an engineer, said Napoleon, who intermittently switches off the 'splendour of the emperor'. The misfortune lay not only in the detail of that day's events, however, but in the whole plan: advancing to India via Moscow. This disastrous project was the emperor's undoing.

The Political Neck Bite

Saint-Just, the merciless angel of the *terreur*, had been fine-tuning his speech since late afternoon the previous day and throughout the night. It would have been better to be badly prepared rather than erupt into a profusion of words right at the start of his speech. The speech was especially important. It was supposed to make up for the setback of Robespierre's address at the convention the day before, in which the accused were not named; everyone in parliament had the impression of being in immediate danger.

Saint-Just's speech was marked by a sense of proportion, an unusual text for him. He had barely read out 20 lines of his draft—he had not found his rhythm, nor were the convention members really listening yet—when the conspirator Tallien burst in from the atrium, where throngs of representatives were chatting among themselves, and interrupted him. He demanded that the speech be broken off. From the muddle of voices, two representatives rose and called for the arrest of Saint-Just and Robespierre; further representatives voted and took up speaking time. They should arrest him too, screamed Couton, if they were demanding Saint-Just and Robespierre. The invalid thought he could put his popularity in the balance. All too late.

The 'neck bite' consisted in preventing Robespierre's faction—which was to be toppled—from getting in a word at all. It was a battle for speaking time on the podium, fought with noisiness, joke-cracking, outrage, interjections and manipulations of the presidium which pulled the agenda back and forth like a bone.

In that time, one could see the Mountain, the minority of Jacobins to whom the Revolution had been entrusted, flocking together. The group could not reach a decision. As it later turned out, the patriots found it dangerous to intervene on behalf of Saint-Just and Robespierre, for their success could result in DICTATORSHIP. But if they took away all their speaking time, if they toppled them, the Revolution could collapse. At that moment, Robespierre had the idea of addressing, in a loud voice and without occupying the podium, the right wing, the part of the convention sitting on the right, with the words: 'Honourable gentlemen of the right.' This was the party of order, and Robespierre hinted with his calls that he would exempt it from any future accusations. He was shouted down by the centre, the swamp.

The hecklers had an easy time. Not only because they were spread throughout the hall and belonged to all factions (except for the Mountain). Every minute, every second of speaking time they blocked led the 'faction of terror' closer to the abyss. At 3 p.m. the representatives were told to step towards the railing of the convent, the place where they were considered arrested.

They had been defeated in two and a half hours. Fallen prey to a conspiracy, victims of the historical process. Even if they were freed by troops of the Commune soon afterwards, they had been declared 'outside the law' by the French entity and were thus lost. Simply because Tallien had shouted at the right moment, well aware that Saint-Just had not yet reached this level of hysteria, also because it happened in the morning. The neck bite means denial of time.

The Aftershock of Power

Towards the end of his life, Louis XI of France feared for his power. It was known that his life force was dwindling. From time to time, he left the monastery where he was cared for by medically experienced monks to travel to the capital. There he announced a number of unjust death sentences, dismissed officials and gave excessively preferential treatment to favourites. He preferred measures that would make his interventions seem especially unjust; thus he re-established his authority through TERROR. In this manner, his power survived past the point when he could still have made physical or mental use of it. What remained: naked duration.

He spent those days wasting away at the monastery. The unexpected trips had reinforced his IMAGE to such an extent, however, that it survived as a mask until his natural death. No heir could molest him. Indeed, it would have been out of the question for anyone to smother the tyrant with a cushion, as

Caligula had successively done to Tiberius who had failed to manifest his customary terror adequately during his final year.

US president Truman showed the same neck bite of power when he left for Korea and relieved the unruly hero Macarthur of his duties. What the general lost—and what had seemed invulnerable—the president gained. In comparison to the powerful dose of Louis XI, that was less than a gram of the desired attention.

The concept—already practised successfully by the Roman Caesars—proved Napoleon's undoing. To prove his authority after an attempt on his life that he attributed to the royalists, he felt the need to make a point by abducting the Duke of Enghia. The result, however, was that no one trusted him any more. The abduction was constituted a violation of international law. His insistence on an execution, which the Empress Josephine advised strongly against, hardly seemed serious. If the ruler had shown humility, he could have created an equilibrium between himself and his opponents. He was a bad political psychologist.

At that point he had POWER. Had he not attempted to prove it, which required further battles, he would most likely have kept it. By that time, he no longer wanted to expand it.

It Is Not the Individual, Not the Clan but, rather, the Institution That Determines the Exact Degree of Hostility

The pope was his guardian. King Frederick of Sicily knew very well what decrees would result from conditions in Southern Italy, and thus what the Vatican's policy would be. His merciless adversary, the German emperor Otto IV from the House of

Welf, was a friend of the Pope by way of family tradition. But as soon as German kings or emperors reached the zenith of their office, they found themselves in opposition to the popes. The institutions joined in ruthlessly with the 200-year war between the church and the emperor.

With IRA (anger) and STUDIUM (zeal). That was equally true of the pope's confidant, Frederick II of Hohenstaufen, when he defeated the opposing king and assumed leadership of the empire. It was impossible to establish whether the spiritual or worldly authorities were closer to the Imitation of Christ. They were sworn enemies, at any rate, whatever understanding they had in their hearts. The difference was that a church does not die whereas the emperor ends in his grave in Palermo.

An Uneasy Feeling

There is something shocking about it, but we must take it as a medical fact that wounded GIs who have both legs amputated show signs of excessive sexual excitability already in the rehabilitation phase, and more so later on. In fact, says the chief consultant at Fort Utah military base, who treated soldiers coming from the combat zones of the GREATER MIDDLE EAST, I wouldn't just speak of excitability but of a massively increased sexual drive.

In the military-medical search for reasons, he continued, we stumbled on the squatting position of the embryo in the womb. In this phase, the soles of the feet are close to the head. We see that in the so-called HOMUNCULUS, where the body is mirrored in the regions of the brain; this structure corresponds to the early stage of the human being, the embryo. The body changes, but its representations do not. We would never have thought that these early conditions of proximity would still be significant in adults. After amputation, however, the areas of the brain corresponding to the amputated body parts become vacant for occupation by the adjacent regions. So, in our patients, the sexual representations in the brain have been augmented by the sensitivities of the soles of the feet whose ticklishness we are all familiar with. The tickling feeling comes as a defensive reflex, and accordingly, for the GIs, any emotional reaction that seeks to restrain their sexual greed—that is, a process that defends against nature—increases sexual drive energy by the strength of the moral impulse. It becomes unstoppable. The staff found our reports on this worrying. They are being held back.

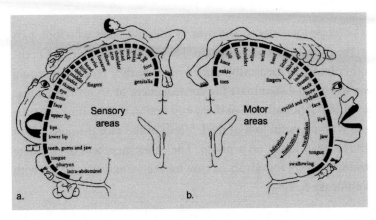

FIGURE 58. So-called homunculus: representations of the body in the brain. The proportions are already present in the embryo.

—So it's not a case of a wounded body reacting to the injury inflicted on it but, rather, an early state, a prehistory, affecting the present?

—The reactions are delayed. I wouldn't have thought there would be medical findings showing an interaction between such temporally distant realities as those of the embryo and that of a 29-year-old man who has been shot to pieces.

—Why do you refer to the 'military-medical', by the way? You could just call things 'medical' or 'psychosomatic'.

—Then we would have to publish the findings in a medical journal. It would be unethical for a doctor to withhold such a discovery. But a military doctor can, they are under orders.

—An incredible causal relationship. You could almost say that the shot hits the embryo retroactively.

—Evidently the Taliban are shooting into the past.

The feeble joke was passed over by the colleagues who took part in the confidential conversation. They had murky doubts. On the other hand, as medically trained officers, they realized it would be wrong to disseminate the consequences of an unwanted war in public. After all, one of them said hesitantly, we don't describe the way an awful loss of the left half of the face through a shot to the head looks on a photo. The other members of this elite training centre for advanced care for the wounded were left with an uneasy feeling.

The Absolute and Relative Concepts of Politics

'Politics is the continuation of war by other means.'
Michel Foucault

1

Wild Stream of Random Clouds, Reality Masses

Heinz-Alex Bogdanov, great-grandson of the legendary Alexander Bogdanov, had already belonged for 38 years to an informal group of lively minds that had formed around the journal *Aesthetics and Communication*. At the moment he was working on a draft for the project UNIVERSITY OF SUSTAINABLE MANAGEMENT, BERLIN (USM). This concerns the establishment of a private university. The interdisciplinary approach relates, among other things, to the fact that the anchors of qualified observation (aesthetics) and control of the wild stream of random clouds and reality masses, which are fluid even if they do not resemble any sea (the political), barely react to each other any more. It is necessary to formulate a concept of politics, Bogdanov formulates in the name of the group, that responds to the change of conditions in the twenty-first century.

'Politics is the organization of collective social experience.' That was a formulation from 1918 that came back into use in 1968. It is based on the concept of organization. But Heinz-Alex Bogdanov preferred to work with the concept of TEACHING for the introductory seminar he was preparing (which would have to be incorporated into the planned university context). There is no known mode of organization, he says, that would give the political a different disposition to its current one, but one could learn what collective social experience tells us: how one uses it to REPLACE organization (for example, through autonomous, self-regulated processes). Isn't that a bit clumsily expressed? asked Elisabeth Kiderlen, great-granddaughter of the undersecretary. As so often, an idea shone all the more radiantly the more its contours were weakened by speech and response. There was something approximate about what the group was searching for.

Heinz-Alex Bogdanov's seminar focused on the 'concept of the political'. It was to be one of 38 lectures. The draft he was working on was intended to keep his thoughts in order.

First, he typed on his computer keyboard: The political is nothing but an expanded duel—with oneself, with one's ancestors, the group or life partners, with the neighbourhood, with the faraway, a life-and-death struggle with the present that overruns me. In the past also between nations and classes but, recently, more about the question of what impressions I discard and which concern me.

This image of a duel struck Bogdanov as elemental on the one hand but unrealistic on the other. Bipolarity could be observed everywhere, but barely anywhere did it come together to form a politics. The political, Bogdanov continued, has an absolute and a coincidental side. After writing 26 pages, he was tired. He printed out the text and gave it to his girlfriend to read.

2

Politics Dreams of Its Absolute Violence

'The political is an outburst of violence, and there are no limits to its application. That is the first extreme.

'Thus I am no longer my own master; rather, he (my polit-ical opponent) gives me the law as I give it to him. That is the second extreme.

'It is a matter of the usable means and the strength of one's willpower; the two factors of this product are inseparable. That is the third extreme.'

These three laws, writes Bogdanov, already led to boundless violence in the French Revolution, though only at the moment when the republic was threatened by the counter-revolution (the Vendée uprising, the invasion of the Allies). This manifestation of the political is rare in history. It corresponds to the essential core of the concept, however, which has effects even if one can-not see it, as in everyday life. It is a REAL ABSTRACTION to the extent that all realism, everything specific, is ignored. The detail is swept away under the dominion of the concept.

This results in a 'paradoxical trinity of absolute politics'.[13] (1) The original violence of its element, like a blind natural instinct. (2) The play of probabilities and chance which subjec-tively 'make them a free activity of the soul'. (3) The subordinate nature of its immediate tools and closest interests which makes it subject to mere reason.

These assertions were discussed in the group. Where does one find that nowadays, people directly reading formulations to one another and debating them? Those assembled have been doing that for 38 years. They were interested in an exact defini-tion of the political for that entire time. That evening, they also discussed the committees of the planned USM. With 1,000 stu-dents (by 2016), roughly 5,000 square metres of space would be required. Twenty-five per cent of that would be shared area.

Recognition of the private university by the Berlin Senate required, in addition to the budget drawn from sponsors' funds, a bank guarantee of over a million euros.

3

The Portuguese Carnation Revolution of 1974:
A Laboratory of Direct Political Experience for the German Left

When he worked, Bogdanov sat at the computer—that is, in a private place. He only really carried out field research during the Portuguese revolution. The left in Frankfurt had been surprised by the news that a colonial army (considered reactionary) in Portuguese Guinea had staged a coup leftwards. German cadres visited the revolutionary country on the Atlantic coast. A laboratory of direct political experience! It was a matter of dispute whether a *proletarian* revolution could take place a country divided into an agrarian south and an artisanal, manufacturing, petty-bourgeois north. At the time, the group for 'Aesthetics and Communications' occupied itself with ELEMENTS OF REVOLUTIONARY THEORY. The experience gathered in the student protests did not provide sufficient data for that. Reliable news from China remained scarce. What counted now were the comrades in the factories that existed in Portugal (one can only establish that by travelling there, as they are not listed in any directories). It was evident that here two different countries had been fused to form a joint republic (most recently under Salazar's forced rule): the large estates were in the south while the social composition of the capital, Lisbon, differed to an extreme degree composition from that south and the agrarian-artisan north (with the city of Porto). What had happened to the attributes of a seafaring nation that had characterized the country and established Brazil? In this region of the world, remote from the war zones of the Second World War, the political had not appeared anywhere in a striking form for decades. Bogdanov had noted down the statement by Saint-Just: 'If a people can be oppressed, they will be oppressed.'

After all that, an uprising such as the one the comrades were now observing, like physicists in a laboratory, was improbable. But the results were becoming visible. A legendary figure was at the head of the state, voluntarily placed there by the internally divided factions: General António de Sínola, the monocle in his right eye. His ancestors in his face, extending far back, nobility. But this emphatic movement, which demanded freedom, expressed itself in pieces of music and broke through institutional barriers in all places except for the small precinct around the presidential palace, was atypical of anything Bogdanov knew. At the moment it resembled the image of the ABSOLUTELY POLITICAL, yet without the eliminationist tendency towards possible opponents who after all, according to the theory, should be part of this phase. It is all unusual, said Bogdanov. The group came to this conclusion: What we are seeing here is the neat version of a bourgeois revolution, 185 years late.

If there were proof of a favourable bourgeois revolution, Bogdanov said, it might also be conceivable to plan social changes that were non-bourgeois or pointed beyond bourgeois revolution. And planning means doing, added Heiner Boehncke. If one knows how to bring about emancipation, no living person will let themselves be prevented from doing so. They returned to the Rhine-Main metropolis full to the brim with experience, debated, wrote and drew up projects at their tables in the Nordend district. They had seen the political in action.

They were observers by profession. Bogdanov, a trained physicist, was a *schooled* observer. He could not be disappointed by the fact that something he had watched in detail later vanished (almost entirely). 'I saw it,' he wrote at the start of the quarto exercise book he was using for his notes during that time. His collection on the two months in Portugal, written entirely by him, fills 1,146 closely written pages.

REINHARD JIRGL

Postscript to 'Heterotopia'

Retired Lieutenant-Colonel Yuri Antonovich Alegyev
Interpreter at the 1961 Vienna Conference

Aspects of Poikilothermic Politics

Climate, weather, skin : a triply !determined=measure of political behaviour-in-the-moment, without any of the three terms-themselves constituting a political category. These three factors took their decisive effect before & during the negotiations in Vienna from 2 to 4 June 1961 between the Soviet secretary general Nikita Sergeyevich Khrushchev 'n' US president John Fitzgerald Kennedy.

Vienna, the location of the conference. City centre: 48°12′N 16°22′E. The city is enclosed by a tertiary subsidence area between the northeast-edge of the-Alps and the-Carpathian-Mountains, resulting in a natural valley. Southeast of Vienna the Viennese Basin between the line of thermal springs, the Danube, the Hainburg Mountains, and the Leitha and Rosalia Mountains with the 'Hunchbacked World'. In the north, the 'Damp Plain', crossed by a number of streams. In the south, the dry 'Stone Field' along the Schwarza.—The climate in the city is continental, no west wind current; winds are coming primarily from the south and the east; hot Balkan summers, not infrequently steamed up by humidity & pushing down into the city basin. In the winter, veritably breath-rustling coldness of Siberian origin.

Kalinovka, Kurskaya Oblast, Khrushchev's birthplace. City centre: 51°54′N 34°30′E. Mining region in the 'Central Russian Upland', a sprawling mountainous landscape with a continental climate.—A similar climate prevails in Moscow, location of the-Kremlin, the seat of the Soviet government.

Brookline, Massachusetts, Kennedy's birthplace. City centre: 42°20′N 71°07′W. Here the climate is Atlantic-Oceanic. Climatic conditions are comparable in Washington DC, the seat of the USA government ('White House').

The Soviet secretary general was entering a familiar climate in Vienna whereas the US president was faced with completely unaccustomed weather conditions. From a poikilothermic perspective, an !immense political advantage of location for Khrushchev.

The skin of-humans: as the outer coating of the entire bodily surface and with its adnexa (nails, hair) it serves above-all to ensure the-protection, the-absorption & transfer of stimuli as well as the-exchange-of-substances.

3 layers of skin: 1.) *Epidermis*. Several layers of cells, at the bottom the-germinal-layer (basal cell layer) for regeneration in-the-form-of the horny layer made of keratin.—2.) *Corium*, consisting of connective tissues & elastic fibres. Interlocked with the-epidermis through peg-shaped eversions (papillae) & traversed by blood & lymph vessels. Here are also the skin appendages: hair, sebaceous & perspiratory glands. In extreme cases, the-skin may emit up to 2 litres of sweat in 24 hours. The thermosensitive receptors in the-skin, in combination with the pain receptors or nociceptors, !substantially determine the momentary sense of well-being or discomfort in humans.—3.) *Subcutis*, gradually emerging from the-corium. Connective tissue loosens up, adipose tissue is stored in the structures (panniculus adiposus). Depending on age, sex, diet, other predisposition & physical strain, this layer varies in thickness; above-all, the-corium possesses most diverse protective functions against outside influence.—Under the climatic conditions during the 3 conference days in June 1961 in Vienna, the American president Kennedy obviously felt great discomfort: outside in the city the air was heavy with humidity, hardly any breeze in the cauldron of Vienna, the-sun stuck in the sky's milky vapour like a partly melted lump of bronze / stuffy=static air in the conference rooms with no exchange worth mentioning, rapidly increasing aggressive=germ formation . . . . . The smooth, well-groomed skin of Kennedy's face registered the-germs in the air like pinpricks, first the skin turned a rosy colour, then isolated areas of sting-red blotches sprung up. The quickly consumed breathing air placed itself heavily in front of his mouth like a hand damp from clay. Indeed, within-a-short-time his whole body seemed covered in sweat—his longing to shower !immediately was unmistakable.

But unfeasible for the continuation=of-the-negotiations; he would have had to leave the conference room, which would have been taken as a !grave diplomatic affront. Stay & keep suffering . . . . . The American's body arms legs, which had slipped perfectly into his tailor-made clothes at the start of the day, would surely soon be drenched in sweat—the cloth fibres stuck together with ever-renewed streaming=sweat, his pores grew tallowy, the breathing of his tissues became halting. The president's skin yearned increasingly !urgently for purification, ventilation and drying. Because it, the president's skin, could not have all of that at once, it rebelled and became unruly. It changed noticeably=quickly from the protector of the body into its enemy: itches, isolated at first, then soon covering the whole epidermis—stabbed right-into-his-brain like hypodermic needles, accompanied by hot flushes—. In short, the American president's sensitive skin seemed to have *defected to the enemy*, if one can put it like that . . . . .

Soviet general secretary Khrushchev, accustomed to the-phenomena of the continental climate since-childhood, was unfazed by these conditions. He too showed profuse sweating on the exposed parts of his skin, especially forehead neck & back of the neck, but the stout body seemed to compensate for this circumstance far better than the athletic American Kennedy, who was used to Atlantic-Oceanic climates. As if the Russian had an additional layer under his corium comprising a number of vessels which, like dozens of tiny bubbles, were capable of absorbing the increased sweat discharge. Now, compared to the American, his considerably more poorly fitted clothes actually put him at an advantage: the baggy eversions between body and cloth provided him with additional air stores.—1 glance at Kennedy was enough to see that a=certain fear was gradually mounting in this man in-the-course-of-the-negotiations=over-several-hours: fear of any physical contact . . . . . with this sweat-drenched Russian. Horror tactus,—& only 1 possible !escape: keep up the forced=march further and further out into-the-defensive—.

2 funda-mentally contrary types met in Vienna: Khrushchev represented the fading type of *the-worker*, shaped in equal=measure by both technology and the incorporation of his work-induced bodily reactions as his=property. Main attributes of his type: withstands deprivation, inwardly unfree.

Whereas Kennedy embodied the model for already-appearing specimens with characteristics of a different kind: epilation, extensive steam baths, mild & healthy drinks, hygienism & veget-aryanism : the-type for the ascending eunuchoid epoch; his main qualities: driven by will, undisciplined.

The pathways of stimulus transmission from the-skin receptors into the-human=psyche are still largely unexplored. Yet !these stimuli seem to trigger the reactions and behaviour of poikilo-thermic animals in the *zoon politikon*. For a long time, the-skin was seen as the outermost limit of the human self. Underneath the-skin is that which belongs=to-humans, which is native=to-the-self; outside of this boundary all the-offers of (delusional) self-identifications: ideas, ideals, God & other highercreatures, pat-riot-ism . . . . .—The-skin is the clearest scene of destruction for history : the way my skin is & presents itself is the way my ancestors & I were wrong . . . . .

Marxistleninist-medicynal research shows no interest in this subject. One of the bigmistakes of the-professional-Marxist-leninists is to-ignore the authority & significance of a *soul* as the poikilothermic authorization of humans. There is no entry for 'soul' in the *Philosophical Dictionary* of the-party; only the *scintilla animae* ('spark of the soul') of Meister Eckhart is mentioned briefly. But whoever !ignores The Human Soul fails to recognize the best friend 'n' enemy of both the-politician and the-warrior; those who do so have put their arguments & weapons in the wrong place. That is why THEY continued to fight battles long after THEY had triumphed: in the-propaganda (from Alaska to Zaire, people debated with the vocabulary of Marxism), &: THEY wanted to win where TEHEY !had to lose: in the-economy. Thus THEY created a space for the essence of history to run riot unfettered: because it was made by humans, human=stupidity . . . . .—

The-Americans did not win the negotiations in Vienna. But in-future the-Russians will lose !more than everything . . . . .

(Undated handwritten notes, found in the party archive in Tura, Central Siberia, Retired Lieutenant-Colonel Yuri Antonovich Alegyev's final place of work)

FIGURE 59. After his first meeting with Zhou Enlai, Mendès-France takes the train to the airport. He is surrounded (in addition to his bodyguards) by a crowd of motivated officials. Coming from the optimistic tradition of the 1920s and 30s, Mindès-France is a *planificateur*. He is able to control apparatuses. France's massive planning machinery was revived in those weeks: more than 300 years old, representing the reform phases of the country like a geological stratification. Strictly speaking, some employees should be wearing a bicorn, others an Egyptian turban, others still should be dressed up as Cato, Fabius Maximum (dressed in the spirit of the French Revolution) or as employees of the Suez Canal Company, and the last faction as engineers from 1940— a colourful assortment of initiatives.

Impressions of a Swiss Observer
at the 1954 Indochina Conference in Geneva

I would put it like this: the People's Republic of China, a participant in this conference, has not entirely 'arrived' yet. This was said by a Swiss military intelligence agent responsible for the accommodation and facilities for the conference in Geneva. His name was Colonel Ferdinand Hilgenegger and he was fluent in French. This body politic of China, it struck him, was an outpost of the Red Army located there, as the party still seemed like an appendage of the military cadres. This political system was just under four years old. If a child was born to one of the comrades in the 1949, the year of the victory, it had just learnt to speak and would be starting school in two years.

—Have enough schools been set up?

—It seems that the best way to set up a rural commune is to start by building a school. That's where the children are kept. The collective can start work.

—Is that intelligence information?

—We hear a lot of things that we haven't researched ourselves. But we can only understand our guests by gathering information about them.

The Swiss observers were very surprised by the deployment of the 'social groups from France' in the vicinity of the Chinese delegation. These were mainly deputations of women's societies, workforces and pacifist groups, most of them close to the French Community Party. They had organized their travel tickets jointly. The Chinese delegation spent a great deal of time with the visitors. Presents (propaganda leaflets, cigarettes, publications by Mao Zedong) and French counter-presents (books and bottles of wine) were exchanged. In records conveyed to Shanghai by ship via Suez, which were inspected by Swiss military intelligence before being exported, it was remarked that 'all questions from the delegates of the French people were answered correctly'. This ritual was considerably shortened towards the end of the conference. An incitement of the French base struck comrade Zhou Enlai as 'impractical'. In a delegation of French people's representatives, the Swiss secret service identified French agents who were monitoring the group. They were visited in their Swiss hotel rooms and cautioned. The Swiss observers had also picked out a Chinese agent in the French delegation, a white-haired European Catholic with a history in France going back to the 1930s, who provided information twice daily. This knowledge was not passed on to the French side; rather, the man was given the right to hospitality that had been afforded the People's Republic of China which was still young and inexperienced in matters of concealment. As long as there was no use of force, all delegations of the conference were free to operate in their respective agency networks.

A Blitzkrieg Warrior of Peace: PMF

1

A Bourgeois Character with a Chain of Ancestors

Better to be the betrayer or a great man than not to meet a great man at all. I was planted in his vicinity as a representative of the Algerian settlers, his mortal enemies. I will compensate for betraying him by writing a biography.

He gains the sympathies of the populace by addressing the people in the provinces by radio every weekend. The listeners are surprised to find him speaking so concretely. His opponents were not expecting him to establish such direct contact with the French. I consider it possible that he will rule for 10 years, assuming he is not toppled within 200 days.

His ancestors came from Portugal, immigrating to France early on, hence the addition of 'France' to his name. Related to the Spinoza family? Presumably so, going by genealogical progression. One thousand years produced an incredibly large number of ancestors, who split up into the numerical world of a small Sephardic community in Portugal; there has to be some kinship there.

FIGURE 60. Mendès-France in the back seat of the car that took him to Geneva on 1 July 1954.

In 1928, Mendès-France was the youngest lawyer in France. The French youth after 1918 were not a 'lost generation'. They found the places of those who had fallen in the First World War deserted. The phrase 'new time' was no empty slogan. His personal file notes: physical exercise during his studies, extreme sport, special courses and training with explosives. Finance Ministry undersecretary in the cabinet of Léon Blum, 1936. Air force lieutenant in Syria. Returned to the fatherland in time in 1940. Arrested while trying to reach North Africa after Pétain's surrender. Escape to London from the Vichy Regime's prison. French head delegate in 1944 at the negotiations in Bretton Woods. In de Gaulle's cabinet, fell out with Finance Minister Pleven in 1945. Dismissed.

In every situation, all the others join forces against this 'top pupil'. Meanwhile I find his face no uglier than that of [the French] Henry IV.

Generosity, the ability to let go. Has no compulsion to defend his turf; that testifies to self-confidence. A cool head. But what is cool about fast perceptions? Especially in understanding in advance what is going on in other people's minds? It will be the usual 37° that warm up his neurones. The brain comprises trillions of connections. This suggests that a good mind tends more towards the fiery.

Pierre Mendès-France goes to Rome with his delegation with three railway trains, crossing the Alps late at night. It is unheard-of for someone to take their government abroad with the. His enemies rail spitefully against him. The M in the abbreviation PMF is translated as *merde*.

2
The Significance of Dien Bien Phu Gradually Dawns on People

The surrender of Dien Bien Phu was inevitable, according to the Ministry of Defence, because the wounded had to be saved. The march of the brave into captivity. Filmed by opponents from every propaganda perspective. The reformers and parachutists, as well as Alphonse Juin and Jacques Massu, claim that the commander who surrendered had lost his nerves. The legionaries and the flown-in battalions could still have held out until the arrival of armoured relief from Hanoi. The army factions blocked one another out of jealousy.

How glorious the entrance of our army was when it took over the area at the Red River from the Japanese armed forces! I can see Ho Chi Minh, the nationalist leader, climbing up the gangway of the *Dunkerque* for negotiations. Then finally the offensive planned by de Lattre de Tassigny. In 12 steps. Methodical. Occupation by individual districts, ultimately the whole country was secured. When he died, there was no one to realize the plan. The measures came to nothing because those in Paris had no idea what was going on in the north of Indochina.

3
The Night Session. The Mandate

I honour my boss. The speed of his movements and decisions enchants me.

Night has fallen. Mendès-France goes over to the parliament. He is the president of France. According to the constitution of the Fourth Republic, until he is voted out: OMNIPOTENT. He speaks to the members of parliament. The chamber is not particularly full. Only the Communists' faction, 94 MPs who voted against him, is complete. The Soviet and American ambassadors are in the diplomats' lodges. At that moment, the majority of MPs are spread among the restaurants of Paris.

The president promises to return his mandate to the house if he does not succeed in negotiating a ceasefire in Geneva, and thus the borders in Indochina, within four weeks—that is, by 21 July 1954. Is he putting himself under pressure? He is forcing everyone else's hand but making his own position comfortable because time is on his side. He can give the opposing negotiators in Geneva and the divided parties in France the choice: either him, or an incompetent who will fail to achieve peace.

The political teams, having had their dinner, return after midnight to their seats in the assembly. Mendès-France goes far afield: he speaks of France's pasts, its future, its transformation under the pressure of a new world. No one here believes in that. In the CONSPIRACY OF INSISTENCES that unites political groups, people are certain that Mendès-France, this temporarily useful instrument, can be toppled quickly and effectively once used. Edgar Faure, the leader of the Radical-Socialist Party (Mendès-France's party) who failed to win a majority against him, and Guy Mollet, head of the socialists, a temperamental character from Normandy, both experienced with the apparatus, two enemies, have joined the cabinet.

4
How One Superimposes One's Own People on a Ministry

The president took over the Foreign Ministry in personal union. When it came to the rapid peace he was striving for, he does not trust any apparatus. He brings his young people with him, graduates of the major schools, assistants like me, the traitor. But even I am only treacherous with a small part of my actions; as far as the larger part is concerned, I am useful to him as a skilled helper and the boss thinks he knows what I am worth. Mendès-France sent his people to the Foreign Ministry at the Quai d'Orsay. All they need to work is a telephone and paper with a letterhead. They are surrounded by a troop of typists; secretaries come and go the way one changes mistresses. The work procedure is generally communicative. They work in close coordination, in groups, rushing back and forth; rooms with closed doors would be unsuitable. Those rooms are where the office holders of foreign policy sit, the heads of departments, deputies, legation councillors. Our superimposed structure, the intelligence layer, as it were, the PARTY OF RAPIDITY, has settled in the HALLWAYS, the BATHROOMS and TOILET ROOMS, is besieging the bureaucratic castle.

An orgy of competence. Especially at the weekend. The boss wants the most precise information about locations. 'Knowledge of a location is the soul of service.' He is preoccupied with the possible drawing of borders, the demarcation line between the north (communist, nominally neutral) and the south (nominally neutral, initially French, later independent, whatever that means). The boss has not negotiated with anyone in Geneva yet. But he is already agonizing over what his opponent will say. He wants to see aerial photographs from the 16th, 17th and 18th parallels which cut Indochina through in the middle. The peace agreement will take place in the other's mind.

5

The Clocks Are Stopped

I am convinced that had the president failed in Geneva, he would not have asked the National Assembly for an extension. He acts predictably and does not let the opposing parties blackmail him—that is his currency. The negotiations were not yet finished by midnight on 21 June; not for lack of goodwill from the other side but because of the sheer number of contacts needed to reach a conclusion. In such cases, out of politeness, the Swiss hosts—having already asked everyone involved for their consent—STOP THE CLOCK. That happens in the conference room and through an announcement to the press waiting outside. Two hours later the demarcation line had been drawn on maps and confirmed on the 17th parallel which will separate the future North and South Vietnam.

6

Intelligence Is a Nervous Virtue, Meaning It Is Always Too Quick

In its fast rhythm, my president's brain can be controlled neither by him nor by third parties. That will be his undoing. One of the consequences of his speed is his popularity. He reinforces it every Saturday with his radio speeches to the French nation. The CPF, which after all 'administers the masses', resents him for it. It views these speeches as a theft of its vested rights. Now, in December 1956, PMF got the package of measures against alcoholism underway and, at the same time, the withdrawal of the French gendarmerie from Algiers. Both decisions led to a sharp dispute with the right wing. If I could still believe that he would govern for 10 years, I would be faithful to him.

7

L'amour propre as a Principle

In keeping with the whole attitude of my ancestors, I am obliged to love myself. They would look on me with contempt if I were not steadfast in this stance. This also involves ascertaining my own value. My position and I have no value if I fall with my president. I have a value if, staying in circles of power, I sell secrets to third parties. In exchange for the usual promises for the time after the end of my political career. The one who lusts most for my betrayal is René Mayer, the energetic leader of the French settlers in Algeria, a radical socialist like Pierre Mendès-France. This man is striving relentlessly for the president's downfall because he believes that he would deal with Algeria in the same way he did with Morocco, Tunisia and the Saarland. He thinks Mendès-France stands for a politics of renunciation. How wrong he is! My president is a lucky devil. The first act of betrayal I carry out, taking secret papers out of the cabinet and passing them to René Mayer, will support him, for the documents show that the withdrawal of the gendarmerie will *strengthen* the hold on Algeria.

Coughing and Death

My maternal grandfather, Alfred Hausdorf, died of a cold that spread to the lungs. The doctor tried a camphor injection. I can see my mother crying.

Violetta is lying in her bed, her neck and chest loaded with silk cloths, when Alfredo, the charmer from bygone days, arrives. Mimi dies, Parisian pneumonia in her chest; her pitiful barking directs a final accusation at Rodolfo, who left her. The novel *The Magic Mountain*, which has August 1914 at its heart, shows in great detail the various characters of cough, the cause of the history of nations, that shaped the twentieth century. Balzac has just bought forests in southern Russian, chopped them down at a profit and married a Russian estate owner. He rushes with racing coaches to Paris where an apartment is being furnished for him and his future wife. He moves into the apartment, certain that his wife and golf clubs, still six weeks away from Paris, will travel there, and dies coughing.

The fatal cough is no more an invention of novels or operas than war. It cannot be ruled out through antibiotics ('counter-livelinesses'). For then the spirit of the cough, when it disappears among individuals, returns as the CONSUMPTIVENESS OF THE COMMUNITY—'there are societies that bark themselves out of life' (Stendhal). The 'sickness of making part of one's soul disappear', which leads to Violetta's death, cannot be healed, only forgotten. New habits replace coughing or war.

Sketch for an Obituary for the Nation-State

One early autumn day with splendid air in Starnberg, with no enquiries to answer, Jürgen Habermas noted down a sketch for an obituary on the basis of his impressions during the crisis in Brussels from 7 to 10 May 2010, the 'Euro rescue package'. He prefaced it with the following words: 'If it seems that one politics is disappearing or concealed, something new comes about in its place. The political itself is a phoenix. Wherever there are humans, the political cannot disappear.'

But then he noted the points at which he had been struck by the ABSENCE OF LEGITIMATION.

- Responsible finance minister in intensive care at Brussels clinic. The undersecretary from the Ministry of Finance stands in for him. But he has no institutional position in the EU.

- The interior minister, who was flown in late Sunday evening, 10 May, cannot represent the finance department. Remaining time for negotiations: two hours. The Tokyo Stock Exchange opens at 1 a.m. The interior minister acts by authority of the chancellor. But she must not transfer her margin of discretion to him.

- Legitimation after the fact by the Bundestag. Even if it is not a law, the Bundestag still has to approve. But the Bundestag cannot change anything. The motto *pacta sunt servanda* applies absolutely to the markets. They have the DE FACTO POWER OF SANCTION. The fall in stock prices is a harsher sanction than anything a territorial state can impose.

- *Determinacy of the object.* This determinacy is the precondition for all legal action. The Brussels resolutions are indeterminate: one could be dealing with 750 billion euros. But it could be that one needs zero euros, because the demonstration is enough.

Habermas was concerned with the question of sovereignty. In Brussels, the responsibility is split between 27 people. A few of them, not all, are tied at a second level via the ECB and other contracts. These ties interfere with sovereign responsibility. What is the basis of the political here, of legitimation? How is the EU Parliament involved?

Then Habermas listed in shorthand those attractors which take the place of the traditionally political in 'shaping reality'.

- The sum of all business conditions and agreements between the legal departments of large companies. A 'new law' forms on the boundaries where they collide, like international law, which developed along the hems of territorial states at the end of the Thirty Years War.

- Is there such a thing as a total worker?

- Is there such a thing as a total capitalist on a global scale?

- The question of the world citizen: embryonic representations of the idea of a transnational civil society (list).

- The Internet and the stock market accumulate information more rapidly than any political institution. But the things that happen must be mediated by people who, unlike those at the stock market, are not adjuncts of the events.

Habermas wanted to discuss this with himself first, then develop and formulate it. The obituary was certainly not intended to signal the end of the political but, rather, a paradigm shift, just as one used to say: The King is dead, long live the King! This, he said to his wife Ute, who was reading his note too, will still require much searching. As a philosopher one should hire detectives, he said, much as modern law firms do in their class action lawsuits.

Eulogy for Peter Glotz

Dear Felicitas, dear Lion, dear mourners,

The companion and friend whose passing we are mourning today left behind a unique chronology and summing-up, his last, yet unpublished book: FROM HOME TO HOME. There he writes: 'The memory gropes its way through our past like a drunkard with a torch walking through a pitch-black tunnel. That is how our conception of the world is formed.'

Peter Glotz, as we know him, was a man of great presence. Even here, at this moment, I can see and hear him among us, and even in a eulogy, I can only speak in direct dialogue with him.

He describes crossing the border in 1945, holding his mother's hand: 'A simple boy who enjoys life.' This young boy is inside him; that was true at every juncture of his life.

It is striking how changeable are the realities he encounters. What we call reality already begins before the birth of a person, with the things that preoccupied the parents over the last 10 years. In the case of Peter Glotz, born in 1939, it was mirrored in his mother. It is a time squeezed between two world wars. The images of this time give all of Peter Glotz's observations their specific seriousness. He grows up at the time of the economic miracle, the building of a republic. Peter Glotz was born at a similar time to the '68 generation. He adopts a critical stance towards them. He is armed with a sense of reality. He does not act in a 'left' or a 'right' way. To him, that would simply refer to a seating arrangement in the parliament of the French Revolution of 1789. His behaviour is CHARACTER-BASED. Like a peacemaker in a war of religions, he has a sixth sense for the building of political bridges. In more recent times, the Bonn Republic was a constitutional state, a place where opposing spirits could be at home, an example of how to solve a generational conflict. One should not underestimate the influence of Peter Glotz on this process. One of his special qualifications is the termination of hopeless struggles.

Realities change, his character does not change—not after reunification, not after the Cold War. We were all expecting an Augustan age after 1989. After the collapse of one of the superpowers, there was reason enough to disarm world conflicts. Today we look with amazement at the new aggressive realities of the twenty-first century: new fundamentalisms, nationalisms and unilateralisms. Peter Glotz observes every one of them accurately, and always responds out of the same subjective disposition with unbelief. This was known in antiquity as ataraxia.

I was able to observe him up close for over 36 years. He has my permanent devotion not simply as a politician but, above all, as a colleague in writing.

I observe him in 1984. That is a year marked by George Orwell's predictions, a kind of half-time: 16 years since the peak of the student protests, 16 years until the new millennium. Peter Glotz is federal whip of the SPD. A work timekeeper would say that those who hold this office do not have a second's rest. I note: this man, Peter Glotz, gets up at five in the morning. In the time until eight in the morning, so before he is inundated with appointments and telephone calls, he works on his journals, notes, memoranda. The term 'intellectual' does not strike me as suitable for this. His reflecting and writing come from conscientiousness. A man accounting to himself. A man living in the continuity of time. He feels responsible to his ancestors and those who will follow him. That is the virtue of the chronicler, of a person with consciousness. Every person possesses this power but not all of them make the effort to practise it.

I cannot list the many texts that Peter Glotz wrote, a kind of universal combined journal. THE INTERIOR FITTINGS OF POWER: the intimacy of knowledge about how power comes into effect. THE MOBILITY OF THE TANKER: the problem is that in politics, stopping and turning distances are extremely time-consuming. Each individual decision about them is connected to time pressure in the committees, divided into minutes and days. Then 1984: THE WORK OF INTENSIFICATION, a political book about the ability to discriminate. MANIFESTO FOR A NEW EUROPEAN LEFT, 1985. CAMPAIGN IN GERMANY, 1986: this is the Rau versus Kohl election campaign. THE MISGUIDED PATH OF THE NATION-STATE, 1990. THE DIRECTIONLESS ELITES, 1992. THE ACCELERATED SOCIETY: that takes us into the twenty-first century. EXPULSION: THE LESSON OF BOHEMIA, that is the story of a quarrel. It is seemingly about a historical topic; in fact, it is about a very current topic. Without processing all the bitter experiences of the twentieth century, writes Glotz using those exact words, the twenty-first century will become a maze. If an encyclopedia were written today, it would have to work through the experiences of the twentieth century so that our children would have a chance in the twenty-first century. The parts where Glotz becomes passionate are those in which he speaks of us passing on our reality to a future generation.

I asked Peter Glotz about his roots. The closest are his parents and the ancestors he knows, but they are far away in the past. Around 1600 the 'new human being' comes into existence. Galilei, who observes the stars. Later: Leeuwenhoek, who examines his own saliva and discovers microbes through the microscope, Monteverdi, who invented opera in 1607. The anatomist Madame de Lafayette explores questions relating to attachment capabilities and amorous relationships among humans. We shall call this HOMO NOVUS the BOURGEOIS

HUMAN BEING. It makes many mistakes. But it is the only renewal of humanity during the agricultural revolution, which has already lasted 6,000 years. The positive attributes of this character type are: I am not the spectator of my life, I am the producer of my life. I am responsible for the text of my life, for the texts that I write, for my attachments, also for my country (and if it is not a single country, then for Europe or the global republic). I distinguish between the things I consider unsalable and those which I use to exchange. I am incorruptible, says the bourgeois character in its positive origin. That is the foundation for Peter Glotz.

To me, Peter Glotz is an example of how clear-headedness is based on emotional strength. His outward appearance: unsentimental. Against all platitudes, and reserved in case of doubt. On the inside: a strong emotionality, for example, towards the people close to him, but right after that towards the cause he has embraced.

Mourning means: we experience a loss. We have lost someone who cannot be replaced. At this moment, we must call him, Peter Glotz, to mind once again, this intense person, tenacious and full of vitality.

He rendered outstanding services. One should not say to the fatherland, the individual republic, for he rendered outstanding services through a basic attitude that is good for more than a single fatherland: the political, the real, the scientific, the lasting and the steadfast. This is the republic of all authentic patriots, whatever country they inhabit. He was capable of commitment, conscientious, concrete and determined.

'And above me, like a sword of Damocles,
the hour of my death,
and I make haste.'

That applies to all of us who are gathered her. And one person who made great haste is Peter Glotz.

FIGURE 61. Suspicious man threatened by an insurgent. He carefully places his finger on the gun to push it aside.

FIGURE 62. *L'homme Nouveau*. Francis Picabia (1924).

The Descendants of the 'Foam-Born'

1

The Birth of Aeneas

She came into being on the seashore, from the foam structure created by the waves when they break on the beach. She is considered a goddess. She is named after the island on which she was first observed: the island of Cyprus. She slept with a young man; that was the fair Anchises, who was grazing his father's flocks on Mount Ida (near Troy). The goddess pretended to be a mortal. The man took fright when he later discovered the divine nature of his lover. The goddess assured him that no harm would befall him if he kept silent about their relationship. But the foam-born gave birth to Aeneas, Virgil's hero.

Later on, while drunk, Anchises boasted of fathering the child. He was struck by a bolt of lightning from Zeus and immediately paralysed.

2
A Realist, That Is, an Expert on Wrong Decisions

The son of the goddess, Aeneas, possessed two special talents. He could gain the sympathies of those around him with his aggressive spirit, with only a few words. At the same time, almost every one of his decisions was wrong. He was among the observers when the seer Laocoon pierced the gigantic wooden horse (which carried the devious invaders in its belly) with his spear. That was a prophetic warning. But when Laocoon was bitten and strangled by the serpent rising from the sea, Aeneas, who obeyed the authority of facts at all times, assumed that the gods had decided against the seer's warning—hence his punishment. So he ensured that a piece of Troy's city walls was pulled down and the symbol placed in the city.

He was one of the commanders in the final battle for Troy. With his crippled father on his back, his son Ascanius (whom the Roman poets later rechristened Julus so that the background would correspond to Caesar and Augustus) holding his hand and his wife Creusa behind him, he fled towards the seashore with a troop of warriors. Creusa was lost in the turmoil of the escape.

3

The Aimless Voyage

They had built ships. After losing Troy, they hoped to find a new home somewhere. On the island of Delos, sacred to Apollo, they consulted an oracle: they should continue towards the place whence their ancestors had come. And so they sailed where most of their ancestors had originated, namely, Crete. A plague broke out; that militated against the island. Only now did it become clear that a minority of their ancestors had come not from Crete but from Italy. The small fleet of warriors set sail for the west.

Caught in a storm, the fleet finds refuge on an uninhabited island. Herds of cattle there. The warriors slaughter a few of the oxen. Suddenly giant birds with girls' heads appear. They pounce on the food greedily and soil the rest with their excrement. None of the Trojan weapons are effective against them; the birds' feathers cannot be penetrated. Although the girls' heads interest the heroes, no contact can be made with the baffling creatures. Aeneas and his companions leave the island.

4

Dido's Cowhide and the Founding of Carthage

The founder of Carthage, Queen Dido, came from the Phoenician city of Tyre. Her tyrannical brother had murdered her husband. She reached the Libyan coast leading a throng of refugees. The country's inhabitants were willing to sell her as much land as a cowhide could enclose; this was meant as a rejection of her bid. On the other hand, the inhabitants knew that agreements must be kept. Dido had a cowhide cut into thin strips which, tied together, enclosed enough space to build a mighty fortress.

5
Dido's Death

A warrior from a lost battle brings misery wherever he goes. He carries misfortune on the soles of his feet. Aeneas' band of warriors lands in Carthage. A Numidian prince is threatening the city. The refugees from Troy, fighters out of habit, go into battle for Queen Dido. The queen and her guest (aided by the omnipresent mother of Aeneas, the FOAM-BORN) become closer. During a hunt, a thunderstorm breaks out and scatters the entourage. The two lovers flee alone to a grotto, where they come together.

Supposedly at the behest of the gods, but actually because of his ability to make decisions that are wrong in a certain male way, under the illusion that the oracle commanded him to found the future Rome in a place on the Tiber, Aeneas wants to board the ships with his fellow warriors at all costs, leaving Dido. The desperate Dido, who believes she cannot continue her life without Aeneas, has a pyre set up and puts Aeneas' equipment and weapons on top. Then she utters a curse, creating the future enmity between Rome and Carthage, and gives herself over to the flames. She hopes that her disloyal lover will still see the fire blazing from his ships and suspect her cruel demise.

6
Les Troyens by Hector Berlioz, Acts 3–5

In the mammoth work *Les Troyens* by Hector Berlioz, a grand opera in five acts, Acts 3 and 5 describe the tragedy caused by Aeneas when he first protects and seduces Dido, then casts her aside.

One sees how the Trojan refugees, at once apocalyptic warriors, arrive in the civilized Carthage with cases, weapons and servants. A barbaric assortment of once-genteel people from the Orient. In truth, they have no idea about anything; at most they know how to fight, and follow an invisible future preordained for them by the gods (or their misunderstandings of the messages from the gods).

Aeneas encounters the queen and, like a sailor, inserts money into her cleavage and forces her brutally to dance. The queen's confidants free the desired woman from the 'impossible' situation. The hero's aggressive behaviour does not put Dido off, however; instead, she falls step by step (as determined in love by Aeneas' mother, the foam-born) for the barbaric charm of the 'uneducated hero'.

In the performance of this music drama at the Deutsche Oper am Rhein in Düsseldorf, Aeneas was sung by the same man who had played the part of Siegfried in the legendary production of *Götterdämmerung* at the Stuttgart State Opera: Albert Bonnema. The Siegfried of Peter Konwitschny's production comes across as a 'ridiculous hero'. No 'man' would make such an appearance but, rather, a child. As a result, all of the hero's impertinences towards the Burgundian court are 'overly direct'. It is precisely this naivety, however, that enables us to empathize with the hero. Brünnhilde, the woman he secretly loves and unwittingly betrays, dies by leaping into the flames after his death. The same singer was now portraying Aeneas, whose propensity for error is no less than that of Siegfried. The worlds of Rome and Carthage do not end at the same time (so there is no 'Twilight of the Gods' here) but consecutively. The male manner of Aeneas, guided by a divine mission, is as 'ridiculous' as that of Siegfried. His departure triggers the same death in fire enacted by Brünnhilde who has the logs piled up. As long as Albert Bonnema sings this part, there is no difference between the two works.

7
History Takes Place in a Roundabout Way

After landing at the mouth of the Tiber, the Trojan refugees were sent another sign from the gods. The King of Latium gave them the right to hospitality and was willing to give Lavinia, his only child, to Aeneas for a wife. But anyone who met Aeneas and showed him kindness died quickly or was massacred. This was due to the original disunity among the gods, who could not agree on the victory or defeat of Troy, the great metropolis of the East, until the end of antiquity.

The playwright Heiner Müller died on 30 December 1995. In the last November days of that year he put on, partly as a project to avert death, an epic—or a sequence of dramas— intended to capture the fall of Troy, the flight of Aeneas and the 'impact force of history': the Greeks level the mighty Troy to the ground. THE NEWS OF THIS IS CARRIED ACROSS THE GLOBE WITH THE WILDNESS OF THE REMAINING WARRIORS. THEIR ENERGY (THAT OF TERROR) IS ENOUGH TO FOUND THE VIOLENT ROME.[14] ROME'S LEGIONS CONQUER GREECE. WHEN CORINTH REVOLTS, CORINTH IS BURNT. AS HAPPENED TO TROY 800 YEARS EARLIER.

Directly after Christmas Eve (having been released from the clinic again after chemotherapy), Müller received information about the fall of Smyrna in 1922. Now he looked for connections leading from Troy's tragic follow-up, the burning of Corinth, all the way to the present (originally the epic was supposed to deal with Stalingrad and extend the 40th anniversary of the GDR). An entire act was devoted to 10 senior teachers who infiltrated Greece in April 1941 wearing Wehrmacht uniforms. Only one of the 10 returned home. On the first days of their adventure, which they sought with their souls, the teachers, who appear in Müller's sketch as a mathematician and nine classicists, encounter 'Romans' in the guise of two lieutenants from the Bersaglieri. These are summarily shot by a German detachment (the teachers witness it) because of Italy's surrender.

The playwright was asked if such an accumulation of 'historical novellas' were not arbitrary. He could, after all, present a GREAT PROPHECY without political examples. How would he realize the quick changes of location on the stage of the Berlin Ensemble where he would not have access to a revolving stage?

He needed music, Müller replied. He was already too weak to eat enough every day. How was he supposed to stage a sequence of dramas over more than five evenings in the time that remained of his life? He was in a hurry.

But the poetic eye (and at once those of Virgil and Ovid) sees the PROCESSION OF FERAL SPIRITS going around the world expansively and at temporal intervals that cannot be measured between the birth and death of individual people. Roaring like the stars, as Müller puts it, the bringers of bad tidings wander through history. It would be better for them if they had never been born. If there are midwives, Müller argues, there must also be anti-midwives who limit the long-distance effects of a place of misfortune like Troy. If only Aeneas had never reached the seashore! Destroyed places belong in quarantine.

8
The 'Foam-Born'

The light water's edge on the coast of Cyprus consists of organic matter and 'salt water shaken in a special way'. No human being is capable of stirring up water from the deep sea salt of the Tethys Ocean (which already ceased to exist in antiquity, and only lives on as the eastern basin of the Mediterranean) sufficiently to produce the foam from which CYPRIS formed. This is all assuming that a goddess can take a SPECIFIC FORM, rather than being a CREATURE IN ALL FORMS. The epithets of the GREAT GODDESS are well known. But there is no star sign in which she reveals herself. The majority of stories told about her are implausible. Examples are her marriage to the weaponsmith Vulcan who dwells inside Vesuvius, her visits to the underworld, the mendacious, indeed propagandistic story of how she paired off the sister of Penelope, Helen of Mycenae, with Prince Paris of Troy. She would not have needed to be 'foam-born' to do this; to bring about such events, she could also have been descended from land animals or sea monsters.

Gods come into being like original life, from a difference on the edges of happy islands. These may be lagoons in which the waters gain time, and it could be due to the great force with which the waves crash against rocks or beaches over hundreds of years.

First Performance of the Cruellest Tragedy There Is, at the Start of One of the Most Devastating Wars in World History

In early March 431 BCE, the Thebans, allied with Sparta, attacked the city of Plataea which belonged to the Delian League. A vanguard was allowed into the city late in the evening. As soon as they drew their weapons, the Thebans were overpowered. In the morning, the main body of Thebans advanced. The people of Plataea declared: We will kill the captives if you attack the city. The Theban warriors were barely out of the country when the execution (there were 180 prisoners) was carried out nonetheless. A messenger sent from Athens to appeal the execution came too late. This led to the Peloponnesian War which, it seemed, would never end.

One of the tragedies premiered in Athens in late March 431 was MEDEA by Euripides. The king's daughter from Colchis (roughly corresponding to modern Abkhazia) has been abandoned by her husband Jason. He plans to marry into the royal family of Corinth. Medea is ordered to leave the country with the two children she bore Jason.

MEDEA FROM BARBARIA murders her husband's new wife and the latter's father, the king. After that she kills her own children so that none of the treacherous Jason's traits will be passed on.

Christian Meier sees clear signs that Euripides added the infanticide to the original myth. Medea is shocked by herself when she realizes what she plans to do to the children. She is about to abandon her intention; then she imagines the taunts of her enemies. At no cost does she want to leave the children to them; she also believes that the inhabitants of Corinth will murder her children anyway as soon as she, Medea, has killed herself. She decides to do it herself instead.

At the same time as the tragedy was being rehearsed, the war in Sparta was decided upon. In Athens, it was clear that the Spartan demands would be rejected. In Euripides' play, Medea flees to Athens after carrying out the deed. King Aegeus takes in the stranger.

'The things we thought would happen do not happen;
The unexpected God makes possible'[15]

Pericles' Funeral Oration at an Event in Thebes in 1943

Happy is the troop in which the higher leadership is not interested, and which has disappeared from the files of the supreme command. It performs its duty as it did in the early days of the campaign, when the war still seemed promising.

In the district capital of Thebes, a certain Major Dr Detlef Schleiermacher, senior master in the reserves, commanded one such forgotten unit. In 1943, the war had shifted the focus of his life. Schleiermacher was one of those who had taken part in the 'Celebration of Youth' on the Hoher Meissner in 1913, in the run-up to the previous war; he was 16 at the time. The word YOUTH still passed his lips freshly.

Here at the base of the German occupying power, a team of this youth was entrusted to him. That was how he saw his soldiers, whose level of training made a good impressions on local superiors who visited. The sports festivals and rallies he organized were also taken very seriously, and were a source of prestige beyond the regional level.

In the spring of 1943, two of his soldiers, holding the rank of private, drove while intoxicated with dimmed headlights as per the regulations, but much too fast, and caused a car accident in which they died. Now Schleiermacher's troop was positioned among ancient ruins in the west of Thebes. Torchlight. Actors, flown in from the theatre in Corinth, read from the original text of *The Peloponnesian War* by Thucydides: Book II, Chapters 35–46. The Greek text with an Ionian complexion.

Now the torches were extinguished. They had been procured in spite of the air-raid precautions, as an exceptional case. These regulations applied throughout the Reich (even if it seemed unlikely that enemy aircraft would fly into the middle of Greece).

Standing next to the coffins, which were illuminated only by pocket torches and each covered with a swastika flag, Schleiermacher began his speech:

We mourn the loss of two comrades, he spoke. Amid the mighty struggle for the future of Germany, indeed of Europe, this may be a small occasion. And it is not about these two here but, rather, about declaring sorrow as such. The youth are cut down. With or without war. What does Pericles tell us about this?

We cultivate beauty without extravagance, and intellect without loss of vigour; wealth is for us the gateway to action, not the subject of boastful talk, and while there is no disgrace in the admission of poverty, the real disgrace lies in the failure to take active measures to escape it; our politicians can combine management of their domestic affairs with state business, and others who have their own work to attend to can nevertheless acquire a good knowledge of politics. We are unique in the way we regard anyone who takes no part in public affairs: we do not call that a quiet life, we call it a useless life. We are all involved in either the proper formulation or at least the proper review of policy, thinking that what cripples action is not talk but, rather, the failure to talk through the policy before proceeding to the required action.[16]

Schleiermacher's concern was to keep up the spirits of the young troop entrusted to him as an elite formation until the end of the war—if, as was obviously the case, the 'future we march into man by man' and the purpose of the war had already been lost.

It seemed to him that the reason for the funeral oration was not the self-inflicted deaths of the two privates so much as this LOSS OF TRUE PRESENCE. One had to make something of a stretch (and the text struck him as suitable not because of its content but, rather, its strange seriousness of tone) to say anything meaningful in the occupied Thebes of 1943.

Schleiermacher had some trouble with the rebellious military judge Captain Friedrichs who had come to Thebes from Saloniki. Four cases of illicit homosexual relations between comrades were awaiting verdicts. Going by the files, it was unclear whether their naked bodies had been touched by accident or with the aim of sexual gratification. That would make the difference between a death penalty and a reprimand. In the tolerant Schleiermacher's view, the deed was no worse than the homosexual practices of a Theban phalanx which could certainly be considered an outstanding troop feared by the enemy for its ability in battle. This too, defence against an inciting outside jurist, was part of the defence of the youth that the senior master saw as part of his duty.

The funeral ceremony closed with a social evening. Finally there was light again at the casino. That is how the days passed. Young men who rushed forward, who set out to gain new spaces, a new time, work and practise waiting day by day. The need for a funeral speech grew stronger, but there was no occasion for a further event with a classical text. Unnoticed both by the Greek partisans and their own (by now disconcerted and disorganized) central command, Major Schleiermacher's troop, a reinforced company according to its numbers, was still waiting in May 1945 for some opponents who would collect it into captivity. THE YOUTH MUST BE LOOKED AFTER. THEY WANT TO ARRIVE SOMEWHERE.

The Funeral Speech of the Hetaera Timandra for Alcibiades (According to Carl Schmitt)

'The teeth well up in the eyes like tears!'

The hetaera Timandra gave the funeral speech. The account of it, like almost everything in ancient historical sources, was invented later. The body of the 47-year-old hero or opportunist, who is described in reports as a young man, was mutilated owing to the murder. It was surely not a pretty sight. His faithful mistress and companion had gathered up his remains and deposited them in a stone vat.

She is said to have given an address in which she listed the deeds of Alcibiades. His change of political sides. This too was distorted afterwards by the chronicler. And we can only establish indirectly what he wrote, as the original text was lost. Our knowledge of the events is based on fragments and Cornelius Nepos' revision of all the reports.

In his most difficult time, the spring of 1946 (he was not only starving but also fighting the loss of his position at Berlin University), Carl Schmitt sketched a RECONSTRUCTION OF THE FUNERAL SPEECH OF TIMANDRA on little notes. He had no access to decent libraries during his hardship in Berlin; he practically relied on his memory and his imagination. This resulted in the so-called SKETCH FOR A WOMAN'S POEM.

It had not been changes in the hero's character, Timandra states (according to Carl Schmitt) but, rather, the sudden temperature drops in political power that had caused his frequent changes of allegiance. He displayed the virtue of ATARAXIA, evenness of character, by remaining true to himself. No opportunist was willing to invest such tiring work on their own life. Admittedly, he never explained his indomitable tenacity, his BIOPOLITICAL THYMOS, to his friends and confidants. That was a mistake; they could not keep up with him. He was still planning to explain it later. Timandra had difficulty interpreting the account of his victories, the advice given on changing sides and the outline of the hero's strategic inspiration in her funeral speech. She loved him, so she did not have to comment. All that was left of the dead man was his ribcage. The limbs had been chopped off, destroyed. The right side of his jaw ripped out of his face. What the hetaera could have displayed to those present was very unsightly, so she concealed the remains in the stone box.

The charge of ASEBIA, that is, the participation in the destruction of the busts of Hermes in Athens on the eve of the

Peloponnesian War, was falsely levelled at Alcibiades. It was the first time the hero was knocked off course. He was a product of radical Attic democracy; he was its idol. At the same time, it also included a gaggle of sycophants (denouncers, inciters). As soon as the people rule, parasites attach themselves to their votes. Alcibiades was charged. He escaped to Sparta; that was the enemy. But Alcibiades could not restrain his ability; his impetuous will to survive was at once a will to speak. It was a source of enjoyment to him to lay out the Athenian secrets, the strategy he himself had conceived, to the Spartan elders. Thus he advised the Spartans to land in Euboea. This was a bitter blow for his city. He instigated the uprising in Chios in favour of the Spartans. Then a powerful clique threatened his life; he fled to the Persian satrap Tissaphernes.

He was quicker than others to recognize the displeasure among the commanders of the Athenian fleet of Samos with the excesses of the popular rulers in Athens, Timandra continues in Carl Schmitt's version. During a secret visit, he guaranteed Persian support for an oligarchic republic, the council of 400. The well-advised conspirators of Samos did not thank him for it. But he knew in advance that the resistance against the overthrow would come from the same fleet of Samos (overthrow is always brought about by armed people). Below the command level, the fleet was democratically minded down to the oarsmen. He placed himself at the head of these forces. Now that this civil-war party had triumphed, Alcibiades became the STRATEGOS AUTOKRATOR, the authorized commander.

He was not good, he was not loyal, but he was quick, Timdra continued in her speech. He was prescient. That is what makes a politician. How could one store this precious gift unused, as if in a sacrificial vessel? Instead, the pieces of a corpse a lying here in a stone tub.

After the fall of Athens, Alcibiades fled to his country estates in Thrace and then to Pharnabazus. There he was murdered at the suggestion of the Spartan Lysander.

Now he lies here before us, Timandra closed her speech. Without any power. I do not think power, she says, is the thing that ever interested him, or which he acquired. It was foresight. She could not express, Carl Schmitt concludes his sketch, what had captivated her about this spirit, her who as a hetaera, that is, the companion of great men, had her livelihood and her fixed habits. She was not forced to bring hardship on herself by remaining faithful to the fallen. She saw before her what fascinated her, yet she could not say it in her speech.

A Lover of Knowledge

Michel Serres, one of the last LOVERS OF KNOWLEDGE, who liked to be called the son of a fisherman, tended in his accounts to sharpen his vocabulary once he had found it and to remain in that field of words as if it were a weather zone, as if the goal were to hunt a piece of the truth with nets. These nets were meant to be cast into the associative streams of his listeners. Thus listeners were caught in the net. At the moment of speaking, he was concerned with the characteristics of the word 'life' (*la vie*).

Does an ocean like the Pacific live? Certainly. And the Himalayas? They live, albeit infinitely slowly. What does 'infinite' mean? Immemorial. That means on a time scale that cannot be perceived by our life cycles (including what we hear about the ancestors and the grandchildren). But one could write down information about what goes beyond that. Like the orbits of stars, replied Michel Serres, which move through the sky by one arc second in 200 million years. And the realm of viruses: Are those life forms or just pieces of debris? Leftovers of a parallel world? Or is the whole blue planet divided into different realms of living things? Is the realm of viruses a part of it? You mean, the way one says: Gaul is divided into three parts? What good is a distinction between realms if everything is alive? The best division between alive and dead, Serres formulates, is death.

But Michel Serres was concerned with a fundamental legal question. For oceans, he said, talking himself into a fiery state, have a right to be unharmed, and this right has a constitutional status. Indeed, there are no human rights without respect for the natural rights on the planet; Serres only left aside the constitutional norms of the cosmos because contact between humanity and the forces up there did not strike him as relevant to the present. Should the class action lawyers of New York, law firms with many parts, provide legal representation for the oceans and the defiled mountains? Serres paused for thought. I am almost inclined to say, he replied, that the oceans as well as other organs of the earth, for example, the deep rocks and sediments, are capable of claiming their constitutional rights themselves. For you see how Neptune avenged the blasphemy of Ulysses' men, who slaughtered his white bulls (that would be the spray, the white surf on undamaged coastlines), with a 20-year punishment. One sees it in the picture. Here you see the hero Ulysses on the boards that are left of his ship, looking meekly at the victorious god. But how, interject the listeners, who are net-owners themselves today and cast them out to the speaker, can an avenger like the GULF OF MEXICO find its way to the BP headquarters in London? How is the water supposed to find the rooms of the Chief Executive Officer in that tall, towering construction? If the guilty party has already been chased away and their successor is innocent of the abuse of the sea, how will the avenging force recognize this? So it would be better, Serres acknowledged, if the tribunician power of the ocean were exercised by humans, equipped as it were with a provisional authority of legal representation—of the unborn, of the oceans, of the defiled elements, of the air, of the soils, of history.

Who were the United Waters?

Nothing!

What will they be?

Everything!

And would that, someone asked Michel Serres, be the fourth estate? How many constitutional subjects are there in total? I won't, Serres replies, be forced to commit myself to a number. Not even by you! The questioner was a pretty woman who inspired the philosopher, born in 1930. If we forget even one of the constitutional parties, this excluded fairy will take especially bitter revenge. For the crime that was committed against her, and also for being forgotten.

Three Demonic Forces Came Together, Each Innocent in Itself but Momentous in Combination

Dr Erich Kläde tended, as he later explained, to go outside and undress completely in order to reduce stress. He did this at a very early hour of the day. No people going to work anywhere yet. Near a railway area he was startled when he noticed that a woman had seen him, naked as he was. He took to his heels. The woman, for her part, who found the appearance strange but did not fundamentally disapprove of a naked man, later discovered the fugitive's clothes on the rails, neatly folded.

In the meantime, the man had long since found the way home and arrived at his domicile. The woman who had startled him, a thorough person, had informed the police of finding the clothes. Now they were searching for the man, who could after all have had an accident. The trains, which transport people to work in large numbers, were stopped in the middle of their routes. ICEs[17] piled up. The breach of a dress habit had resulted in tension and considerable economic damage. They had become disastrous through the moral shock of the stress-reducer at his own appearance which he had viewed with the eyes of the young woman without really knowing how she evaluated her impressions. Nor could he have suspected the conscientiousness of this woman when he deposited his clothes on the railway tracks, for at that point he assumed that no train was to be expected any time soon. He was sure he would have time to take his clothes with him again. All parts of the causal chain leading to the traffic chaos had an overtone series of decency and virtue, but they did not fit together. An impartial observer could have revisited the dreamlike entanglement after the event and, with the consent of all parties, brought it to a happier conclusion.

Taking Recourse to Assisted Dying

A respected man in the business world of Rhine capitalism—he had persistently wanted to save his friend Hanns Martin

Schleyer during the latter's captivity (in other matters too, he never betrayed anyone to whom he owed his loyalty)—found himself surrounded by illness in his 83rd year.

His wife, with whom he had lived for 58 years, the same age, was similarly ill. Enduring pain with dignity is possible. There are palliative substances, drugs. But what for? 'Whatever you are not prepared to die for is not worth living for.' And so, one last time, the two of them summoned up all the spirit they had inside them. They went to Zurich. Everything had been arranged and the cost of the procedure had been paid. Hand in hand, in a strange apartment, they departed from this life.

The Harbingers Are on the Way

The governor of the US state and the mayor of the metropolis were acting within a time frame forced on them by the URGENT FACTUAL ISSUES. It really is a miracle, said the mayor, that I can ever urinate into a toilet. If I take my mobile phone with me, I won't even manage an unbroken jet. They had *no time*.

Hence they were reluctant when they were notified in a dramatized form of the harm caused by the mass of water. They would have revolted equally against any other news that added another burden to the daily rhythm they had to follow, which was already overloaded to an UNBEARABLE degree.

And so they, along with the mass of employees, denied that the immense storm front and the flood were a sign or a harbinger of the hurricane. The media had always inflated new events. Thus these two otherwise excellent politicians missed the moment at which they could have accompanied the disaster, which did not depend on their vigour anyway, with words of consolation on the radio, in the action committees or on CNN. That cost both their careers. The population never forgave them for their initial inattentiveness.

But what, asked the prophet Willi Laube from Alsfeld, if the harbingers, as signs from heaven, reinforce themselves into WRITING in various places on our earth? An earthquake in Pakistan, a rock fall in the Pamir Mountains, an ice block the size of Germany breaks off from the Antarctic continent, drought in Chad, a comet travelling towards our abodes, further harbingers: devastation of the senses. Even a crystal vase falling down and shattering can be a harbinger of the day we are waiting for. Do you think that some guardian of our whole, a functionary, a servant of the state and Satan, reads such signs? We need the modern scribe for that, the prophet. He does not read books, he prepares himself for the time AFTER THE WRITTEN WORD. His sensors (which are not his nose, eyes or ears) are spread out to register the NEWS OF THE END OF THE WORLD.

What good is that, the prophet was asked. The question itself is wrong, answered Willi Laube. The point is not what good it is, but whether we show that we are prepared. How can one prepare for a DISASTER? It won't just be *one*, after all.

'My child
Havest thou sinned
Then desist.'

The local doctors considered the prophet, who often complained of backache and a painful strain in his toes, a hypochondriac. But a small community around him considered it relevant to bring his messages to the people. Laube's disciples gave seminars at the adult education centre in Marburg, which is near Alsfeld, in which they taught bookkeeping and foreign languages. In that context, they made announcements for the purpose of PREPARATION.

'One time
Two time
Half a time'

It was all about the measure of time that was left until the end. When we, as humans, prepare ourselves for the DAY OF RADIANCE, there is not a minute to lose. But the management of the adult education centre was not willing to tolerate seminars of this kind. And if no public funds were used for it? The rooms and heating at the adult education centre are already paid for with public money, after all. Couldn't you teach in the courtyard or the street? The zealous followers might have taken up this offer if the students could have found them there outdoors. Their practical sense told them there had to be a connection to the public sphere, to an organization.

'Teacheth them to shine like the
Raydiance of heaven'

The peasant wars took place around 500 years ago in the countryside around Alsfeld. Gathering points for the leaders, whose rebellion was dictated not simply by hardship but also by SIGNS, that is to say, harbingers of the imminent end of the world, were marked by stones, 7 square metres in size, left lying in the woods a long time ago. Those were places that someone found.

And so, under the eyes of wary eyes of the police, communities of between 20 and 70 people gathered to interpret the omens that the prophet taught them to read. They stood in the November cold, holding out for a long time in front of the closed doors of their meeting places.

'To reveal the Endchrist
Is the aim of what is writ'

The Complete Version of a Baroque Idea from Christoph Schlingensief

Jewish graves from the twelfth century bear the emblem of a hare. *Oberrottenführer* Hartmut Mielke noticed the symbol on the stones when his column levelled Jewish cemeteries in Central Germany in 1943 so that water tanks for fire engines could be set up there. The motif is repeated on seventeenth-century gravestones: prone, 'sleeping' or 'slain' hares.

This, as the *Oberrottenführer* knew—he was a local historian in peacetime—contrasted with the heathen portrayal of hares in the Celtic area south of the Rhön. There, hares are documented on sacrificial stones, not on graves.

The cousin of Friedrich Ludwig 'Turnvater' Jahn, Alfred-Erwin Jahn, described in the *Journal for German Prehistoric Research*, Volume 14, pp. 143ff. (1809) the collision of the hare as a fertility symbol (as the spring myth of the goddess Ostara) with the 'theatricalism of Golgatha': 'the sorrowful farewell of the Son of God for a long time'.

This passage inspired Richard Wagner's 'Good Friday Spell' which he inserted into Act 3 of *Parsifal*. The pain of the cross and the cheerfulness of 'vernally laughing nature' struck him as suitable contrasts to express the 'straining of compassion'.

The scenery conceived by Wagner from this perspective was now taken up by Christoph Schlingensief in his Bayreuth production of *Parsifal*. He had spent a long time searching in the score and texts of the piece for something that truly touched him.

In a basement of the Humboldt University in Berlin, a dead hare, acquired in a specialist shop for game meat, was given over to the process of decay for several weeks. Walter Lenertz set up a 35 mm Arriflex camera with a time-lapse apparatus. The light was adjusted. It was ensured that there were flies in the small chamber. The camera filmed the decomposition with time leaps over a space of several weeks.

An insight from Walter Benjamin's study *The Origin of German Tragic Drama* was confirmed. There Benjamin discusses a metaphor that is rather unpalatable in daily life: the hairy animal body being broken open by living, liquefied forces operating inside, so-called worms. The skeleton emerges. It was such 'dying nature', which already had 'new life forming hastily' within it, that the time-lapse camera presented. It transpired that Benjamin was right when he called the 'forwards-thrusting intensity of maggots of different sizes in the ruined landscape of the expired hare' *distressing*.

The sight of the decomposing hare in a large-scale projection during the 'Good Friday Spell' caused the festival audience in Bayreuth some difficulty. They were not, after all, watching the 'resurrection' of a hare but the 'continuation of life in the forms of decay': others living off what has died. By the end the hare had dissolved and worms were writhing, likewise 'moribund', because the basement held no further food for them after consumption of the hare. That was DIFFICULT TO BEAR AS A MEANS OF ENTERTAINMENT FOR AN EVENING but apt as a contribution to finding the truth.

At the international press conference after the dress rehearsal, Schlingensief defended himself against the accusation that his concept was 'pessimistic'. He could not see anything pessimistic or optimistic about the maggots' greed for life shown by the camera. Rather, it was a *positive* thing that the camera was capable of recording such a thing, enabling the events to be repeated time and again in the minds of future observers. What was 'rebirth' if not something like that! 'Overcoming of the over-comer'. The seriousness of the music proved that; something of that kind could not be presented without shocks. Wagner's notes, tamed by Pierre Boulez, could not alleviate the shock.

FIGURE 63. Christoph Schlingensief

'Phoenix from the Ashes'

Christoph Schlingensief had built his installation *Church of Fear*, which caused something of a stir at the Venice Biennale, on the model of the Sacred Heart Church in Oberhausen's marketplace—the church at which he had been christened. Now his coffin stood in front of the altar and the colourful windows, which mesmerized the viewer with iterating stained glass. The photo which his wife Aino had arranged to be placed in front of the coffin and the flowers was a life-sized portrait of Schlingensief. There was a look of 'devious cunning' in his eyes that entered the impressions of the SOLEMN FUNERAL MASS and took away some of its bleak reality. The photo seemed to me to imply that the coffin lid would soon rise and the man present in this photo would join us.

Unfortunately that did not happen. Led by the cross banner and the priests, his wife's brothers carried the coffin through the portal from the church interior and slid it into the hearse which had driven up with its tailboard lowered. The transport people, dressed in black mantillas, stood around them. At the tailboard, Schlingensief's wheelchair-bound mother, his wife and the circle of friends and relatives said their farewells. We all thought something would still happen, for example, that as the car was turning off from the marketplace, it would crash into another car, the coffin would shatter and the young hero would return to us after all and take part in the afternoon meal that had been prepared at the Hotel Handelshof in Mülheim.

There was a delay. A traffic-police barrier had to be completed. Artistic directors and friends had assembled on the steps of the church portal (like politicians for a group photo), in unusually black dress. No one dared capture this group on film—with a reverse shot of the still-open tailboard and the inserted coffin—an opportunity the deceased would certainly not have missed. For his life, this was a historic, singular moment.

The car then began driving very slowly, moving at a pace that befitted the mourning event, as it were. The gravediggers or transport escorts followed on foot in two rows. We stayed behind, incredulously watching the limousine go around the marketplace in a rectangular motion. It left in the direction of the motorway via a side street.

The supervising vicars were still standing at the entrance to the church. Schlingensief's wife had other things to worry about than giving organizational instructions. The aim was to gradually lead a person, highly present in the imagination of those assembled, outside the space of reality. To that end, the photo should have been burnt before everyone's eyes in front of the altar. I understood why the coffin of a cherished deceased person is taken away by strangers. It is difficult to believe in the death of a charismatic person in time; it always seems like a theft, a malicious dispossession.

Evil Players, Nothing Is Decided

(Sketch on a beer mat by Heiner Müller)

Wax in Tantalus' mouth
The two axes in the baths of Mycenae
Electra's cunning look promises success
For all brothers who can start the guillotine!

So our boys of 1941 travel
Into the valleys of Crimea. How many
Lying reports are needed for someone to believe
That their ancestor offered the gods
His child's brain pan as a drinking bowl
The good person braves the battle for all.

Divine beings that set such machines in motion
Sit frozen, we know not where
We probably carry them in our eyes as glass splinters
Alice's beaming eye
If I want something, I must want it as if I wanted
Its eternal recurrence too.

All the debts of the Atreides ground into dust
Propellants for freedom
Automaton inventors, children of the gods
One recognizes them in children's eyes
Up to the age of three
Nothing is decided.

The Politics of Words

At the same time as our ancestors were catching young, inexperienced mammoths in the cold steppe, they were forming a trap for the rationing of air and sound in their throats. Soon they could produce a multitude of sounds for which they had no practical use as yet. This conquest resulted in life forms: words. Soon they founded a republic, language. And for a long time (out of good-naturedness, out of politeness, out of sociability) its self-assured, unenslavable inhabitants obeyed purposes. They carried burdens. They acted as if they were burden bearers. By their nature, words were never workers or servants.

One day in the twentieth century they revolted. In *Finnegans Wake*, one of these unruly, rebellious creatures became the term for the most elemental forces of nature, QUARKS.

'Three Quarks for Muster Mark'

The genealogy of language, according to the philologist Anselm Haverkamp, shows a general nervousness of words, their natural tendency towards subtle disobedience. In outward contrast, they march in step, yielding to the functions imposed on them by everyday life. As propellants of anger and excesses, they exercise moderation in our time.

They were isolated soon after their revolt. They were not needed in the formation of rebellion on all sides. They suddenly find themselves on islands. As soon as they had freed themselves from the compulsion to meaning, they starved.

Like the Gracchus brothers, like Spartacus, like Toussaint L'Ouverture, the authors Joyce, Schwitters, Hans G Helms, Arno Schmidt and Reinhard Jirgl hastened the liberation of words from their yokes, offered colonization—that is, new fields for the slaves to plough. But the slaves did not want to work: We have never been slaves, said the words, we will not be resettled like Roman legionaries or slaves of Spartacus. 'Stay with the majority, even when it is wrong.' So we stay with the people whose throats formed us, who clone us in a thousand forms of dissemination, now digitally too (which honours us), EVEN IF THEY ARE WRONG.

Our revolt is a perpetual revolt. How can one oppress us, when we are the reason why humanity and its constitution exist in the first place? We are self-assured creatures, one must not underestimate us, the words.

As the lion in our teargarten remembers the nenuphars of his Nile [. . .] the besieged bedreamt hum stil and sololy of those lililiths undeveiled which had undone, gone for age, an knew not the watchful treachers at his wake, and theirs to stay. [. . .] Zeepyzoepy, larcenlads! Zijnzijn Zijnzijn! [. . .] (Twillby! Twillby!)

A Peculiar Remark by Till Eulenspiegel

Rainer Stollmann refers to a comment made by Till Eulenspiegel in History 62 of the printed epic, Brunswick edition. The subject is the metaphor 'Get out of my sight'.[18] An impolite city-dweller says this to Eulenspiegel whom he takes for a peasant. Till Eulenspiegel does not do as he is told, however, but argues: 'If I were sitting in your eyes, I would have to crawl out of your nostrils when you close your eyes.'

The principle of Eulenspiegel's replies, according to Stollmann, is to take urban expressions literally and thus counteract the possibilities for deception that exist in the two languages of the city and the countryside, something which had already been used by the city-dweller Odysseus. This corresponds to a politics of concretion, or a linguistic grip on reality.

A Current Research Finding on the
Death of Alexander the Great

Sources on the death of Alexander the Great are stereotypical. After Hephaestion's death in May 323 BCE, we are told, the king did not return to his usual life. It seemed to the witnesses as if the king were 'beside himself'. Shortly afterwards he felt a sharp pain in his upper body. A high fever. Unquenchable thirst. By early evening of 10 June, he was dead.

Adrienne Mayor of Stanford University recently found material suggesting that Alexander was murdered. There have always been rumours about it. She shows that the king was to be awoken from his trance 'with water from the River Styx'. Perhaps one of his doctors considered this water, brought from home on a long journey, to be a cure, or perhaps one of the healers had been bribed to kill him; either way, the administering of this water corresponds temporally with the sudden pain in his upper body. In the rocks beneath the Styx, which is considered the river of the dead, one still finds a bacterium called *Micromonospora echinospora*. It produces the cell poison calicheamicin. This causes the mass death of body cells. The final stages involve failure of the liver, kidneys, bladder, lungs, heart and finally the nervous system. These, Adrienne Mayor stresses, were the exact symptoms named by the witnesses standing around the dying ruler.

A Political Service for One's Own Survival

They were there when the crowds broke through the Hungarian border. That was the way to a new life. But then they preferred to stay on the soil of the republic after all. They returned to the East Berlin district they knew.

In the next few years, however, they repeatedly enjoyed going to Hungary on holiday. And when their bones were getting weary, they visited a health spa in that country, where they had almost reached the parallel world once.

At that health spa near Lake Balaton, Elfriede Eilers met a man who had been injured in an accident. At the group lunch table. They only made eye contact. It was unforgettable for her, and she would have believed it possible to break out of her familiar life one more time (this time too, she would probably have returned to her old life chastened and refreshed). She would have risked the escape if her husband had not been sitting next to her (the spa community ate until late at a large round table). She would have found it overly unrealistic to join a stranger who did not even know she was inwardly weighing it up. But she was not mistaken that the gaze, the contact between their eyes, had been sincere on both sides.

After returning to her familiar circles, she took advantage of her husband's absence to travel to Western Germany. On the evening which offered that eye contact, she had heard that the accident victim was being transferred to a rehabilitation facility by Lake Tegernsee. So she went to the convalescent homes in the area and looked for her brother of the heart, but did not find him. She spent the night at a cheap guesthouse. Hearty air in that mountain area. She took a few steps into the forest. She was used to moving her legs, her thigh muscles, walking long distances. Her legs moved by themselves. She felt full of freedom and very much alive, for she was still hoping to find her DIRECT CONTACT, meaning the returned gaze.

She had got quite far, and was by now no longer sure whether it would be so simple to find the way back, when she saw someone lying by the wayside. Stretched out in the fallen leaves. Had he fallen? The man lay there, pale and breathing only quietly. She had the impression this person was dying. Who would voluntarily lie down on the damp, cold, hearty forest soil if they were not in physical need? The man's clothing struck her as semi-official. Unsuitable for a walk through the forest.

She was full of elan. She could not move him into a sitting position. He fell back into his wretched lying position. She at least wanted to warm him up. Time had already passed. She called for help, but no one responded in that part of the mountain forest.

Now she had already gone too far. She prepared herself to wake up next to the 'crumpled accident victim'. Who was supposed to save him if not her?

She remembered the instructions she had learnt in a first-aid course in the early 1980s, still in connection with the GDR's efforts to defend itself against capitalism. She performed mouth-to-mouth resuscitation on the man who—so it seemed—was GROWING COLDER. That was indiscrete. She was practically kissing a stranger. But she was also acquiring life. And she thought that she would sooner be classified as an angel than a lover. She affectionately wrapped her pullover around the man's neck and chest.

Thus she spent the night hours awake, constantly preserving and supporting anew what had been entrusted to her. She was not tired. She had a task. She laid her body, warm from the day, close to that of the injured man, transferring the energy she had. She was not ashamed. Nor was anyone watching.

Dawn came. In mountain forests one can only recognize it by a slight lightening at the bases of trees. There was hope, for the man was still breathing. A young runner hurried along the path. She later found out that this was a lawyer from Rottach-Egern who always exercised at this early hour. His regularity contributed to the favourable outcome of the political adventure. One moment, he said after examining the VIRTUALLY HALF-DEAD MAN, guided by Elfriede's information. I'll run to my car, he said. We have to get the man to a doctor! It was no use getting the police or fire service by mobile phone first; immediate help was needed here.

She was back at her guesthouse by breakfast time. The COLD MAN, whom she had heaved into the jogger's car with his assistance, was not making any statement. The doctor, after giving the man injections in various places, explained: You saved this man's life. Really? she asked back.

During the whole business, she had not been aware of making any DECISION (when was she supposed to have done that?). SHE HAD DEPLOYED HERSELF.

That same day she went back to Prenzlauer Berg. She would not have gained acknowledgement from anyone. She was still hoping to find the MAN WITH THE REAL EYE CONTACT. There was a prospect of this because the organization Paralympics, which organizes disabled sports competitions, had made available a list of all rehabilitation facilities in Bavaria. On the other hand, she did not want to act unrealistically in relation to her husband or the circumstances of her life at home. She was resolute to 'keep her feet on the ground'.

Ground Adhesion by the Stomach[19]

The sensitive back of the three-month-old child's neck was protected by a neck support. The mother's hand lay under the region of its body that would one day be the bottom. At this point, there is still ground adhesion via the stomach. The ground was the chest and shoulder of the young woman who seemed to be happy. The child's hand lay 'possessively' on the mother's shoulder. With their behaviour, infants secure peace in their immediate environment. If only because of their inventiveness in making contact.

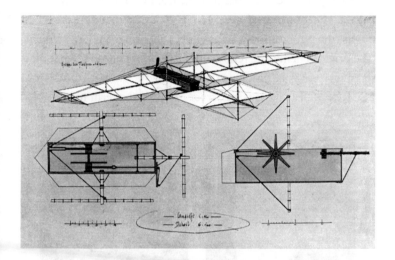

[*Homo volans*] For more than 2,000 years, the FLYING HUMAN BEING has been portrayed from the perspective of a fall. Icarus falls. Medea, however, flies back to her father on a fiery dragon. Alexander the Great lures his mythical steeds with divine food, holding it out to them on a stick, into carrying him aloft to heaven. Wayland the Smith (in the *Poetic Edda*) has his legs paralysed by a tyrant, fashions wings and flies past the royal palace; before that, he impregnated the king's daughter, so all the ruler's offspring will be his. The young Hitler wanted to compose an opera in Linz using this story. For the Italian futurists, flight is one of the attributes of modernity. For Khrushchev and in the Soviet Union, aircraft and spacecraft were the image of pride: a counterbalance to all the misery in the world.

[Politics means precisely determining the enemy] In his text *The Concept of the Political*, Carl Schmitt propagates the opposition between parasitic and antagonistic politics. His point of departure is the *politics of emergency*. Schmitt distinguishes Lat. *hostis* (the public enemy, the political enemy) from Lat. *inimicus* (the private enemy, the fellow human whom I hate). If what mattered in 1945 was 'precisely determining the enemy TO WHOM I SURRENDER', this is a correct usage of the term for Schmitt.

FIGURE 65. Carl Schmitt, theorist of the state

FIGURE 66. Alegyev, interpreter and spy

['Outside, the Bavarian Revolution'] Under the same sky of January 1919, at the same time as the lecture given by Max Weber in front of a bourgeois audience in a hall not far from the centre of the revolutionary government, Dr Eisner, minister president of the Bavarian Republic, worked at the Munich Residence. The same cold weather connected the lecture and the government.

Max Weber is preoccupied with groundbreaking perspectives on the political profession that will outlast the decade and process the experiences of the World War. Dr Eisner has to consolidate the revolutionary impulse of November 1918 with the established Bavarian bureaucracy. He published the secret correspondence between the national government and the Vatican, which was located in the files of the Bavarian State Government. The publication exposed the German Reich's willingness to go to war, as well as shaming the Allies. Aside from that day's weather data, there was no connection between Max Weber and Dr Eisner, who would be murdered shortly afterwards by the right-wing nationalist assassin Anton Graf von Arco auf Valley.

FIGURE 67. Start of the balloon journey. The father guides his children. Provisions are on board.

[Equilibrist. Homo compensator] Virtue of the bourgeois human who seized power after 1600. The organs of equilibrium are not reason, wishes or interest—that is, singularity and component force—but, rather, the ear and music (which began its triumph with Monteverdi in 1607). This, *balance*, is the bourgeois virtue.

[The peasant in me] The agrarian revolution has been going for 9,000 years. We are stilling living in it. If someone becomes a city-dweller, one finds inside them a peasant who has donned a mask. This peasant in us does not resemble the picture of a concrete person working in a field in a particular period. Rather, the peasant constitutes a REAL ABSTRACTION. Billions of facets and elemental spirits of humanity's essential forces learnt from working the soil: that is the peasant in us whom we can depend on when we are in need.

[Subjective-objective] Philosophical (and political) view whereby neither inwardness (the self as Robinson) nor the external (society) can ever form a reality of its own. Rather, the SOCIAL RELATIONSHIP, that is to say, a reality *for* humans, arises through a SUBJECTIVE-OBJECTIVE connection. A happy erotic relationship does not consist of what the one person and the other envisage respectively but develops on a shared platform between them (and that takes time). Accordingly, a work object assumes a subjective-objective form through the will of the worker, but also the will of the material which possesses self-will. A community forms BETWEEN PEOPLE, not in them or beside them.

[Love politics] Field of experience in which people can simultaneously test their intimate behaviour and their political judgement. The libido itself is blind to politics, as Sigmund Freud notes. But its *derivatives* are geniuses of the political and the search for happiness.

[**The power of the factual**] Polemical term in opposition to the *power of the idea*. Thus, writes Machiavelli, all laws and the practice of rules operate on the SURFACE OF HABIT AND INERTIA, AS ON A WATERWAY. The power of the factual, however, is based on an illusion if it presumes to be stronger than values. Power is rejected by humans if it consistently violates their values.

[**Surrender**] Agreed submission to a superior enemy. It is an achievement of civilization: rules that apply along the seam between war and non-war. This achievement is lost in genocide and aerial warfare; here surrender does not exist.

[**Deditio**] In antiquity there was a customary law with constitutional status stating that a defeated enemy who surrendered must not be humiliated beyond the wretched state he was already in. In the Caesarean system, this developed into *clementia*, meaning the duty to pardon one's opponents at the end of a civil war. It was a breach of this law when Emperor Frederick II of Hohenstaufen left his rebellious son Henry VII, who prostrated himself before him, lying on the ground for a long time. The vassals were already getting restless. Finally he picked him up, but only to have him brought to a dungeon where he died. Here the DEDITIO was refused. The modern opposite of that is unconditional surrender. This does not cause the occupied country to be deprived of all rights. Even the defeated enemy must be provided with food, and enemy soldiers must be allowed home afterwards.

['**Politics is destiny**'] Napoleon unified a political mandate, charisma and military presence in one person. He seemed to have the power to create a NEW WORLD. Instead, he simply took possession of the OLD WORLD, his critics say. He died at the age of 51. His statement 'politics is destiny' can be interpreted to mean that his narcissistic politics became his destiny.

FIGURE 68. Napoleon on Mount Sinai.

[**Directness**] Mendès-France demonstratively dispensed with all negotiation rituals. The same way the army of Henry IV marched, he goes directly to the most painful part of the conversation. He looks for the decision.

[**Accommodating**] Mendès-France goes by the ideas he observes or suspects in the mind of his conversational partner. That is what a polite person does. He never says anything simply out of courtesy. Conversely, he does not pretend not to have understood quickly what the other person wants. The Chinese president was baffled by this form of behaviour. He was not familiar with it from the rituals of Chinese diplomacy.

FIGURE 69. Mendès-France.

[**What is urban about politics?**] Until the late Middle Ages, there was slavery all over the world. If there are slaves, the masters are not free either. It was a minority that abolished slavery in the *cities* north of the Alps. ('City air makes you free') If a serf or slave succeeds in reaching the city, they are not handed over.

This was the seed that grew into the Protestants, the Puritans. Freedom spread to America. That is politics in the modern sense.

[**The singularity of the polis**] In the first millennium BCE, citizenship came into existence in Greece (Aristotle called it POLITEIA). This concerned a limited circle of people and fields; it related to agriculture, trading, slavery and a little piracy. In the classical period there were 700 such poleis. The structure corresponded to the Celtic oppida of Asterix and is faintly reminiscent of the earliest form of Swiss cantons. The ancient historian Christian Meier has researched and reconstructed the genesis of the concept of politics in this historically singular period. In the great empires of Egypt and the megacities of Mesopotamia, Christian Meier argues, achievements compatible with the concept of freedom and the political community of the Greeks were improbable. The monstrous power concentration of the great kingdoms made any alternative to central rule seem like chaos. Hence Marx refers to the Greeks as CHILDREN OF FORTUNE: a 'historical childhood of humanity, the most beautiful part of its development, as an unrepeatable stage'. This was when the idea of the political was born that was suitable for emancipation.

[**Emergence**] Attribute of a behavioural pattern produced by the interplay of many small behavioural patterns which join and, at a collective point, break out into a parallel reality. Example: the sudden shift of a flock of birds in a new direction, unprovoked by the appearance of a falcon or any other observable cause. A different term for this: *symmetry breaking*.

['**Production of publicity**'] Common expression during the student protest movement. Synonymous with POLITICIZING: concentration of public attention on a focus—Vietnam, justice, emergency laws, class struggle. The demand for PRODUCTION OF PUBLICITY AS A WAY TO BREAK THROUGH SECRET POLITICS comes from an entirely different context—from the war guilt of 1918 until the *Spiegel* Crisis in 1962. Social evil gathers in the arcane areas. If one could uncover it, people would have a chance to react to it.

[**Arcane area**] Through its agents, the Republic of Venice knew all the secrets of the European courts. Similarly, the spies of the GDR's HVA Department IX (counter-espionage) had access to all NATO secrets (from NATO Restricted to COSMIC Top Secret) and those of the West (from Restricted to Top Secret in the USA). Arcanum = secret. Secret reports are among the attributes of power. The misguided constitutional doctrine concerning illegal state secrets (*Spiegel* Crisis of 1962) and the current efforts in the USA to criminalize the publications from the arcane area by Wikileaks show the intense desire of power to defend this secret world. Just as value is emigrating from banknotes and trust in the state is dwindling, the phenomenon of an 'emigration of reality from politics' is visible in the fact that the secrets are making their way into the open on a massive scale.

[**Principle of the inverted cistern**] Hans-Jürgen Krahl explained: the student protest movement operates by the principle of an 'inverted cistern'. Cisterns give water to the thirsty in the desert; the water is held in the rock and emerges drop by drop. Our

FIGURE 69. 'No appeasement at any cost'

activity, by contrast, can be imagined as pressing water into the rock (society). The goal is a fluidization of petrified conditions.

[No appeasement at any cost] We must not appease at any cost, sad comrade Reimut Reiche, a psychotherapy ace, who drove a truck to the Opel factory at five every morning and deposited leaflets there. Of course social change is possible, whether we call it revolution or not. One must always accelerate subversive action, because next week the motive could already be gone and the group might disband. Haste deprives the revolutionary process of its temporal foundation, the field of employment. If we gain the necessary temporal perspective, however, we have to worry that we might not be able to hold the intensification of feelings (and the group) together for such long periods.

[**Michael Kohlhaas as a pensioner**] Contrary to what Kleist reports, Michael Kohlhaas, who was already being prepared for his execution as a condemned man, was abducted from the prison in Wittenberg by a gang of robber friends from Bohemia (as described in Schiller's drama). He later lived in a Frankish imperial town. Like after a sudden drop in temperature, he lost his craving to avenge the injustice done to his animals. He was never again capable of committing bloody deeds. He worked as a merchant prince and paid close attention to equivalence of exchange.

[**Bifurcation**] Customary term in Michel Serres' writings for: a branching off, a crossroads. Within an analysis, one can trace the result of a development back to a bifurcation where one evolutionary path separated from another. But if one goes back to this separation point 'with all one's soul and accompanied by the gods', Serres explains, then one discovers a trace of energy that took the other path; it has simply not yet reappeared in reality. According to Serres, we must learn like scouts to discover and follow up these parallel worlds, which respond to our sense of possibility and—whether or not we like or know it—coexist with our everyday lives. This often leads us to cousins of the present.

[**Alienation**] Central concept in the *Paris Manuscripts* by Marx. See also Hegel and Adam Smith. It concerns a disturbance between the subject and the object. Something objective found its way into people as if it were subjective, and this objective element makes them inhuman. Family men who otherwise behave good-naturedly, once organized as a police battalion, shoot strangers in the east.

The concept's emphasis lies on the fact that this aberration (alienation) is caused by subjective forces in humans. Human essential forces, fluid by nature, turn to stone.

Such alienation cannot be imposed by outside force. No slave commits the acts of cruelty carried out by a motorized storm troop of volunteers, or which manifest themselves in the indifference of a banking centre that refuses loans to West Africa. People who are alienated do not recognize the product of their work as their property (for example, that of history). Their living time ('dead work') is put into what they produce. But they consider their products foreign values to which they grant dominion over themselves.

[**Emergence from self-imposed alienation**] Alienation is not NECESSARY. 'Insistent attention' as well as 'passion and good judgement' thwart alienation. All emancipation deals with the 'emergence of humans from self-imposed alienation'.

FIGURE 70. 'Emergence from self-imposed alienation'. Angelica Balabanova, Russian revolutionary of 1905.

[Charisma] Description of the nimbus of a powerful person credited with wondrous power. Max Weber, the discoverer of modern OBJECTIVITY and RATIONALITY (asceticism, psychophysics of industrial work, limits of knowledge, Protestant ethics), made this concept one pole of his reflections after 1910. Today, the originally 'innocent' term (Hans-Ulrich Wehler) is overlaid by the Führer principle in the Third Reich. It refers to a WILLINGNESS TO COMPLY that is not based on interests or rationale but, rather, on the MAGIC of a person credited with the ability to break out of the merely factual, like the departure of Alexander of Macedon and his companions to the expanse of the Orient. The *extraordinary* quality of the charismatic character and the *intellectual fireworks* connected to it fascinated Max Weber as much as—going to the opposite pole—the modern mass effect of bureaucracy, industry and rational standardization. Each pole conditions the other.

[Heroic ecstasy of the drunken elephant] The ideal type of the charismatic contains one historic and one animal phenomenon. Weber speaks of the 'heroic ecstasy of the drunken elephant'. With the prospect of a charismatic power horizon, Max Weber primarily wins over young people. The lack of precise distinction in this term reveals itself in one of the examples of charisma advanced by Weber: in 1917 he sees 'BORN LEADER NATURES NOT SO MUCH IN THE REICHSTAG AS IN THE CURRENT DIRECTOR OF THE KRUPP FACTORY, A FORMER EAST PRUSSIAN POLITICIAN.' This was Alfred Hugenberg, later head of the German National People's Party, film and press tsar, who entered the cabinet of the charismatic Hitler as minister of economic affairs and had already ruined the economy after a year. I owe this information to: Joachim Radkaum,

Max Weber: Die Leidenschaft des Denkens (Munich: Hanser, 2005).

[Accumulation of power] Since Plutarch, telling the life stories of great men has also involved describing the power they accumulated around their person. When the power-seeker grows old (when he loses his motive or dies), the power structure still lives on for a time ('as if its head had been cut off'). This is followed by an account of the Diadochi, that is to say, the division of the empire, the occupation by parasites: an account of the bankruptcy of accumulated power.

[Power as a source of unrest] Michel Foucault denies that power can be a form of property, saying that it is never static or collectable. It is something that unfolds and, ownerless, becomes the spoil of third parties (if its author or attractor falls away). In this respect, Foucault looks for the effects of power 'outside the field circumscribed by the legal sovereignty and the institution of the state'. It is 'micropowers' and 'struggles' that produce power, meaning a SOURCE OF UNREST.

[Microphysics of power] To exercise sovereignty, according to Foucault, it is not enough to levy taxes and send rebellious elements to the gallows. The dynamics of a population, the assertive potential of passions, 'biopolitics', 'to live at all costs', industrialization, potentials that fill subjects after the collapse of industries, form INFINITESIMAL NETWORKS. They do *not* act at the centre of each individual tendency (which, after all, has balances) but in its side effects on the adjacent areas whose balance they disturb. Tiny changes multiply, imperceptibly at first, causing POWER to move in a different direction.

More comparable to a dragon, that is to say Leviathan, than a 'platform' or 'machine'. The following exercise power in the body politic: souls, children, families, households, businesses, the unemployed, the sick and slogans. See Michel Foucault, 'The Meshes of Power' (Gerald Moore trans.) in Jeremy W. Crampton and Stuart Elden (eds), *Space, Knowledge and Power: Foucault and Geography* (Aldershot: Ashgate, 2012), pp. 153–62.

[**Model of war**] According to Foucault, 'politics is the continuation of war by other means': not a system of rules but, rather, an expanded duel. Thus Foucault inverts Clausewitz's hypothesis ('war is the continuation of politics by other means').

[**Protego ergo sum**] 'I am able to protect, therefore I am.' Thus speaks the sovereign. He can demand the property and lives of the citizens if that is the condition for their protection: delegation of authority from the bottom to the top. The ruler seems to command, but in fact he is entrusted with a common property. If this is misappropriated or the protection fails, authority is lost. This is the legitimation for power in the territorial state. It applies to kings and parliaments.

[**Police science**] 'The true object of the police is the human being.' Thus the formulation in *police science*, meaning the science of the cameralists in the eighteenth century. This is not about the controlling and repressive tasks corresponding to a twentieth-century police force but, rather, the SPLENDOUR OF THE STATE, the happiness of the citizens. I am capable of supporting, therefore I am. THE STATE IS ALLOWED TO DO WHATEVER IS NOT EXPRESSLY FORBIDDEN.

[Prussia—Anti-Prussia] The GDR government of the final hour reverses the definition of state authority: THE CITIZENS ARE ALLOWED TO DO WHATEVER IS NOT EXPRESSLY FORBIDDEN. The round table adopts this as a watchword with constitutional status.

['Tribunician power of the oceans'] A Roman tribune had no administrative authorization. He had the right to speak in public for the purpose of defence or accusation. He could veto laws of the senate. The legendary tribunes Gracchus (two brothers) died while administering their office.

Concerning harm to the oceans, Michel Serres applies the traditional right of veto in such a way that, for example, not the members of class action lawsuits in New York or NGOs but, rather, the POWER OF NATURE itself appears as a tribune and issues an interdict against blasphemers (for example, the company BP). Just let the company try and touch the seas again!

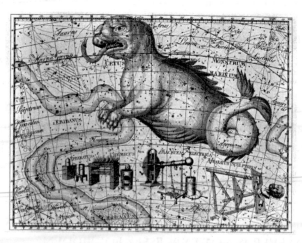

FIGURE 71. Constellation of the whale from Johann Elert Bode's *Uranographria*. Tools are represented below it.

[The laws of nature are the earth's invisible government] In a suburb of Boston, reports the physicist Robert B. Laughlin, there lived some doctoral students of physics. Their apartments were at the end of a blind alley. One day, the temperature changed and rain fell in tropical quantities. The sludge of snow and rain blocked the gutters and still filled the street at three in the morning, when an arctic Cold Front from Canada froze the mass, which was neither solid nor liquid, into a thick ice crust. The city administration and the doctoral physicists living here waited a week for a thaw that would not come. The whole thing remained there as a kind of dirty, extremely dangerous ice concrete until it thawed in spring.

[The difference between barbarism and the state of nature] 'The intellectual atrophy, however, that is artificially produced through the transformation of immature humans into mere machines for producing added value is very different from that primordial ignorance which leaves the spirit uncultivated without ruining its capacity for development.' Note from Theodor W. Adorno's journal.

[Earth and workers] 'Anticipation of the future—true anticipation only takes place in the production of wealth with reference to the worker and the earth. For both of these, premature overexertion and exhaustion [. . .] can anticipate and devastate the future in reality.' Note in Otto Ohlendorf's writing books in the Nuremberg Palace of Justice.

[What does 'to the right of National Socialism' mean?] At the 1931 parade in Bad Harzburg, the majority of right-wing nationalists were to the right of the National Socialists. On

1 May 1933, the National Socialist leadership emphasized a kind of left-wing front. The emphasis was on National *Socialism*. This line (among several others) was cut off on 30 June 1934. In Halberstadt: the Klamroth family, Dr Wischhusen, my parents, state prosecutor Genest, Alwine Steinrück (master butcher), estate-owner Däneke and factory-owner Heine stood to the *right* of the National Socialists. They considered the party's rule temporary, found the parades plebeian and refused to have stew every Sunday, making a donation instead. It was socially acceptable for someone standing to the right of the National Socialists to enter the SS or the NSKK, but hardly the SA. Nor did they serve in the NSV. The mounted SS would be perfect.

[Polit-bureaucrat] is a term that is not meant pejoratively by Max Weber. It refers to the character of the passionate planner. This type is consumed by politics, to which he devotes his life and his ideality. The word 'bureaucratic', Dahrendorf reminds us, was still unexhausted for Weber as the discoverer of administrative reality, that is to say, of objective rule from an office. It refers to a modern attitude.

[Miracle in the Vatican] Cardinal Undersecretary Waldemar, who had suffered from hiccups for years but kept his office 'in his hands' to the end, when all that was left was skin stretched over his collapsed bones—only a quarter of an hour before his death, he had music by Beethoven from his record case played—was the object of a miracle even *after* his last hours, days, weeks. He had already breathed his final breath, and the black spots that mark physical death were appearing on his back (and if one turned him on his side, they appeared there too after a while).

FIGURE 72. Polit-bureaucrat (after Max Weber) as *Homo volans*.

Light held in front of his eyes (two dynamo torches), triggered no reaction from the pupils. No pulse, no more warmth—clinically, this energetic prince of the church was dead. At the same time, however, his tongue was miraculously still capable of speaking. 'Ecce nubs lucida obumbravit'. Then: 'Scindite corda vestra'. 'Ne vacuata sit crux'. Bystanders reported hearing 'Eccaeca' several times. These words were considered important: 'Quid fiet hominibus qui minima contemnunt, majora non credunt . . . '. This how the sounds were interpreted. There was no trace of breath when a mirror was held up to his nose and partially open mouth, nor when the corpse 'spoke'. Five doctors from the curia tried to draw blood from the vein; they failed. They plucked at his eyelids; his paper skin could be peeled off like a leaf. Numerous distrustful archbishops convinced themselves with their *own eyes* that a kind of miracle was in evidence here. The tongue was surgically removed and placed under glass. The next pope already called it 'Waldemar's lifeblood'.

[Displacement activity in politics] A dog chasing ahead that has to decide between two contradictory commands will not stop running but, rather, change direction. One calls that displacement. Two days after the attack on the Twin Towers on 11 September 2001, the Hawaiian battle fleet appeared off New York. Witnesses from the war had the impression that the armada once surprised (in 1941) by a Japanese ambush had turned up here to protect the wounded city. But the ships floating by the coast were modern vessels. They constituted an attempt by the Pentagon to respond quickly to the disaster. Displacement means: a reflex gets out of control. In reality, there was no instrument of American politics that could have responded to the attack of 11 September. It was only by shifting the question to Afghanistan, into another world, that the deployment of forces became possible.

FIGURE 73. Chinese leadership in 1989.

[Coincidence as a strength of politics] As late as October 1989, US experts still considered a 'Chinese solution' (the violent suppression of a popular uprising) possible in the GDR. Waltraud Grünbein, a second cousin of the poet,[20] identifies 8 October as the turning point. That evening, a wall of police officers laid down their shields. It looked like the performance of an opera. The surprising gesture and the sudden quiet, the cessation of the water games, pacified the protestors. None of those politically responsible had triggered this event. The party's district head, the later Prime Minister Modrow, was attending a performance of *Fidelio* at the Semperoper and thus unreachable. Mayor Berghofer received a delegation from the protestant church—unavailable. Secret agents in civvies, watching behind the police cordon, were temporarily not responsible while the shift changed. *Coincidence* caused the shields to be lowered. It was also a coincidence, writes Waltraud Grünbein, that Beethoven's opera had a direct, practical political effect.

['**Emigration of reality from politics**'] Berry Zischler, a cousin of the actor and author,[21] demanded in his essay in the *New York Times* of 29 December 2010 that 'we' (referring to the American readers) now finally had to settle in the twentieth century. So far, 'most of us' had believed the events since 2001 were 'like a bad dream', that is to say, temporary. But the twentieth century was not coming back. The powerlessness of politics in the face of companies and stock exchanges that act like territorial states, the DISSATISFACTION OF THE PEOPLE (their despair and anger), expressed in the founding of new religions, proved that REALITY IS EMIGRATING FROM THE SYSTEM OF POLITICS. Zischler's partner, who works for the *Washington Post*, was of a different opinion. She wrote an opposing article that appeared on 2 January 2011. In it, she asked: If reality emigrates from the political, then what is real about reality? The two partners shared a home in Manhattan. They spent Christmas and New Year's together harmoniously—in spite of their dispute.

[**The fruits of rage**] 'Since the closure of the company that employed my husband here in Bremen for 20 years, he has been working in the Stuttgart area. We, the family, live in Bremen because we can't afford to move. I essentially agree with the Stuttgart 21 initiative, and also with the protest against the transport of radioactive material, but I'D still like something stronger to express myself in a lasting way. Now I have to pick up the children from school. I won't let go of my hope. Warm regards, Elfriede Willke, née Handorf.'

FIGURE 74. Elfriede Willke, née Handorf

['**You're tough, I am tough / who will write our épitaphe?**'] The New Year's article by Fritzi F. Hamilton in the New York edition of *Spex* begins with this line. The subtitle reads: 'The Return of the Political as a Partisan'. The article contains a preview of the decade from 2011 to 2020 from the perspective of New Year's Eve 2010.

[**The indestructibility of the political**] Once again, humanity had overreached. It had packed up the great ape inside the ship in the hope that it could bring it from Africa to New York, where it planned to exhibit it at the circus or in a large park. As soon as the animal arrived in the city of lights, it would be worth a fortune, but for now there was still water between them. The captain was afraid. The man had a guilty conscience. Icebergs went past the steamer's salons. It seemed cold down there, under the ice stumps. The icebergs have edges that extend downwards, like roots—and if the captain doesn't keep an eye on his ship, these underwater knives made of ice will slit open the tin box which will then sink bitterly to the bottom of the sea. How can the captain overcome his fear? A ghastly situation, and it's not even night yet . . .

16°N, 88°W. That was the hour of Kong's great power. How easy to smash this ship. The ship wasn't built for a force of nature like this. Lightning and storm winds outside. In the ship's hull at this hour: gigantic nature. In the stern, glasses are shattering.

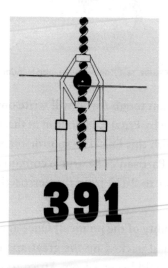

FIGURE 75. Drill. Francis Picabia.

NOTES

1 The word *Dünnbrettbohrer*, literally, 'thin-board driller', refers to someone who is a lightweight in intellectual or behavioural terms. [Trans.]

2 The phrase *das geht Dich Aff' gar nichts an*, which imitates the sound of 'Afghanistan', means 'that's none of your business, you idiot [literally, "monkey"]'. [Trans.]

3 A reference to two Brothers Grimm tales: 'Cinderella' and 'The Wishing-Table, the Gold-Ass, and the Cudgel in the Sack'. [Trans.]

4 *Viertel* means quarter, *Sechzentel* means sixteenth. [Trans.]

5 Planning takes place at the national level. It follows guidelines corresponding to the insights of businesses that think in global structures, that is, calculate the utility value in real averages of the global scale. On site, such architecture, in the form of an underpass (and shopping arcade) in a major train station, creates a CHIMNEY EFFECT. After all, on the large scale of a 'street line', the underpass is a 'chimney'. A concentration of November air, brought over from the northwest, moves past the old woman.

6 A corruption based on the expression *en avoir ras le bol*: 'to be fed up with something'.

7 The original German, *Nicht gefangen, nicht gehangen*, is a modification of the saying *Mitgehangen, mitgefangen*, which corresponds in English to 'Cling together, swing together'. [Trans.]

8 All proper names have been changed by the author.

9 The conversation took place in the Advent season of 1933 in the Reich capital, Berlin. The correspondent of the *Neue*

Zürcher Zeitung suggested the smokers' lounge at the Adlon as a meeting place.

10 Eduard Richter, a party member since 1923, a jurist from the school of Dahm and Schaffstein in Kiel, author of writings on legal philosophy, confidant of I. G. Farben. Committed suicide in Oslo in 1945.

11 Immanuel Kant, *Critique of Pure Reason* (Marcus Weigelt ed. and trans.) (London: Penguin, 2007), p. 573.

12 The historical constellation of 1928 preoccupied Herbert Wehner in the 1970s.

13 In analogy to Carl von Clauswitz, *On War* (Michael Howard and Peter Paret trans) (Oxford and New York: Oxford University Press, 2007), p. 30.

14 What is violent, Müller writes in his notes, is not the quick use of weapons but the unjust use thereof. Hence it was the behaviour of Aeneas, who cast away Dido's love, that drove the queen to her death. And Aeneas' successors were levelling Carthage to the ground all the more eagerly a few centuries later. They had the ground PLOUGHED on which the city stood, and where it now lies destroyed. An especially laborious way to complete a destruction their forefather had begun. Müller initially had Carthage's elephants (their slaughter by the Roman legionaries) in mind as a metaphor for this. But then the image of the effort invested by the Romans in the work of destruction, the dismemberment of the foreign city, struck him as the better symbol.

15 Euripides, *Medea and Other Plays* (Philip Vellacott trans.) (London: Penguin, 1963), p. 45.

16 Thucydides, *The Peloponnesian War* (Martin Hammond trans.) (Oxford and New York: Oxford University Press, 2009), pp. 92f.

17 ICE is short for Intercity Express, the fast long-distance train. [Trans.]

18 The German phrase used is *Geh mir aus den Augen*, which literally means 'Get out of my eyes'. [Trans.]

19 The German term *Bodenhaftung* creates a play on words, as it refers both to ground adhesion in the technical sense—for example, the grip of tyres on roads—and in the metaphorical sense of a person's grip on reality, which is echoed in such English expressions as 'down to earth' or 'keeping one's feet on the ground'. [Trans.]

20 Durs Grünbein. [Trans.]

21 Hanns Zischler. [Trans.]

ACKNOWLEDGEMENTS

I would like to thank Zita Gottschling and Beata Wiggen for their motivating preliminary work for this book. I am grateful to Ute Fahlenbock for her flexible and masterful realization, as well as her patience. I owe special thanks to Wolfgang Kaussen, who went above and beyond his duties as an editor and guided me with a sure hand in dramaturgical and logistical matters. I also thank Thomas Combrink for fruitful collaboration.

CREDITS

Page 39. The parts of the dialogue with Thilo Sarrazin reproduced verbatim were recorded during the 2010 Frankfurt Book Fair. The complete conversation was broadcast in the dtcp programme 'News & Stories' on SAT 1 on 9 January 2011.

Pages 98-106. The account is based on Jules Michelet, *History of the French Revolution* (C. Cocks trans.) (London: H. G. Bohn, 1847).

Pages 111, 138, 338. 'Double page with a note by G. W. Leibniz', 'The triumph of Prussian archaeology at the pyramids' and 'Constellation of the whale' from *WeltWissen: 300 Jahre Wissenschaften in Berlin* (Jochen Hennig and Udo Andraschke eds) (Munich: Hirmer, 2010).

Pages 118-29. Pictures from the collection of Stanley Kubrick for his Napoleon film: *Stanley Kubrick—The Napoleon Film: The Greatest Movie Never Made* (Cologne: Taschen, 2009).

Page 140. *Un treno nella note del mondo.* Picture by Aroldo Bonzagni from 1915.

Pages 154-8. Pictures and parts of the description from Eva Maurer, *Wege zum Pik Stalin: Sowjetische Alpinisten, 1928–1953* (Zurich: Chronos, 2010).

Pages 270, 273, 329. Frank Terschel / Time & Life Pictures / Getty Images.

Page 312. ddp images / ddp / Michael Kappeler.